SIGNS OF LIFE

DENNIS JUNG

Signs of Life © 2018 Dennis Jung

Praise for Dennis Jung's Novels

Mr. Jung did it again. Wonderful, engaging and spellbinding.
----Katseye

I waited so impatiently for this book, because I love the author's work! I read it cover to cover without stopping, My only complaint was that I just didn't want the story to end. I'm fascinated with the characters. Thoroughly enjoyed it, and recommend "The Language of The Dead" without hesitation! It's my favorite book that Dennis Jung has written. Well done.
----Erin M Coyle

I just read "Language of the Dead" and thought it was a great addition to the series featuring the photojournalist Harper Harris. She has taken me on an amazing journey around the world, not only in this story, but in the previous works by this author. Even places considered to be tourist destinations have their gritty side exposed by Mr. Jung. As an avid traveler myself, I enjoy being vicariously transported to places that I wouldn't venture into other than through Jung's uncanny ability to describe the sights,sounds, smells and feels of the those places. As if that were not enough reason to read these books, the story lines include characters that you find intriguing and in situations that involve events that are today's current affairs. A must read for anyone who enjoys a story that engages on so many levels.
----T. Foster

Also by Dennis Jung

Still Life in a Red Dress

Morning of the World

Jack of all Trades

The Language of the Dead

Acknowledgements

All of my stories, this one being no exception, take flight from a germ of an idea, always inspired by a real person or event; in this case, an incident related to me second hand by my friend Erin. Her account of a brief, intense and tragic encounter lingered in my mind for several years before I managed to find a way to exploit the repercussions of that event into a suitable plot. I hope I captured the nuance and complexity of that episode in a satisfying manner.

My thanks to my friends Maureen and Sara whose critiques and feedback have proved invaluable.

And to Mary for her gracious stewardship while we wandered amongst the living and the dead through the streets of Oaxaca during the Day of the Dead. That experience proved very germane to the ending of this novel.

The Mexican film director, Guillermo del Toro, when describing the character of the Mexican people, said "No one loves life more than we do, in a way, because we are so conscious about death." The celebrations depicted in this story, the Burning of Zozobra and Dia de los Muertos, are affirmations that we must honor the darkness to truly appreciate the light. The cycle of life and death deserve nothing less.

SIGNS OF LIFE

Dedicated to those whose remorse is far greater than their misdeeds, and to Kathleen, my wife and life partner, for her everlasting support, and the patience she grants whenever the "evil twin" appears.

PART ONE

"Rightly or wrongly all remembrance of things past is fiction."
-Hemingway

1

Santa Fe, New Mexico
September 2016

There are no accidents.
Wasn't that the last thing she had said to him? And his response had been what? For the life of him, Quist couldn't recall his rejoinder. No doubt some smartass quip born from his gin infused, carnal stupor. He opened his eyes and allowed the painting hanging on the far wall to slip into focus. In the dim light all he could make out were the vague outlines of an adobe structure. In the almost twenty hours he had been sitting here, every minor detail of the image had become imprinted on his memory: the muddy brown stucco walls, the rank of red geraniums lining the rumpled parapets, a towering cascade of the cumulus cloud as the back drop; and a lone figure cloaked in a native blanket hunched against the wall, his or her features muted in the shade of a cottonwood.

He stared at the image for a moment before lifting his cell phone from his lap and flicking it on. Ten fifteen. What had they been doing at ten fifteen the night before? It would've been about the time they walked back along the river to her hotel. He dropped the phone into his lap and looked over at the figure lying on the bed. Her face appeared unnaturally slack except where the tape that held the endo-tracheal in place pinched her cheeks. He could just make out a hint of the tiny scar on her left cheek peeking from beneath the tape. It made him think of her other scar: the angry web of purple that ran down her forearm to the crook of her thumb. He recalled sliding his finger along its smooth ridge that night in the hotel. She hadn't revealed the nature of either of her wounds, all the while interrogating him on his own varied disfigurements.

He listened for a moment to the rhythmical soft whoosh of the ventilator before glancing up at the monitor perched on the shelf above the bed. Blood pressure eighty-eight over fifty, oxygen saturation ninety-eight, respirations eighteen, pulse sixty. As he studied the screen, the jagged row of heart beats hiccoughed, jiggled and then returned to its relentless rhythm. PVCs the nurse called them. Pre-ventricular contractions. Not unusual for someone in her condition, she said matter of factly. I even get them if I drink too much coffee, the nurse added without bothering to make it sound like anything but false reassurance.

He dropped his gaze back to her face. For the first time, he noticed the fine delta of wrinkles around her eyes; her makeup and the bar lighting the most likely explanation for him having not noticed the night before. The halo from the overhead light made her hair appear more auburn than he remembered. It was shot with gray around her temples. There was one other thing he hadn't noticed. A small mole peeked from her hairline just above her left ear. He found it oddly disconcerting all these features he had overlooked. Maybe it wasn't just the bar lighting or the martinis. And later, in the dim light of the hotel room, their frenzied coupling hindered anything more than casual inspection. Or maybe you just see what you want to see.

He reached over and fingered a lock of her hair that had fallen onto her forehead. A flicker of some nascent memory caused him to pull back; his face buried in her hair, the smell of it, lavender and sweat, the shiver of sexual excitement. And then it was gone, only the ethereal glimmer of something lingering, and then the sudden remembrance of the challenging glint in her gaze when they first exchanged glances at the airport the day

2

before. That had been ... what? Not even forty-eight hours ago, he thought slumping back in the chair. He closed his eyes and thought back to their first meeting.

2

The airport lobby didn't appear much larger than the sitting room of the eight hundred dollar a night suite Quist's client had been staying in for the last week. Trevor Ritchfield was the client's name, not that anyone would be familiar with it except for perhaps the denizens of Wall Street or Silicone Valley. Quist had Googled him before signing the contract. The guy was some kind of social media tycoon who had graduated into adulthood selling computers at Best Buy. Now he dealt in the vapor cloud of what passed for information. He was one of those achingly handsome, square-jawed guys that you saw on the pages of some slick magazine modeling expensive men's cologne. The slicked back hair and two-day old beard completed the persona.

It's just a business trip, was all Ritchfield offered when he first engaged Harlan's services. I'll be taking meetings all week was how he put it. He made it sound like the meetings were merely an opportunity for vassals to come and pay tribute. Ritchfield had emerged from this tribute taking on only two occasions, and then only to play a quick round of golf.

This left Quist with not much to do but surf the cooking channels and drive Mrs. Ritchfield into town every afternoon to shop. On some level, this trivial task irritated him to no end. It would be one thing if Ritchfield's wife was even remotely personable, a quality he had decided was securely out of her grasp. A good decade younger than her husband, she was expertly spackled with silicone and botox, and with the requisite sense of entitlement of a sorority girl turned trophy wife. In later retrospect, he should have seen it all coming. Babysitting women like

4

her rarely went well.

Quist waited in the airport lobby as Ritchfield checked his golf clubs. The place seemed busier than the one other time he had been here. It's because of Fiesta week was how the bartender the evening before had explained the crowded bar and the lack of downtown parking. It'll be that way for a couple more nights the bartender had added as Quist had settled his tab.

The crowd filing off the last arriving flight appeared somber and anything but festive, much like his own state of mind. As they drove to the airport, Ritchfield had sat mutely in the rear of the rented Mercedes, not bothering to reply to Quist's casual remarks about the traffic or how astonishingly blue the sky was in New Mexico. Mrs. Ritchfield had departed earlier that morning for Taos in the seemingly capable hands of an older Native American looking gentleman whose stoic visage Quist imagined would only fossilize as the day wore on.

Clients like the Ritchfields were like a tooth going bad, and you find out your dentist's playing golf somewhere in Florida. You learn to live with the discomfort and the aggravation by numbing yourself with mindless television and too many martinis. An ex-girlfriend, a former beauty queen turned New Age financial advisor, referred to it as Quist's version of mindfulness. The ingratiating attitude he had to at times project only made it worse. So he often found himself in overpriced hotel rooms, lying in the dark and taking inventory of his options, slim as they were.

After ATF had let him go, he had gone through the motions of putting in applications with different cop shops from Sacramento to Boston. But it was like he was radioactive. The guy's a loose cannon, someone had scribbled at the bottom of one rejection letter. After that, Quist figured he might as well assume a whole new identity and past, something he had found himself seriously considering. There was no way to hide his history, not these days, and especially when you were on every federal agency's do not hire list. So after turning down several jobs in various rural sheriff departments, he drifted into freelance security gigs.

At times, it was lucrative and sometimes even entertaining, like the time he accompanied a washed up, sun dried seventies rock star on a week-long mai-tai binge in Jamaica. Most of his assignments weren't even remotely dangerous, at least if you discounted the occasional temptations of some client's girlfriend or a neglected wife. And because he resolutely shunned such enticements, his jobs were mostly without the kind of edge he thrived on.

He leaned against the wall and watched as Ritchfield began conversing with a tall, beefy young man who had joined him at the check-in desk. The young guy's suit was too small, or more likely he was too big for it. Everything about him screamed ex-jarhead; the shaved head; the biceps the size of Quist's calves. He had the shuffling, thigh- chafing gait of someone who spent an inordinate amount of time in the weight room.

In a sudden burst of clarity Quist could see what was coming. Ritchfield strolled over to where Quist was waiting, the jar-head in tow. Ritchfield offered a brilliant, toothy smile.

"I told you I'd be flying back tomorrow," he said, his voice louder than it needed to be. "But I won't be requiring your services any longer."

"Was there a problem? I mean, I'm more than happy to make sure your wife gets to where she needs to go this evening."

Ritchfield, still grinning, looked away and then back, the grin abruptly gone. "Well, I don't believe that will work out. You see, she told me when you picked her up last evening you had been drinking and you drove rather recklessly."

"Whoa. I had one martini while I was waiting for her."

"The bartender said it was three. Regardless, here's your salary," he said, handing him an envelope. "I'm being more than generous. You can leave the Mercedes in the parking lot and leave the keys with security," he said and hurried off for the departure gate, the jar head in close pursuit.

"Did she tell you she made a pass at me?" Quist asked, just loud enough for Ritchfield to hear. "I must've hurt her feelings when I turned her down."

Ritchfield barely paused, glancing and nodding at his new

body guard who turned and shuffled over to Quist. Granted, the guy was awesomely huge, but not huge enough to prevent Quist from goading him.

"You best be careful Mr. Ritchfield doesn't step on your knuckles when you're walking behind him," Quist said.

"Listen, hambone…"

"Hambone? I assume that's your feeble attempt to disparage my southern heritage. Let me give you some advice since you appear to be new to this line of work. Never underestimate a threat. Didn't they teach you that in that online course you took after your janitor job at the gym? No? So, listen here, meat sack. Best you lope back to your handler before I plant you face first in that pot of cactus over there."

The guy reached over and planted a massive paw on Quist's chest.

"You're really serious about having a go at this?" Quist said softly, thinking his only chance would be if kneed the guy in the balls right about now.

"Tommy," he heard Ritchfield yell. "Leave it."

Tommy scowled and nodded before walking off with his tight, lumbering gait. Quist glanced around the lobby to see if anyone had taken notice. If so, they had quickly lost interest. He briefly considered which of them came off as a bigger asshole, quickly acquitting himself. He had to admit the adrenaline rush far outweighed the risk of getting his ass kicked. Was he really that bored? What was it someone had once told him? Being alive wasn't the same thing as living. That sounded about right. His heart still pounding, he exhaled deeply and headed for the restroom.

He washed his face with some cold water before leaning over and studied himself in the mirror. An old girlfriend had once described his face as lupine; the high cheekbones and long jaw line; the narrow, almost slanted eyes a vestige of some Cherokee heritage on his mother's side. His eyes were dark, so dark people often remarked that they couldn't see his pupils. He still wore his coal black hair short and spiked with hints of sideburn. He studied his profile for a moment longer and then reached up and absently stroked the pinkish welt of scar beneath his right eye, a souvenir of the African debacle that had cost him his ATF job. He should've learned from that experience not to poke the bear.

"Okay, Harlan. Now what?" he muttered to himself.

He could always go back to working for the drilling outfit out of Houston, providing security on Venezuelan oil rigs. Two weeks on and then another couple off lazing around on one of those barrier islands; good beaches, cheap rum and plenty of accommodating if not always beautiful Latinas. Some of them might even be happy to see him back. It was hard times down there, and a few greenbacks and a smile bought you a lot. It would also give him time to work on his Spanish which was only slightly more advanced than that of a mildly inebriated college kid who had taken two years of high school Spanish; in other words, his proficiency was highly suspect and subject to context and his level of concentration.

Or he could start surfing the internet and see what turned up. He took the envelope Ritchfield had handed him, opened it and fingered the crisp bills. It looked like the full five thousand Ritchfield had agreed to in the contract. Good pay for one week. That would at least buy him some thinking and drinking time. The work had been steady all year, and thanks to expense accounts and his frugality, his bank account showed a little over two hundred grand.

Maybe he should just take a vacation, maybe go back to Jamaica. There was a woman there he had met when he was working for the rock star. He called her up occasionally at wholly inappropriate hours. She was married with a kid and her husband worked nights as a security guard. Maybe he would call her tonight, he thought as he walked out of the restroom.

He almost knocked over a woman leaving the adjacent restroom. She was a small but sturdy woman perhaps somewhere on the generous side of forty. It was hard to tell. She wore her auburn hair piled high on her head like a Jehovah Witness. The lack of any noticeable makeup confirmed this impression, not that she needed makeup, for her face projected the kind of natural beauty some women seem to easily get away with. Good

8

bones and a hard to forget mouth. She wore faded, ill-fitting jeans and an equally faded, red, short-sleeved, pearl buttoned Western shirt. One hand clutched a water bottle; the other held a small beat up leather valise. Her arms were deeply tanned as was her face; an outdoor face. He hazarded a guess. A rancher's wife, although the frayed, weathered tennis shoes she wore suggested something different. He noticed her belt was undone, the ends hanging un-notched.

She glanced up at him briefly and muttered what sounded like excuse me and started to turn away.

"M'am. Your belt," he said.

She turned and looked at him as if he had spoken in some foreign language before offering what almost resembled a smile.

"Not used to it. Wearing belts," he thought he heard her say. "You mind holding this?" she asked, handing him the valise without waiting for his reply.

Her voice had a soft lazy accent that was hard to place. The valise weighed next to nothing. It couldn't have contained more than a toothbrush and a change of underwear; a couple of paper backs, maybe. And surely no cosmetics. He waited as she un-selfconsciously tugged at her jeans and notched her belt.

"Thanks," she said, looking up at him and reaching for the valise. She again attempted a smile but it seemed to come hard. Still, something about her face told him that once upon time she had smiled often and easily.

He noticed her eyes then; the pupils a burnished brown like you might see on one of those old timey China dolls. They had a washed-out quality to them, as if they had perhaps seen too much for one day.

"You're welcome," Harlan replied and watched her as she walked off. Something in her stride seemed guarded and tentative. He waited until she made her way through the now nearly deserted lobby and out the exit before following her.

The bright autumn sunlight momentarily blinded him. In just the few days he had been here, he had grown enamored with the New Mexican sky. Everything felt closer here, the dry, burnt landscape dotted with yellowing flowers, the gray, rumpled peaks of the Sangre de Cristos, and the stacks of ever-changing clouds that scudded overhead across the brilliant expanse of blue stretching the horizon in all directions. It made him feel light and almost part of the air. He slipped on his Ray Bans and glanced in either direction. The woman was hailing a cab. He thought again of her empty valise. There was a lot to be said for traveling light, he thought as he reached into his pocket for the keys to the Mercedes. Screw it. He would get himself a nice hotel room off the Plaza and stay a few nights, he thought, twirling the keys and staring up at the impossibly blue sky. He could always bring the Mercedes back tomorrow.

3

You know you're not supposed to be here."

Harlan slipped the blanket off his head and blinked. The nurse, a tall, high-hipped young black woman, was the same one that had warned him earlier that day, and now seemed duly disappointed he hadn't taken heed.

"If my supervisor comes by, I'll catch holy hell," she said as she stripped on a pair of latex gloves.

"You're still on?" he croaked, his voice thick with sleep. "Christ, don't you have a union or something? What time is it?"

"My shift is done in thirty minutes. I guarantee you the next nurse won't cut you any slack. We call her the hell bitch," she said, allowing herself a brief smile. "I was told she used to be a nurse in the marines." She had an obvious southern accent.

"Tell you what. Put me on your speed dial and let me know when that supervisor of yours shows and I'll hide in the shower."

She shook her head in obvious disapproval. It was the same look she had given him when he told her, "No. I'm not her husband. I'm not her boyfriend either. Not even a relative. I'm an acquaintance," he said, after pondering it a moment.

"I know who you are," she had replied, arching her eyebrows. "You know we get the gossip from ER. And I'm sure they told you too that if you're not related to the patient, you can't be up here."

Quist had simply nodded. He watched as the nurse began suctioning out Carlotta's ET tube. Carlotta, Charlotte or whatever her name really was. Charlotte was the name on the passport and the Visa card he found in the valise. He had inspected them while waiting for the ambulance. Consequently, there had been some confusion at the admitting office when they queried him the night before. The admitting clerk had asked him twice whether his friend's name was Carlotta or Charlotte, and both times he had merely shrugged.

The passport and the credit card wasn't all he found. Twenty-two thousand dollars were stuffed in the bottom of a shopping bag in the closet. The cash had been bundled in bank tape and swaddled in a pair of red panties that still bore the sales tag. Still wrapped in the unworn panties, it was now safely ensconced beneath the spare tire in the rented Mercedes' trunk.

Quist grimaced at the sound of the suctioning. Carlotta-Charlotte never flinched.

"That doc ever come by?" Quist asked.

The nurse took a moment to answer. "Not since the afternoon. You know it's against policy to tell you anything. You not being kin and all. It's a HIPPA violation." She disregarded his look of bewilderment. "Maybe you should know something though. Even if you're not invested," she added icily, "I can still probably tell you. Prognosis doesn't look good for the lady. I saw the MRI films. I'm sorry, but I wouldn't be holding out hope for her making it. That aneurysm must've been big as a plum. Most folks don't ever recover from something that size rupturing. Maybe that might oughta figure in whether you stay or go."

Quist didn't say anything, but simply watched as the nurse finished her suctioning and turned her patient on her side. The nurse moved to his side of the bed and crouched down to inspect the urine bag strapped there.

"Where are you from?" Quist asked. "If you don't mind me asking."

"For' Worth. How about yourself?"

"West Virginia."

"I sorta figured somewhere up about those parts. Can I ask you something?"

"Sure."

"This lady. What do you know about her?"

"Hard facts? Not enough to fill a couple of Post-Its."

"She must mean something to you," the nurse said when he

didn't offer more. "You know, with you staying here like this all day."

"You're fishing now, darling and that hole's been overfished. Afraid you need to move on." He fell silent as he watched her stuff a pillow between Carlotta-Charlotte's knees.

"Being alive isn't the same as living," he muttered.

"What's that?"

"Nothing," he said, finally. "Just something that occurred to me."

The nurse turned and looked at him. "I think I know what you meant. About living. And by God, this surely isn't it."

Before Quist could say more the door opened to reveal a rotund Hispanic looking guy in a tan three piece suit, a whitish polyester shirt and a bolo tie.

"Might you be Harlan Quist?" the man asked.

"That would be me."

"Could I have a word?"

"Are you her doc?"

"No," he said simply, parting his suit coat to show the badge clipped to his belt. The belt didn't match the suit. It was tooled black leather with a turquoise and silver buckle the size of a large ash tray.

"I guess the jigs up, Nurse Ratchett." Quist flung the blanket aside and rose stiffly. He glanced down at the inert figure on the bed, wondering if this might be the last time he would see her, and then walked past the cop into the hallway.

The cop jerked his head, motioning for Quist to follow him. He didn't turn or say anything until they had reached the foyer in front of the elevator. Reaching into his suit pocket, the cop pulled out what looked like an inch of business cards wrapped in a rubber band. He stripped one off and handed it to Quist who squinted at it in the dim light. Henry CdeBaca. Homicide Detective. Santa Fe Police Department it read.

Somehow, CdeBaca didn't look like your average homicide cop. He wore his thick black hair slicked back in what resembled duck tail from the fifties. One of his front teeth was capped in gold and he had a woman's full sensuous lips. The kind of guy

Quist envisioned on weekends straddling a Harley and wearing a wife beater shirt.

"You understand why the hotel called us, don't you? Standard procedure under the circumstances. A nude, unresponsive woman. The guy in her room not a registered guest. From what you told our patrolman, you had only known the woman a short time. Is that correct?"

"Pretty much. Look…"

He stopped Quist with a raised hand. "Hold on. No judgment here, but it's routine we look into these things. Especially when there are some, what you might call oddities."

"It's not odd for a couple of people to hook up in bar. So I assume you're referring to the fact the lady was traveling light."

CdeBaca stared at him a moment. "What's your business here, Mr. Quist?"

"You mean here in this hospital or in your fine town?"

"We looked you up. You used to be in law enforcement, right? An agent with the ATF. So you know how this works. You do private security now, right?"

"The last refuge of the fallen you might say. If you're wondering about that Glock back in my hotel room. I've got a permit."

CdeBaca shook his head. "I assume you already know there was some discrepancy about the woman's name. You gave the EMS people one name, her passport says something different." CdeBaca pulled a small notebook from his suit pocket at glanced at it. "You said her name was Carlotta. Her passport and the name she registered under at the hotel is Charlotte Aucoin. You know anything about that?"

"What can I say? Carlotta, Charlotte. I might've got it wrong. It was loud in the bar." He shrugged and smiled sheepishly. "You ever get a girl's name wrong?"

CdeBaca stared at him without expression. "Are you on a job down here, Mr. Quist?"

"I was. Now I'm just on sabbatical. I figured I'd take in Fiesta."

"Are you sure you didn't know her real name? I mean, you

didn't go through her things before EMS or security came?"

"Why would you think I'd do that?"

"Because you're a cop."

"I was a cop. Besides, a gentleman doesn't rifle a woman's purse. So what are you getting at?"

CdeBaca shrugged. "Anyway, the name on the passport matches the name we got off the prints we took last night."

"Prints?"

"Yeah. It's routine with a discrepancy like that. It seems up until a few days ago Miss Charlotte Aucoin was a guest of the Louisiana Department of Corrections."

Quist grunted. "You don't say?"

That strange tan of hers was the first thing that popped into his mind. Sure as hell not a beach tan, he had thought upon first seeing her nude the night before. Pale legs and tan halfway down her arms. A farmer's tan, they called it. Or an inmate's, he thought in retrospect.

"What was the rap if you don't mind me asking?"

"Second degree murder of her husband and felony murder of her kid. Concurrent. Served fifteen years. Got out early for good behavior."

"She killed her kid? If I recall felony murder means unintended."

"Splitting hairs. Killed is killed."

"How old was the kid?"

"Four or five as I recall. So she never said anything about being in prison?"

"What do you think?"

CedeBaca gave him the lie detector stare. "How about did she happen to say anything about why she was here in Santa Fe? Visiting somebody, maybe?"

Quist shrugged. "Never came up. Maybe she was here for that Zozobra thing you guys do. That big ass puppet you guys burn up. Supposed to burn up all your troubles, right? That makes as much sense as anything given the lady's history."

"Maybe. How about her mentioning any travel plans? This passport of hers was issued two months ago."

"Issued while she was still in prison? That's seems sorta unlikely, wouldn't you say?"

"I thought the same thing, but it seems she was a trustee at the prison. I was told she had a fair amount of privileges, so it's feasible she was able to apply for a passport. Have the warden vouch for her and hold it until she was released. She had a credit card, too. Seems just about anyone can get one nowadays. Even if you're in lockup. She made quite a few charges on it before she met up with you. Three hundred bucks at a fancy clothing store downtown. Another hundred and fifty getting her hair and nails done. A couple pair of shoes. Her purse still had the sales tag in it from a tourist shop on the plaza."

"Yeah, I noticed. The shoes and hair I mean."

CdeBaca nodded in confused agreement before going on. "She charged the flight to here from New Orleans. And here's the kicker. Just before she showed up in that bar she bought a one way ticket to Leon, Mexico. She was supposed to leave today, but that surely isn't happening," he added.

"Mexico, huh? She never mentioned anything about Mexico."

"Alright then. You've got my card. Call me if you think of anything." He reached past Quist and pressed the elevator button. "One other thing, I'm supposed to tell you have to leave here. You know, not being a relative and all."

"Have they found anybody? You know, like a next of kin."

"Not the last I heard, but we're still working on it."

"I'll get my things and I'll go," Quist said, turning away.

The nurse was standing outside the room jotting notes. Quist motioned for her pen. He tore off a piece of paper from a scratch pad and jotted down his cell number. "You'll call me, right?" he said, handing her back the pen and the slip of paper.

"Sure."

He went inside, grabbed his jacket and turned to leave, but instead plopped back down in the chair next to the bed.

"You could've told me. It wouldn't have mattered, you know. My mama used to say we're all lambs in the eyes of God. Some maybe more than others though, I should hasten to add."

16

He suddenly thought of the money in the trunk of the Mercedes. Should he tell CdeBaca or hang on to it and see what happens? The only reason he had taken it in the first place was past experience told him large amounts of cash had a curious way of disappearing. His intention had been to simply safeguard it until she was recovered. But now he'd have to give it some thought.

He stood and leaned over her face, brushing the hair from her forehead, and then planted a kiss on her one eye. It tasted salty. "Catch you later, Charlotte Aucoin."

4

Twenty-four hours earlier

Quist pocketed his cell phone and popped another morsel of calamari. No answer again and her mailbox was full. He tried to recall the time difference between here and Jamaica; two or three hours at the most. The chances were she would still be working. He turned at the sound of someone shouting a greeting. A young guy with a Rastafarian hairdo carrying a trumpet size instrument case climbed up on the small stage opposite the bar and exchanged some words with an older man dressed in jeans and a sport coat who was setting up a microphone.

The first time Quist had ventured into El Meson had been while waiting in the bar as the Ritchfields spent the better part of the evening in the adjoining dining room. On that occasion, a small jazz ensemble played Tango music. The tables and chairs had been cleared from the small dance floor just enough to allow a half-dozen or so couples to pivot and dip without overturning someone's drink.

Some years ago, he had taken a couple of Tango lessons back in D.C. He entertained the illusion he had gotten the hang of it, but a weekend at a Tango retreat in the Adirondacks had quickly dispelled him of that notion. His deficiencies might have presaged his marriage to the woman he met on that same dance floor. Back then, Eva, his ex-wife, had been high-spirited and more intoxicating than the secretaries and the occasional fellow agents he romanced. Intoxicating, and also off her meds, he realized much too late. Three years of marriage was just about right, he had ultimately concluded. The kind of moderately conservative investment you could always walk away from is how his ex-girl friend and finance advisor put it in an effort to console him.

He finished off the last of the calamari, chasing it with the last of the Albariño before reaching into his jacket pocket and retrieving his phone again. He was in the mood to chat. There must be someone on his contact list that would listen to him. He scrolled past a couple of ATF agents he used to work with, guys he occasionally called up. They were the kind of friends that had always been willing to return his calls even when the African thing had rendered him a hazard to their careers. He squinted at the number of an old girlfriend in Houston, but he doubted the number was current. He scrolled down further and paused over Harper's name. It had been a couple of years since their last conversation. Quist always thought it odd for two people to have gone through what they did that time in Sierra Leone and not ever hook up again. Not that they hadn't spoke on the phone with some regularity for at least a year afterwards. Her career as a foreign correspondent frequently put her out of touch, a fact he used to rationalize their lapsed connection. He started to tap the call button but hesitated at the sound of a woman's voice from several seats down the bar.

He leaned back and craned his neck to peer past the couple sitting next to him. The owner of the voice stood surveying the room for a moment before climbing up onto the high barstool. She wore a pair of stylish khaki colored linen trousers topped off with a turquoise, double buttoned silk jersey. Harlan caught a brief glimpse of her face, her profile partially hidden by a wave of shoulder length hair. Something about her, something Quist couldn't quite put his finger on, led him to think he had seen the woman before. Maybe at the Ritchfield's hotel, he thought, turning back to the bar. She dressed like she might stay at a high dollar hotel. The bartender, a young Hispanic in his twenties with eyes too soft to be a guy's asked if he wanted another glass of wine.

19

"No thanks. I'll have a martini. Up with olives and make it with Hendricks," he added as he thought again about Harper. That had been her drink. Fortunately for both of them, he wasn't drinking back then, otherwise things might've become more complicated. He contemplated his phone for a moment longer before putting it away. Quist leaned forward as the bartender moved down the bar to take the woman's order.

"I'd like some mezcal," he heard her say. He was positive he knew her from somewhere, he thought leaning back as he filed through his memory. He doubted any of the women at Ritchfield's hotel were the mezcal drinking type.

"How about Del Maguay," the bartender replied. "It's our best."

"Sure. And some limes, please."

He was still sifting through the possibilities when the couple seated next to him stood to leave. His view now unobstructed, he openly studied the woman as the waiter placed a shot glass of mezcal and a plate of limes before her. She stared at the glass for a long moment as if it was an object she had never seen before, and then delicately lifted it to her lips and sipped. She picked up one of the lime slices, took a bite and downed the remainder of the mezcal in one swallow.

Quist nodded in appreciation. He plucked his martini from the bartender's hand, took a healthy swig and turned to the woman.

"Excuse me, ma'am. But do we know each other?"

The woman, startled out of some reverie, turned and glanced at him. Even in the dim light, he could see her eyes were damp and red as if she had been crying, an assumption seemingly confirmed when she swiped at her nose with the back of her hand. After a moment's hesitation, she shrugged. Her smile tugged at his memory.

"Are you okay?" he asked.

"The mezcal," she murmured after a moment, her voice thick.

"God, I do know you. I just can't place from where," he said, sliding over one seat.

She picked up her drink and lifted it to her mouth before

realizing it was empty. She shook her head in mild annoyance and turned to look at him. It occurred to him then where he had encountered her and it momentarily confused him. He almost couldn't believe it was the same woman. Her eyes and her mouth gave her away. But everything else was different; the clothes, the stylish coiffed hair, the eye shadow and lipstick. It still took a moment before he was able to say anything.

"The airport," he said. "I held your bag while you did your belt."

She sniffled and stared at him a moment. "Oh. Yeah," she said with some hesitation. "Of course. I remember. "

The drawl sealed it; somewhere in the South.

"Can I buy you another one of those?" he asked, pointing at her empty glass.

She seemed to consider his offer for a moment before nodding. "Sure, I wouldn't mind another," she said with barely a whiff of conviction.

"You look different," he said, gesturing to the waiter to bring her another.

She didn't reply and when it didn't seem she would offer more, Quist slid into the seat next to her. Seeing her up close, she reminded him of some movie actress from the 50's whose name he couldn't recall. The actress had been a favorite of his mother's. Susan Hayward, maybe.

"You mind the company? I won't take offense if you tell me to get lost."

She looked at him as if she were critically appraising a grapefruit before sighing. "I don't usually... Yeah. Sure, why not? Excuse me," she said, leaning over and motioning to the bartender. "Is there any chance you have some Ibuprofen or Tylenol?"

"Sorry, ma'am. I sure don't."

She swung her gaze down the length of the bar before looking at Quist. "I've had this headache from hell all afternoon. The altitude, I guess. I doubt this mezcal is helping matters any."

"There's a hotel in the next block. I'd be more than happy to run over to their gift shop and get you something."

She smiled for the first time. "That's very nice of you, but

I'll manage." She eyed the glass of mezcal the bartender placed before her. "Make sure and cut me off after this one," she said to no one in particular, taking a sip. "Well, maybe not this one, but for sure the next one. It's been a while," she said, glancing away. When she turned back, she seemed uncomfortable, almost as if caught doing something illicit.

He waited for her to say something more, and when she didn't, he said "You know when two people meet like this in a bar, you know, strangers and all. Well, they start with the usual small talk. Breaking the ice is what they call it. Right? Talk about the weather, what they're doing here in a place like Santa Fe. Some people start talking about their spouses or maybe their pets. By the way, do you have a spouse? No?" he asked when she didn't reply. "How about a pet? No? Then let me tell you about my pet raccoon."

She laughed, a raucous bellow that made a couple at the far end of the bar look up from their tapas. "Jesus. I can only imagine how much luck you must have with that line," she said, shaking her head and suppressing a grin.

"More than you'd think."

She lifted her glass to eyeball what remained. He noticed then a tangle of what appeared to be scar tissue that enveloped her right hand and snaked up her wrist and into her sleeve. It reminded him of a scar he had seen on a fellow GI in Iraq who had attempted to pull a buddy from a burning HumVee.

"I imagine next you'll ask me if I want to come up to your room and see your raccoon."

"No, he's in my car."

She laughed again and shook her head. "My father had a pet raccoon once. He kept it caged in the storeroom of this bar he used to own."

"Oh, yeah? Where was this bar? Maybe I've been there," he asked, fishing for the origins of her accent.

"Galveston. It's where I grew up. Have you ever been there?"

"Matter of fact, I have. Some friends and I boated out of there once to do some fishing. Back maybe ten years ago. We stayed at some seedy hotel on the seawall."

"That must've been back before the hurricane. They tell me Ike washed all those godforsaken places into the gulf. Now it's all these big resort type hotels. Or so I've been told."

"What kind of bar was it? The one your dad owned?"

She downed the last of her mezcal and rubbed her temples. "It was this little dive down on The Strand. Down by the wharves. It was the kind of place where sailors came to drink and pick fights with the locals. It burned down," she added.

Quist shook his head in amusement. "Is that so? My mother always told me I would most likely die in a bar fire."

"My dad was passed out drunk in the back. He forgot to put out his cigarette."

"Oh, Jesus. Sorry to hear that."

"Don't be. He really wasn't worth the sentiment." She pivoted in her seat and gave him the once over. "Let's talk about something else. What do you do? For a living, I mean."

"Cleaning up after that coon is a full time job. But mostly I watch over my brethren."

"What? You're a minister or something?"

"No. An overpaid security guard, but personal security has a nicer ring to it."

"Personal security? You mean like a bodyguard? Really?" Her demeanor seemed to suddenly change, as if she had slipped away to somewhere else.

"How about yourself? This morning at the airport I had you pegged as a rancher's wife."

She motioned to the bartender to bring her another mezcal. "Don't say a word. It's my last one."

"So? Was I close? About being a rancher's wife?"

"Why a wife? Why not just a rancher?" she said with obvious irritation. "If you're talking about what I was wearing when you saw me at the airport. Well..." She paused before going on. "It was all I could find in the closet. It's been awhile since I bought any nice stuff. You were close though. Not about the wife part. I was living on a... a farm. I didn't have much need for nice clothes."

"A lot to be said for that kind of life," he said, raising his drink. "I'm Harlan, by the way."

23

She looked at him for a beat or two before replying. "Carlotta. You're not allowed to smoke in here, are you?"

"Doesn't appear so, but we could step out on the street."

"Do you smoke? No? Even better. I gave it up."

"All that healthy farm life, I suppose. Fresh air and milk cows."

She shot him a look that he had difficulty deciphering.

"Are you here for Fiesta?" he asked.

"Not exactly."

"Shopping trip?"

She looked at him, her face reflecting a mixture of emotions. "No," she said after a moment's hesitation. She twirled her shot glass between her fingers and shook her head. "I actually came here to kill someone. I'm kidding," she said in reaction to the look of surprise on his face. "I do admit to having murder in my heart. At least at first. But now it's just..." She shook her head and looked at him. "I don't know why I'm telling you this. I don't know you from Adam."

"Sometimes it's better that way. Confessing things to a stranger. Safer."

He waited for her to say more, and when she didn't, he motioned for the bartender. "You should eat something. The calamari was pretty good. I was thinking of lamb chops and some mushrooms stuffed with manchego and chorizo. Care to share?"

She smiled and nodded. The smile telegraphed some melancholia mixed with acceptance. "Lamb chops sound good," she said. "And a salad would be nice. I haven't eaten anything but weeds and month old iceberg in god knows how long."

"They didn't feed you well on that farm?"

"Not that you'd notice," she said with what sounded like bitterness.

"Well, then let's make an evening of it. It's on me. I'm unencumbered, and as it happens, flush with cash."

"Well then, Harlan. Why not?" she said, hoisting her glass.

He grinned and raised his glass in a toast before finishing it off.

5

A jazz trio had taken the stage and played some reasonably good covers of Coltrane and Davis as Quist watched Carlotta polish off most of a tapas plate of lamb chops, another of mushrooms stuffed with chorizo and manchego and a salad of spinach, goat cheese and pears. A whole basket of sourdough also fell victim to her predations. True to her word, she had stopped after her third mezcal but had eagerly agreed to a glass of white wine. The mezcal had done its work, loosening her tongue to the point she rambled on about her childhood in Galveston. Curiously, it seemed her life, or at least as far as she was willing to relate, ended around age eighteen.

The alcohol also had the effect of softening her features. When she first began to talk, he sensed a reticence of some sort, a camouflage he had become adept at perceiving, this intuition an artifact of his previous life. Being undercover and ferreting out illegal gun transactions among a commune of Aryan Nation types in the backwoods of Idaho had required honing an ability to read people and register duplicity. With Carlotta, for whatever reason, this sense failed him. Whether it was truly duplicity on her part or simply a reluctance to share intimacies with a total stranger, he couldn't be sure. She held back even when her mouth and eyes said otherwise.

Her eyes had taken on a different hue than he remembered from the airport. It was more than just the dim bar lighting. Maybe it was only the mezcal, but her pupils appeared lighter, her gaze more direct. Her mouth, the first feature he had noticed that morning, at first seemed to curl into a smile that almost seemed too easy. Practiced was the word that came to mind; the kind of smile that one offered more out of artifice than amiability. But as the evening wore on her smile seemed more relaxed and genuine.

Quist noticed she had barely touched her wine. "You want another mezcal?" he asked.

"God, no. I should've stopped after the second one."

She shot him a smile. Yeah, Susan Hayward was who she reminded him of. Maybe it was the auburn hair, or something g about her eyes.

"So where did you develop a taste for mezcal?"

She considered the question for a moment before replying. "A long time ago on a lost week in Cozumel. It was..." Her voice drifted off. "I think I'd like some coffee," she said after a moment. "Maybe it'll help this headache." As she pushed her plate away, she knocked over a candle, the flame almost igniting her napkin.

"God, I'm beginning to think my mother mighta been right," Quist said, tamping out the smoldering napkin. "You know. About me dying in a bar fire."

She smiled. "It sounds like your mama didn't exactly have high hopes for you. Tell me about her."

"My mother? Why would you want to know about my mother?"

"Because it says a lot about the child. About the man. About who you really are, Harlan...?"

"Quist. Harlan Quist." He finished off his wine and motioned to the bartender. "Two coffees, please." He turned and looked at her. "My mother , God rest her soul, died some years back. Suicide. The how isn't relevant. Seems she was always the nervous type. Her people were generally known for that. They were all nervous. Going back generations. She was a real pretty woman. Delicate is the word that I believe some people like to use. You know, in that nervous sort of way. She always wanted to go to college and study art, but then my brother and I came along." He related all this in the kind of neutral tone one might use in reading aloud a newspaper article.

26

"One of my first memories of her is of her painting. Our garage was full of her canvases, dozens and dozens of them. My brother and I used to spend hours looking at them and making up stories about them. Oddly enough, there wasn't a single goddamn landscape among them. A lot of them were these portraits of people we'd never seen. And then she painted these weird pictures of people doing strange things. You know, sharing beers with a two-headed dog or breaking up furniture with a sledge hammer. We conjured up lots of good stories, mind you." He smiled at the memory. "She was actually pretty good. I even kept a couple of them. At least the ones she didn't burn up. I've got them in a storage locker in DC."

Neither of them spoke for a moment. Quist avoided her gaze even though he felt her eyes on him as she waited for more. What the hell. Might as well, he thought. Didn't I just tell her it was easier confessing things to a stranger?

"My father was a lawman. The sheriff of Mingo County, West Virginia. He died in the line of duty you might say, considering he got shot in the back. Some years later, my mother took up with one of his deputies. This guy seemed to make her happy, or at least as happy as she could be. She even smiled on occasion. She started painting again. But then she found out this guy…" He wiped his mouth with the back of his hand. "This guy, this deputy. It turned out he and my mama's brother, my uncle, had been the ones that killed my father."

He looked at her to gauge her reaction to what he had just said, but there was nothing there. Not shock, not empathy; if anything her eyes reflected a disturbing curiosity.

"This uncle, he always took me hunting. He taught me how to shoot. Gave me my first rifle. We were close like that." He nodded at the bartender as he brought them their coffees. "I was the one that found out the truth about what they did to my father. I was the one that told my mama. Thinking about it later, I probably shouldn't have."

He waited for her to say something and when she didn't, he picked up his coffee and looked at it before setting it back down. "You know you choose the lies you like to tell yourself. I

27

always told myself she killed herself out of some shame that she had fallen so hard for the man who killed my father. A guy she mighta loved. Truth be told, I've always felt she killed herself because she couldn't bear to look at the person who told her and robbed her of the goddamn illusion of happiness. It was all she had left. And I took it from her."

"You can't believe that," Carlotta said, after a moment. "You have to realize things happen that you can't always control. Fate. Seems it always comes down to fucking fate," she said with obvious bitterness. She took a swallow of her coffee and looked at him. "How old were you? When you told her?"

"Fifteen or so."

"Not a good age to deal with stuff like that. But you endured, didn't you? You went on living. But then again living isn't the same thing as being alive."

"Well now. I told myself that very same thing this morning. Aren't we the goddamn philosophers?" he said with unintended sarcasm. "Can I ask you something?" he asked, not bothering for a reply. "I was talking to this bartender the other night. He said people come to Santa Fe either looking for something or running from something. Something tells me that with you it might be a little bit of both."

She didn't reply.

"You come in here looking like you do. So different than this morning. Maybe I'm wrong, but you seemed upset about something. You say you had murder in your heart. Wasn't that how you put it? If nothing else, you've got my attention. So assuage my curiosity and tell me what it is you're about."

She looked at him and grinned. "Assuage? I haven't heard that word since my last semester in college."

"Some of us southern crackers do go to college and learn big words."

She downed the last of her coffee. "If you don't mind, I'd rather forget about today for a little while. I need some air. Maybe it'll help my headache. Let's walk."

"Sure. And then you can come see my raccoon," Quist said, motioning to the bartender for the check.

6

Quist's dream was always the same; though in truth it was more a nightmare than a dream. The rubber sandals scuffing the grimy pavement inches from his face. The smell of asphalt, dog shit and garbage; the usual smell of Baghdad streets, only close up. The strident yelling of the crowd; their language unintelligible, and the sudden suffocating fear he was about to be trampled to death. He tried his best to regain his footing, but people kept pushing him down. And then the whoosh and the sudden heat of the explosion, the acrid stench of burning fuel, the shattering of glass, the panicked crowd stumbling over him. And Nell's screams. Or had he always only imagined that?

Quist opened his eyes, his breath coming in short gasps. The room was dark, the only sound the hum of the air conditioner; and something else; a periodic chirp. It took him a moment to realize it was his cell phone signaling he had a message. He turned his head and squinted at the clock on the nightstand. 7:06 AM

After leaving the hospital the night before, he had given into his insomnia and drove fifty miles north on the interstate before turning around. The creature comforts of the Mercedes had lulled him to the point he briefly considered driving on all the way to Denver; to put as much distance between reality and the life he liked to conjure up when situations as this arose; an alternate self was always a nice fall back position. Instead, he returned to his hotel room, cracked the seal on a fresh bottle of Grey Goose and reacquainted himself with Harlan Quist.

He pulled the blanket over his eyes and lay there another

moment and let his tongue navigate around his dry mouth in search of any errant saliva. He finally propped himself up on one elbow and reached for his phone. It was a text message. He could see that much. He switched on the lamp and squinted. Neither the name nor the number seemed familiar. He fumbled for the reading glasses he had left on the night stand and opened the message.

Your friend died during the night. I'm sorry.

He scrolled down, hoping there was more but that was all. He turned off the lamp, pulled the blanket back over his head and went back to sleep.

He awoke again sometime later to the sound of someone knocking on his door. It was most likely housekeeping. He lay there and tried to recall if he neglected to put the Do Not Disturb sign on the door. He waited for another knock before swinging his legs to the floor and dropping his head into his hands.

"Yeah, give me a minute," he yelled as he rubbed his eyes and shot a quick glance at the clock. 9:35 AM. He grabbed his T-shirt from a nearby chair and stripped it over his head before surveying the room for the first available pair of trousers, in this case, a pair of sweats. As he climbed into them, he eyed the half empty bottle of vodka on the night stand. No wonder his mouth was dry. He stood stiffly and shuffled to the door just as the knock came again.

"Yeah, hang on, I'm coming."

He took a deep breath, unlocked the security bolt and flung open the door. He expected the short, elderly Hispanic maid he had seen in the hallway the day before. Instead, before him stood a woman dragging a carry-on bag in one hand and clutching a large plastic bag in the other. The first thing he noticed was her clothes. She was dressed like one of those civilian nuns; a plain gray, below the knee length skirt topped with a plain white blouse beneath a black sport coat that made him recall his third-grade teacher. Dropping his eyes to her feet confirmed it; the sensible flats and dark nylons.

"Yeah," he muttered, trying his best to focus his desiccated eyes on her face.

"You're Harlan Quist?" she asked, her voice hoarse as if she hadn't had a drink of water in a while.

He studied her for a moment before replying. Something about her face hinted at something familiar, but the grim set of her wide mouth made it difficult to place. She had almond-shaped eyes that were the color of dark honey, and he struggled to determine if she was peering at him or past him at the disarray of his room. She wore her chestnut hair pulled in a tight bun and wore no makeup to speak of; a pair of simple gold ear studs her only adornment. Somewhere in her late thirties, he guessed. Five eight, a hundred and twenty pounds give or take.

"I'm Quist. Do I know you?"

The grim lips feigned a smile. "I'm Royale Aucoin. This cop at the hospital said you knew my sister."

7

Royale Aucoin cocked her head and looked around the hotel room. Discarded clothes were strewn haphazardly on the floor and several cartons of what appeared to be takeout were heaped on both the dresser and the small table in the corner. On the night stand sat what appeared to be a half empty bottle of clear liquor. The room smelled fusty with an underlying bouquet of leftover chow mein. She wrinkled her nose and turned her gaze back to Quist. He was unshaven, and his black spiky hair was matted on one side, giving his face an oddly uneven appearance. His mouth was open, in befuddlement or abject stupidity, she couldn't be sure. So this was the creep Charly spent her last night with?

He stood there a moment staring at her before raising one finger as if requesting a timeout before turning toward the bathroom. He closed the door behind him and few seconds later, she heard a fit of retching followed by what sounded like vomiting. A silence followed, then the flush of the toilet. When he reappeared, he was wiping his face with a towel.

"You're not sick, are you?" she asked.

He looked at her with bewilderment. "Oh, you mean that?" he asked, gesturing to the bath room with his thumb. "What? Doesn't everybody do that when they get up in the morning?"

She shook her head in revulsion mixed with barely suppressed amusement.

"You coming in?" he asked, tossing the towel onto a nearby chair.

"I'm not sure. Maybe I should have the health department give it a clearance first."

His smile rearranged his face in a way that made her reconsider her first impression. She could suddenly see what Charly might have seen in him.

He looked around the room. "Yeah. Well housekeeping has been a bit remiss in their duties. I guess I should've taken down that Do Not Disturb sign a couple of days ago." He looked back at her. "I see the resemblance. You're taller, darker. She dressed nicer," he said with obvious sarcasm. "Okay. How about we start over? Give me time to clean up and I'll meet you downstairs. I need some breakfast."

She hesitated for a moment before replying. "Sure. Is it okay if I leave my bag here?"

His eyes seemed to focus on a thought and then he nodded. "I'm sorry about your sister. I only found out a couple of hours ago."

Royale allowed her eyes to again survey the room. Something about Quist's intense gaze made her uncomfortable. Maybe this was a mistake, but she needed to know what her sister was doing here; and why she had spent the last night of her life with this guy. She could understand why Charly hadn't called when she was released. Ten years and people grow apart. But there were so many questions, and now she was afraid she might never know.

"All right then. I'll see you in a bit," she said, wheeling her suitcase inside the door and stepping out into the hallway. She stood there a moment after Quist closed the door and thought about what the cop had told her. There's something off about him, the cop had said. I don't think he's dangerous or anything, but I wouldn't trust him either, he added.

33

8

The dining room of the La Fonda Hotel was packed with the brunch crowd so she put her name on a waiting list and wandered out the hotel's front entrance. The crush of tourists with their cameras in one hand and a Starbucks in the other reminded her for a moment of Canal Street but everything else seemed foreign; the mud colored buildings, the crisp air, the slumping gray line of mountains on the western horizon.

She had been here once before, a crazed forty-eight hours in the company of a male acquaintance who had promised to take her to Hollywood but instead had dumped her in Santa Fe when the money and the coke ran out. She remembered the cathedral and its seemingly unfinished façade, but not much of anything else thanks to the prodigious amounts of cocaine in which she had indulged. It had been meant to last them as far as the California coast, but a sudden snow storm had marooned them in a cheap motel room on the outskirts of town.

As usual, Charly came to her rescue, wiring her the money to return home to Galveston along with the usual admonishment about her choice in men. At the time, Charly had just begun dating Bisco, goddamn him to hell.

"That motherfucker," she hissed under her breath, causing a boy of about six being towed by his mother to turn and stare back at her as if he had just happened upon something deliciously vile.

The girls' father, in one of his rare moments of clarity, and to his everlasting credit, had called Bisco a carpetbagger to his face.

"Face it, he's all fart and no ass," he had told Charly.

"You called him a carpetbagger?" Charly had asked him, barely able to contain her rage and embarrassment. "Just because he moved here from Brooklyn? He's a businessman."

"Oh, yeah? Businessman, my ass," her father replied, pouring another glass of Jack Daniels from the private bottle he kept beneath the bar. "You know what he is. A dago from Brooklyn who's in the import-export business. Come on for chrissakes. Think about it Charly. There just ain't a lot of olive oil groves in Central America. Mexico, neither. Stay away from him. He's gonna be nothing but trouble."

And for once their father was right, Royale thought, ducking into a doorway to let a throng of elderly women pass. For some odd reason, she always associated ducking into a doorway with lighting a cigarette. She could use one about now. She gave up sneaking them eight years ago, but not a single day went by when she didn't crave one. Bisco, she muttered to herself. I should've been the one that shot him, not Charly.

She turned and leaned her head against the glass shop window, overcome with a sudden deflation, her grief mixed with guilt and regret. A moment went by before she noticed a young shop girl watching her from inside the store. Behind the girl was a sign that read 'Street Feet'. It took Royale a second to realize this was the store where Charly had purchased a pair of shoes. She had seen the sales slip amongst Charly's personal belongings. Dabbing her tears away with her sleeve, she went inside.

"Excuse me," she said, approaching a gray-haired woman who was stacking a pile of shoe boxes onto a nearby shelf. "A friend of mine bought some shoes here two days ago. I was wondering if you might remember her. Auburn hair, fortyish, about this tall," she said, gesturing with her hand.

The woman looked at her and smiled. "You say two days ago? Honey, I have trouble recalling if I watched the evening news last night. I'm sorry but I don't remember anyone like that."

"I remember her."

Royale turned and looked at the young woman who had

been watching her through the glass.

"You were on lunch break, Ramona," the girl explained. "The woman bought a pair of ankle boots. Fawn colored. She didn't have to think about it either. Just slipped one on and then said she'd take them."

Royale reached into her purse and fumbled through it for a moment before pulling out the photograph. It was faded and folded in two. "Is this her? It's an old picture, twenty years at least, but the likeness is still good," she said, handing the girl the photo.

The girl studied it for a moment. "Yeah, I believe it's her. She definitely looked older, but you did say this was an old picture."

"Can you tell me anything about her? I mean, how did she seem to you?"

"What do you mean?"

"I don't know." Royale shook her head. The truth was she wasn't sure what she was searching for her. Why in the hell hadn't Charly called her?

"She seemed a little upset if that's what you mean. She looked like she had been crying and she was, I don't know, like not really here. Distracted, I guess you could say. Like I said, she barely tried on those boots."

Royale nodded. "Thanks." She turned and started for the door.

"There was something else funny about her," the girl said. "She wasn't dressed like someone who spends two hundred dollars on a pair of shoes. She was dressed like some… I guess I mean to say, and don't take this wrong, but she was dressed like someone lower income than we usually see in here. Maybe she needed them for a special occasion or something."

Royale thanked the girl and walked outside. "Charly, what the hell were you doing?" she muttered as she made her way back to the La Fonda.

9

The La Fonda's dining room was a large, airy atrium, most of the walls comprised of glass panes decorated with painted designs. She decided not to wait for Quist and ordered a coffee, but only a minute later she looked up to see him entering the restaurant. He saw her immediately and began to stroll leisurely in her direction. He paused to catch their waitress and ordered a coffee. Make it a pot, she heard him say to the waitress as she walked away.

She allowed herself to be surprised at the transformation. Quist wore a pair of French cut blue jeans and a pressed white dress shirt topped with a dove colored linen sport coat. He had shaved, and his spiky coal black hair had been combed in a fashion that made her recall an old poster from the fifties her father kept in the storeroom. It advertised a show at the Balinese Room on the Seawall featuring some rockabilly star. Eddie Cochran if her memory served her correctly. She couldn't imagine Quist's appeal to someone like her sister, even after fifteen years in prison. She shouldn't judge, she told herself, eyeing Quist as he pulled up a chair.

He gazed around the room for a moment before meeting her gaze. "Sorry about earlier. I didn't have a good night, but then again I imagine you didn't either. My condolences."

She held her silence, waiting for him to go on. She was good at that; waiting for her clients to go on. Except she rarely thought of them as clients. That was part of her problem. She didn't know how to think about the women that sat across from her. Or how they saw her. Confidante? Mother? Sister of the same cloth? Surely not a friend.

"I imagine you want to know what happened," he said, nodding at the waitress as she brought their coffee. When he realized Royale wasn't going to reply, he went on. "It wasn't what you think."

"How do you know what I think?"

"You talked to that cop, didn't you?"

"And he told me Charly died of a ruptured aneurysm. What the two of you were doing beforehand really isn't any of my business. Unless you drugged her or something."

Quist clicked his tongue in annoyance. "Look. I only met... Wait, what did you just call her? Charly?"

"That's what we called her."

"I only met... Charly a few hours before. We struck up a conversation over dinner. I went up to her room later and..."

"Had sex with her. I'm not totally naïve. I know how those things happen."

He smiled. A shit eating grin was what her father used to call that kind of grin.

He let his eyes drift over her plain blouse and her rumpled jacket. "Anyone ever tell you that you dress like a nun? You remind me of Sister Thomasina from the third grade. She was shorter though. Friendlier, too. Didn't have any tats either," he said, nodding with his chin at her right wrist.

She tugged at her sleeve in an effort to conceal the constellation of crudely tattooed shooting stars she had acquired one Dexedrine and tequila fueled night after her senior prom. She and some girl friends had driven all night to Matamoros Mexico to spend the dawn cruising the sketchy bars that lined the wharves. They awoke mid-morning in the back of her friend's pickup truck beside some railroad tracks somewhere outside of Brownsville parched and amnesic but otherwise intact.

"Your sister seemed to be a really nice person. I only wish I could've gotten to know her better."

She allowed herself a moment of distraction before meeting his gaze. "I have to say you're pretty good at faking conviction."

"Look, Miss Aucoin. It seems you and I have gotten off on the wrong foot here. Now I can see you thinking I maybe took advantage of your sister, but something tells me she could take care of herself."

No, she couldn't, Royale thought to herself. Big sisters always think they can take care of everything. "You're right, Mr. Quist." It suddenly occurred to her that maybe Charly had taken advantage of him. That would be Charly. She sighed and shook her head. "Would it surprise you if I told you my sister and I haven't spoken in over ten years?"

He arched his eyebrows but said nothing.

"You already know about her being in prison. Yeah, that cop said he told you. What you don't know is…"

"Ten years? You two didn't talk for ten years? Why not?"

"It's not any of your business."

"None of my business? Then why did you bring it up? By the way, what do you do?"

"Do?"

"Yeah, are you a school teacher. Or maybe a church lady?"

"Are you a misogynist, Mr. Quist?"

"I'd like to think not, but if you keep it up I might be persuaded to change my mind."

"You're right. I'm sorry. We have gotten off on the wrong foot. Look, I just want to know if she told you anything about what she was doing here. Or where she was going."

"She never mentioned it. It's what I told that detective Cde-Baca."

"You don't know anything about her going to Mexico?"

"Didn't I just say that? Look, it was mostly small talk. You know, strangers striking up a conversation. She was easy to be with. I even saw her smile a couple of times. What can I say? We were both lonely, I guess. It happens. You meet someone. You make a connection and one thing leads to another."

She looked away, measuring what she should say that might get her the answer she wanted.

"You want to know what I do? I'm a social worker in New Orleans. I work with prostitutes mostly. Battered wives. People whose lives didn't work out the way they thought they would. One of the reasons I dress this way is because it makes them open up, believe it or not. They think what they see is what they get. No costumes, no makeup. I'm not one of them. But I'm not their mother either. Or their kindergarten teacher. I'm there to listen. Not to judge, but to listen."

"Does it help them?"

"I like to think so."

Quist nodded. "I have to give you credit. That's hard job. I used to know someone that used to do that kind of work. She ended up jumping off a bridge. It seemed it was easier to help other people than herself."

Quist picked up the menu and took a sip of his coffee. "Migas. That's what I want. Christmas. How about you?"

"Christmas?"

"It's how the locals order their chile sauce. Half red, half green."

She glanced at the menu. "I'll stick to the plain egg white omelet. Mr. Quist…"

"Harlan. Call me Harlan."

She hesitated for a moment and then leaned down and picked up the plastic sack CdeBaca had given her. She pulled out Charly's valise, set it on the table, and then reached inside.

"On the cab ride over from the hospital I went through her things. I threw away the cosmetics and some other things at the hospital. There wasn't much else in here except a paperback. Graham Greene. The Tenth Man. She liked reading the older stuff." She flipped open the book and pulled out a slip of paper. "This was stuck inside. Somehow CdeBaca must've missed it." She showed the slip to Quist who started to reach for it, but she quickly pulled it away. "It's the name of a nursing home here in Santa Fe. There's a number written on the back. A room number is my guess. I called there and asked whose room it was but they wouldn't tell me. Did she mention anything about a nursing home? A place called Placita de Vida?"

Quist shook his head. "No, she did not. You figure she went there?"

Royale shrugged.

"Why are you telling me this? Why don't you just go there

and ask if she was there?"

"I plan on it."

They paused as the waitress took their order. Royale could tell Quist was considering something, almost as if he was holding something back. She knew waiting might be more productive than asking him outright. Quist poured himself another cup of coffee and looked at her.

"I'll tell you this. She did say something about starting off the day with murder in her heart. I'm pretty sure those were her exact words. But I got the impression something happened to change her mind. Or her heart, I guess. But that's all she said. Well…" He stared past her for a second. "Back at the hotel, she asked if I had ever lost something, and then found it and regretted it. I got the impression she was talking about someone, not some thing."

What in God's name were you doing, Charly, Royale asked herself for perhaps the twentieth time. She must've come here to see someone. Two days out of prison and she comes here. But why? Who was here?

"Were you two close?" Quist asked. "I mean ten years go by and not speaking to one another."

"Yeah, we were close. At least until she went to prison. I suppose CdeBaca told you why she was there."

"He did. Let me guess. It's like that line you hear in those old westerns? The guy she killed needed killing. What about her kid?" he asked when she didn't say anything.

Royale hoped her face didn't betray the sudden pain that she felt in her gut. "It was an accident."

"Felony murder they call it. When someone dies in the course of…"

"I know what it means, and you don't know what happened. It wasn't right convicting her of that. It's why she… It's why things turned out the way they did. How in the hell do you punish someone who's already so full of guilt. " She looked away. When she looked back, Quist was staring at his coffee.

"I visited her every week for five years and then all of a sudden she wouldn't talk to me anymore. She wouldn't meet with me. She cut me off," she said, surprising herself with her bitterness. "Like she was dead. Already dead," she said, her voice breaking.

"So you're thinking Charly went to see someone yesterday and you want to know why. How about I go with you? It's the least I can do."

"This isn't really any of your business."

"Miss Aucoin. You may not believe this but I used to be a federal agent. Yeah," he added to her obvious look of disbelief. "ATF. That's Alcohol, Tobacco and…"

"I know what it is."

"All I'm saying is I could be helpful. Besides, she was…" He ran his hand across his mouth and looked away. "Let's just say, she made it my business," he added, meeting her gaze.

"I appreciate the offer, but I don't know you from Adam. What?" she asked in response to his smirk.

"Funny, but your sister said the exact same thing."

"Yeah, and look where that got her."

Quist smirked. "I bet back in kindergarten they called you a biter."

"Okay, I'm sorry. That was uncalled for. I'm tired and a bit confused about all this."

"Offer still stands."

Royale looked at him for a moment before nodding. "Okay," she said, surprising herself. "But only as far as this goes. Like I said, it's not really any of your business."

"Fair enough. Now Miss Aucoin, I say we enjoy these eggs," he said, nodding at the waitress as she placed their plates before them.

"You can call me Roy."

"Roy? Something tells me your dad was hoping for boys."

"That's not the half of it. Do you have a car?"

"Indeed, I do, but prudence requires me to exchange it. Meantime, try some of this salsa on those sorry looking eggs of yours," he said, sloshing a spoonful of green sauce on her omelet before she could object.

10

Royale waited outside the Avis car rental office and watched as Quist made arraignments to exchange the Mercedes for a medium sized Ford sedan. When she asked him why he was switching he just said the Mercedes wasn't really his. On the drive over, she asked why he wasn't with ATF any longer. He took a long time answering and provided details in fits and starts, almost as if he was making up the details as he went along. He offered that he had been a criminal investigator in the Army, had served a tour in Korea, then one each in Afghanistan and Iraq, and once discharged, was accepted by ATF. When she asked why he left ATF, he said he had gotten overly involved in a case in a way that displeased his boss.

"I had to go off the reservation, and I was already on a short leash. Then I ended up missing in action and laid up in a jungle hospital in the back woods of Sierra Leone, West Africa. What can I say? They let me go and here I am."

She sensed there was obviously a lot more to this story, but she also guessed he wasn't about to provide any more details. The rental agency was located on Cerrillos Road, a busy four lane commercial strip a few short miles from downtown. Again, nothing looked familiar even though the motel where her and her boyfriend had holed up was most likely nearby. But then again, there was so much of her memory of those years that had been lost to the drugs and alcohol.

She shoved these thoughts aside as the rental agent pulled up with Quist's sedan. Quist came out and popped the Mercedes' trunk and began rooting around in the compartment that held the spare. He retrieved a paper sack which he juggled in his hand for a moment before walking over and handing it to her.

"Hang on to that while I sign on the dotted line," he said casually.

Whatever was inside was bulky but really didn't weigh that much. When Quist was done with the paperwork, they both got in and Quist started to drive off. He stopped abruptly and stared straight ahead as if considering something.

"You better look inside the bag," he said, his eyes still focused ahead.

She unfolded the top of the bag and peered inside. It was money, hundred dollar bills from the looks of it, and a lot of it. She glanced at Quist who still sat stone faced, eyes forward.

"What is this?" she asked, peeling back the top of the bag. The bundles of money were loosely wrapped in what Royale realized were a pair of red lace panties. She pried a stack of the bills loose and held it up to see it better. Each of the inch thick pack of hundreds was banded with a paper strip that said Iberia Bank, New Orleans. There were a dozen of them at least. She looked at Quist who finally turned to meet her gaze.

"Charly had it. I took it out of her valise the other night before EMS got there. Don't ask me why. It just seemed a good idea at the time. Cash left on the floor of a hotel closet tends to end up missing. If you're wondering if I was considering taking it, the answer's no. I didn't think she was going to die," he added.

"How much is here?" she asked, removing the bundles one by one.

"Twenty grand. Twenty two thousand to be exact. There's something else you should know. I don't think she had it with her when I first saw her at the airport. The only reason I know that is I held that valise for her while she notched up her belt. I noticed her belt was undone and I told her," he added in explanation.

"Where would she get this kind of money? She was broke. All the legal fees…"

Quist nodded. "You notice the bands on those bills are from a bank in New Orleans. I already figured somebody must've given her that money the day she got here. I just had no idea who. But now you bring up this Placita de Vida place, and I think whoever's there might know something."

She looked at him. "You didn't have to tell me about this. You could've kept it. No one would've known."

Quist shrugged. "Maybe. If Charly died and no kin showed up. Yeah, I would've kept it. Though not for myself if that makes you more inclined to think kindly of me. I have a friend in Jamaica who could surely put it to good use."

Was he for real, she asked herself as she stuffed the money back into the sack. For all she knew there could've been fifty grand in Charly's valise. And who would be the wiser? Maybe he was conning her after all.

"So I guess we go to this Placita de Vida," he said as he slipped the car back into gear and started to edge out onto the street.

"Wait," she said, grabbing his arm. She reached into her bag and took out the photo of Charly and held it up in front of Quist's face. "You need to see something. This is who Charly used to be. I need to know what happened. I need to know what she was like when you were with her the other night. I need to know what my sister was doing. Shit!" She started to cry. Quist turned away as if embarrassed by her outburst, but then reached over and picked up the photograph.

"She looked happy here. When was this taken?"

Royale didn't reply for a few beats. "It was taken in New Orleans. Right after Lana…"

"Lana?"

Royale glanced out the window. When she looked back it seemed she was about to cry again. "Her daughter. It was taken at Lana's one year birthday party." She plucked it from his fingers and stuffed it back in her purse.

"You want to know what Charly was doing? If I knew I'd tell you. All I can do is tell you about the other night, but I doubt that'll give you any answers." He backed the car up beneath a nearby locust tree and cut the ignition. "You're sure you want to hear all this?"

She looked at him and nodded. "Everything. I need to know everything."

11

A thunderstorm had passed through while they were in the restaurant and the street glistened in the street lights, the night air cool and redolent with ozone and pine. They strolled for a block without speaking until they reached the edge of the small plaza where a band played beneath a gazebo, the young female vocalist belting out a bluesy rendition of the Door's "Light My Fire".

Quist had bummed a cigarette off of one of the waiters and offered it to Carlotta, and after a moment of contemplation she grudgingly accepted it, allowing Quist to light it with the matchbook from the restaurant. They lingered at the edge of the crowd as she smoked the cigarette down to the filter. To his bemusement, she extinguished the butt by lifting her shoe and grinding it into her sole and then field stripping it.

"Last time I saw anybody do that was back in the army. You served?"

She glanced at him and shook her head. "I served, just not in the military," he thought he heard her murmur before she turned back to watch the band that had now slipped into some country ballad bemoaning about a woman done wrong. They watched in silence a moment longer before she nudged his arm. "Let's walk," she said.

The route she chose led them past the adobe façade of the La Fonda hotel and down a cobblestoned side street lined with Native American style jewelry and curio shops. Quist sensed she didn't want conversation as much as to just mindlessly gaze in the shop windows, so he held his silence.

"Would you like to come up to my room?" she asked, her

gaze fixed on a display window full of Western hats. The tone of her voice was not unlike someone asking directions of a stranger.

He met her eyes in the reflection of the store front window. "Miss…. What is your last name by the way?"

She didn't reply. The first thought that crossed his mind was that she was married and was worried he might try to look her up someday.

"Well then Carlotta, maybe you need to tell me what it is you're proposing so there aren't any misconceptions here."

She turned and looked at him. In the dim light it was difficult to gauge any emotion in her face. "If you don't want to, just say so," she said

"Look, I'm as big a hound as the next guy, but it's just that I like to know things about people, especially people I get close to."

"Who said anything about getting close?" she said with obvious irritation. "All you need to know is that it's been a while since I was with someone."

He shook his head in amusement. "You could start off by telling me what kind of a farm this was that you were living at? Was it some kind of religious cult? A convent maybe?"

"Yeah, something like that."

He had to admit he was curious, not just about the proposition but about the woman herself. He liked a bit of mystery in a woman. It always left something new to discover.

"So why me?"

She shrugged. "You seem decent enough, and the truth is, I don't think I want to be alone right now. Is that so hard to understand?"

"Maybe. But you give me pause. Hell, you might be one of those Black Widows."

She laughed in spite of herself. "At least see me to my web," she said, taking his arm.

She led him down a street that he realized ran parallel to the creek the locals mulishly referred to as the river. He recognized the skunky odor of chamisa wafting up from the dark unseen riverbed overlaid with the tang of riparian rot. The chorus of frogs almost drowned out the faint music drifting from the plaza.

"I don't want you getting the wrong idea," she said.

"Too late. I already have lots of wrong ideas. Most of them are pretty good, too."

They held their silence as they crossed a street and strolled though the thick-walled gateway of the Inn at Loretto. High dollar, Quist thought to himself as they walked through the entranceway. He waited off to the side as Carlotta retrieved her key from the concierge. The concierge, a young Asian woman, gave him a long glance as she handed the key to Carlotta.

Carlotta walked past him towards the elevator without meeting his gaze. Neither of them spoke until they reached her door.

"So? Are you coming in?" she asked.

He hesitated for half a beat. "I believe I will."

The room's walls were tinted a deep rose giving the room a warmth in spite of the cool night air coming from the open double French door across from the bed. The profile of the spotlighted, blocky spire of the cathedral filled the door's opening. She tossed her small handbag onto the desk and walked over and closed the French doors before sitting on the foot of the bed.

Quist surveyed the room from a vantage point just inside the door, for once unsure how to proceed. It all seemed a bit odd. Sure he had picked up women in bars before but something about Carlotta seemed off. Perhaps it was just her presumption of anonymity, even though that in itself wasn't all that unusual under the circumstances. It was more like simple intuition, a gut sense that it was unlikely he would ever plumb the depths of who she really was.

"I won't bite. I promise," she said, still sitting primly on the bed. When he made no effort to approach, she slipped off each of her shoes and then flopped back on the bed. She stared at the ceiling for a long moment, before sighing and turning her face towards him. She had a look that telegraphed first degree felony wistfulness, something with which he felt too well acquainted.

"Have you ever lost something?" she asked. "I mean like something you're sure is gone forever and then one day you find it. And you're not sure you really wanted to find it in the first place. Does that make any sense?"

"Just who might we be talking about here?"

"You seem wiser than the usual jackass," she said, her voice betraying more melancholia than sarcasm.

"Are you sure you want me to stay?"

She didn't reply, but looked back up at the ceiling.

"What I meant was it didn't seem you were talking about a piece of misplaced jewelry," he said.

"Please," she said so softly he might have imagined it.

Quist walked over to the bed and sat on the edge with his back to her and removed his shoes and his jacket. He lay beside her, pulling her into him. She didn't resist but instead clung to him. They remained like this for perhaps a minute or two before she turned her face up to his.

"No questions," she whispered. "I just want to be able feel something again." She undid one of his shirt buttons and slipped her hand inside. She patted his chest as if she were reassuring a child and then craned her neck to meet his lips with hers.

Her open mouth sought his, her tongue forcing open his lips. She tasted of mezcal and cigarettes. Before he was even aware of it, she had undone her blouse. As she sat up and stripped off her blouse, he noticed again the deep tan lines on her arms and neck. She was toned and buff like an athlete or a dancer might be. With one hand, she reached behind her and undid her bra. Then reaching across him, she turned off the lamp, leaving the room in darkness. She straddled him, and for a moment, seemed to hesitate before leaning over him to kiss him again. He cradled her with his arms and pulled her down atop him. She seemed to momentarily resist but then he realized she was merely struggling to remove her pants. They both sat up and hurriedly fought their way out of their clothes.

Nude, she fell onto her back, scooting towards the head of the bed, her hands gripping his. She tried to encircle him with her legs, but he pulled free.

"Wait," he said, gently pinning her arms to her side. He leaned down and kissed each of her breasts, his lips tweaking her spongy nipples. She made a sound as if she was coming up for air and he felt her shiver. With his tongue, he traced the contours of her ribs, her stomach, and the crease of her hips. She seemed to relax then, opening her legs to him. He kissed each of her thighs in turn before caressing with his tongue the soft cleft on either side of her vagina. She arched her hips, lifting her pubis to him. He tasted the salty tang of her labia and began to devour her with an intensity that almost seemed to make her pull away, but then he realized she was only opening herself still further. Reaching between her legs, he explored her with his fingers. It took a mere half a minute before she climaxed in a fit of un-restrained ecstasy and what almost sounded like laughter. She finally pushed his head away and gasped.

"There's a God after all," she whispered.

He slid up and laid beside her, spooning her, his arms encir-cling her waist. She shifted so she could face him and started to reach for his penis.

"No. Just stay still."

He placed his hand over her mons and held it there tightly much like one might caress a piece of ripe fruit. Her heat sur-prised him; a flash of memory of the same sensation and feel caused him to wince.

"What?" she whispered.

"Nothing. Cat ran over my grave."

"My mama used to say that."

"She passed on to?"

"Giving birth to my baby sister."

"You have a sister?"

She didn't reply for a long moment. "I guess so. We haven't spoken in a while."

"Because?"

"No reason. What happened here?" she asked, fingering the pockmarked scar on Quist's chest.

"I got shot."

"Oh yeah? And this one?" she asked, grazing her finger over the scar below his right eye.

"A bar fight of sorts. How about you tell me about yours?" he asked, touching the scar on her wrist.

"Kitchen fire. Tell me about your gunshot."

"Some other time."

"There won't be some other time." She started to pull away and instead reached down between his legs. "Ships passing in the night and all that crap. That's all. There's the here and now and that's all there is."

"A simple twist of fate. That's it? Some accident?"

"There are no accidents. If you want to call it fate, go ahead. It's just things happen. No matter what you do. Or don't do. "

She began to fondle his flaccid penis. Before he could respond, she rolled over on top of him. Crouching, she took him in her mouth and began a slow dance of fellatio. Once he was engorged, she withdrew and mounted him, her legs straddling his hips. She reached for his hands and brought them to her breasts as she lunged into him. The fury and intensity of her thrusts made him feel like he was being attacked by some hungry beast. It was all he could do but to hold on as she rode him wildly. In less than a minute, she climaxed again, her face contorted in joyous agony. She suddenly froze as if struck dumb, grunted, and collapsed on his chest.

"You've been saving up, haven't you?" he asked, caressing her buttocks. She didn't reply but just lay on top of him, her arms limp at her side. After a moment had passed, Quist reached down and lifted her face to his. Her eyes were closed, her lips moist with spittle. Her head felt heavy and as he slipped his hand from beneath her chin, her head dropped heavily on to his chest.

He clicked his tongue and looked up at the ceiling. He recalled a girl in college he once bedded that always fell asleep immediately after sex, but never before they were both satiated.

"Carlotta," he said, patting her buttock. When she didn't respond, he slid from beneath her and brushed the hair from her face. "Carlotta. Hey," he said softly, flicking on the lamp.

Her mouth was open now and it almost appeared that she had vomited something. He sat up and quickly rolled her over. "Wake up! Carlotta," he said, shaking her shoulder. She didn't respond.

"What the hell?" He leaned down and placed his ear on her

chest. He could hear a heartbeat, faint and slow but it was there. Glancing down at her, he could see her belly rise ever so slightly.

"Shit! Shit!" He looked around the room in some pathetic hope of…What? Help? An explanation for what had just happened? "Come on, don't do this," he said jumping to his feet. There was no telling what happened to her; too much booze. Maybe she had taken some pills. He glanced down at her once more and realized he better get help. He started for the phone, then leaned down and rearranged her on her side, propping her with a pillow so she wouldn't choke.

He dialed the operator who answered him so quickly he wondered if she somehow knew what had happened. "I have an emergency. Could you please call 911? I need paramedics. Room…Christ, I don't know."

"I have your room number, sir. What's the emergency?"

"A woman… A friend. She's collapsed. She's unconscious but she's breathing. Hurry. Get some EMS," he stammered and slammed down the phone. He collected his clothes and quickly dressed, his eyes never leaving Carlotta's inert form. She was still breathing. He could see that; shallow and slow, but still breathing. He covered her with a sheet before studying the room. He wasn't sure what he was looking for, but there had to be an answer for what had just happened. It had to be an overdose of some sort.

He picked up her small handbag. It was empty except for a small wallet. No pills. The same was true for the drawer next to the nightstand. Not even a Bible. A quick inventory of the bathroom revealed nothing either, just the usual cosmetics, and an almost full bottle of Tylenol. He flung open the closet. It looked empty except for a couple of blouses, a skirt and a pair of jeans, none of them appearing to have ever been worn. A sales tag dangled from one of the blouses.

Glancing down, he saw a pile of clothes in the corner. Rummaging through it, he realized it was the same clothes she had worn at the airport earlier that day. There was something else on the floor. The valise. He picked it up and opened it. There was a paperback, an envelope and a package or something wrapped in what appeared to be a pair of red lace panties. He pulled out the bundle and peeled off the panties.

"What in the hell?"

It was cash, and a lot of it; all of it wrapped neatly in bank bundles. He wrapped the money back up in the panties and stuffed it under his arm. Opening the envelope, he slid the contents into his hand. It was a passport. It looked new and never used. Flipping it open, he saw her photograph and beside it, her name.

Charlotte Louise Aucoin. Her date of birth, 18 Aug 1976. He stared at it for a moment before reinserting it into the envelope and dropping it back into the valise. Someone would come soon; if not EMS, than most likely hotel security. So should he leave the cash for them to find? Almost without thinking, he unwrapped the cash and began stuffing the bundles into his waist band. He was lucky he had recently lost some weight for the waistline of his pants gave him just enough room. He crammed the panties into his back pocket and pulled his shirt tails over his pants just as someone knocked on the door.

"Hotel Security. Miss Aucoin. Are you okay?" a voice yelled.

He glanced at her once more and moved to open the door.

12

There were details he didn't tell Roy; obviously not the sex. He thought it better to start at the end, relating the arrival of EMS, their triage and efficient evacuation of Charly to the emergency room. He glossed over the police interrogation at the hotel, alluding only to their curiosity regarding his presence in a hotel room with an unconscious nude woman and the fact he wasn't a registered guest. He did impart to Roy the hours he spent waiting for word in the ER and the vigil at Charly's bedside. But in the end he left out the details of the fifteen minutes he and Charly spent in her bed.

Now they sat there in the car in silence, Roy with her head against the window, Quist absently watching a family of tourists loading their gear into a SUV.

"Why did you stay with her? At the hospital?" she finally asked.

Quist fumbled for the right thing to say. He knew why he had stayed. Because she was alone, and no one should be alone when they're dying. It was a resolution born mostly out of his guilt. Nell had been alone in the trunk of the car. She would've heard the glass breaking, the screams of the mob, Quist calling her name as they dragged him from the back seat. Did she smell the gas? Or hear the explosion? Regardless, she had been alone. The bottom line was he didn't want Charly to be alone.

"I guess I stayed because there wasn't anyone else. Simple as that."

She nodded. After a moment, she said, "She told me I should forget about her. That I should stop coming to see her. She told me that on the last day I saw her." Roy turned away, and Quist could hear she was trying to stifle her sobs. "Shit. I forgave her."

"You forgave her. For what? Sending you away?"

Roy sniffled but didn't reply. "I think you should just drop me off at the nursing home," she said finally. "I appreciate your…" She fumbled for the words. "Your concern for Charly. But this really isn't any of your business."

Quist could still hear a twist of bitterness in her remark.

Quist shrugged. "That's where you're wrong. She made it my business when she invited me up to her room. And you showing up this morning made it my business. It's like I said, I'd be lying to you if I said I knew her. I guess I knew her as well as anyone can in four or five hours. Don't give me that look," he said when she shook her head. "How about then I say I would've liked to have known her. Shouldn't that be enough?"

She shook her head. "God, that sounds like a line from some day time soap."

He allowed himself to laugh. "Could be. I watched my share of them this past week. So? Do we have a deal?"

She turned and looked out the window. "I keep asking myself why Charly would've invited you to her room. What she saw in you." She looked back at him. "It's just that she wasn't right about too many things and sure as hell not about men. That said she was my big sister. I trusted her. She took care of things. She took care of me and…" She shook her head as if she were trying to shut something out. "But she could be stone blind when it came to men and money. Maybe she trusted you, but I haven't quite made up my mind."

Her eyes suddenly revealed a certain coldness. "You don't know me, Mr. Quist. You may think you do, but you don't. You didn't know her either. You best be careful. Maybe it's like you said, I'm a biter." She offered him a smile. "So take me to Placita de Vita. At least the name sounds hopeful."

Highly unlikely, Quist thought as he started up the car.

13

They found the nursing home on the edge of town at the end of a stretch of poorly maintained asphalt bordered by a scrubland of dense juniper and yellowing chamisa. The home, a rambling two story mish-mash of faux adobe and fake wood siding, stood a bit forlornly amidst a handful of dilapidated sheds and outbuildings. Hopeful was decidedly not the word that came to mind, Royale thought as Quist pulled up into the space labeled "Visitors" at the edge of the graveled parking lot. They exchanged glances and as Royale started to get out of the car, Quist reached for the bundle of cash.

"Best leave it here. No sense complicating matters," he said, stuffing the money beneath his seat.

Inside at the reception desk, a young Hispanic woman with a bad case of acne greeted them cheerfully and inquired if they were here to see a resident. Royale retrieved the card from her shirt pocket and handed it to the woman.

"A friend of ours was here a couple of day ago to see someone. I believe this was the room number," Royale said. "Anyway, before our friend left town she asked me to drop off something for this person. I'm sorry but I forget their name. I know I wrote it down somewhere but I must've misplaced it."

The woman glanced at the card. "Oh, yes. Mr. Eloquin. You know, I remember your friend." She hesitated. "Is she okay? She seemed pretty upset when she left here."

"Do you know why?" Quist asked.

The woman hesitated and looked around. "I know I shouldn't be saying this, but Mr. Eloquin is... I'll just say he can be difficult. Then again, he's not well."

They both waited for her to say more, but the woman most likely realized she had already said more than she should.

"We can see him though?"

"Sure, why not? You're only the second visitor he's ever had. He's been here three years and now two visitors in two days." She shrugged and pointed down the hallway to her right. "There's an elevator at the end. You'll find his room easy enough."

"Does the name Eloquin mean anything?" Quist asked as they walked away.

Royale shook her head. "I'm not sure. It sounds vaguely familiar. I guess I should've asked her his first name."

"You want me to go back and ask?"

Royale turned and looked back at the reception desk. The receptionist was nowhere in sight.

"Sure. If you don't mind. I'll wait for you at the elevator."

She waited until Quist reached the lobby before hurrying up the stairwell. Eloquin. She knew that name from somewhere. She was still filing through her memory when she stepped onto the second floor. Room 201 was just to her left. The door was open and what sounded to be a television turned to full volume blasted out into the hallway. The interior was dark even though it was almost noon. She lingered in the doorway for a few seconds to let her eyes adjust before entering. The room held the smell of sour body odor and something vaguely medicinal.

The figure reclining on the bed appeared not to notice her, his attention focused on the flickering blue gray screen of the TV. She approached the bedside and squinted in the murky light.

"Honey, would you get me my Pepsi?" he croaked.

"Who are you?" she asked.

It was only then he looked at her. She could now make out his face well enough. He didn't appear so much old as ravaged. His patchy, salt and pepper hair was shorn close to the skull. His sunken cheeks and eye sockets called to mind a photograph she had once seen of a German concentration camp survivor. He wore no yellow star though, just a faded and threadbare New Orleans Saint's T-shirt that hung on his cachectic frame like a piece of dingy laundry. Even in the dim light, she could see his eyes shone with a brightness that belied his other obvious frailties.

He studied her for a moment and then smiled. "I'll be. First she shows up and then you. I remember you. They used to call you Roy. Right?"

"Who are you?" she asked again, stepping away from the bed.

"You don't remember me, do you? I'mTommy. Tommy Eloquin," he said with a leering grin.

It came back to her then in a slurry of emotion. Bisco's bodyguard. At least that was how he always referred to himself, the reality being he was nothing more than a drug-addled go-fer and hanger on whose practiced menace came across as comically pathetic.

She stood there speechless, her stomach roiling with the memory of those days; images and snap shot vignettes of Charly and Bisco and her. And Lana. But Eloquin; she hadn't thought of him in years. He had disappeared from view and no one missed him or cared.

She glanced over her shoulder at the sound of someone in the doorway. Quist slipped in, shooting her a look of annoyance.

Eloquin shifted his gaze past her to Quist. "Who's your friend?"

"Why did she come here?" Royale asked.

Eloquin nodded and glanced back up at the television. Royale scooped up the remote control from Eloquin's lap and without taking her eyes from him, turned off the TV. "I asked you. Why was she here?"

He looked back at her and licked his lips. "My Pepsi. Then we'll talk."

"Quist, would you get this fucking asshole his Pepsi?"

Quist smiled, obviously amused by her outburst of profanity and walked out.

"You don't look so different," Eloquin said. "Filled out a little. You two still resemble each other though. I always thought you were the prettier one though."

She remembered his salacious leering, how he would undress her with his eyes. The Prince of Creeps is what Charly called him. Quist came back with a can of Pepsi which he opened and handed to Eloquin, who snatched the can, his hands shaking like a drunk. He took a long pull and smacked his lips.

"I suppose you're here for more money. There ain't none. That was the last of my blood money. I told her that."

"Blood money? What are you talking about?"

"She didn't tell you? That don't surprise me none." He looked up at them, his eyes bleary and bloodshot. "I'll tell you like I told her. They say I'm running out of time. So I figure it's time to make amends. Besides, I can't take it with me." He laughed, a dry chuckle that ended in a coughing fit that lasted the better part of a half a minute. He snatched a Kleenex from a box beside his leg and cleared his throat, launching a wad of phlegm into the tissue. Wiping his mouth with the edge of the sheet, he groped his hand along the side of the bed until he found the oxygen mask. Slapping it over his face, he took several deep breaths, all the while his eyes never leaving Royale. He dropped the mask and panted.

"See, I got the lung cancer. Doc gives me maybe a couple of months. I do believe your sister would've liked to hustle me along sooner." He smiled. "About two o'clock this morn I sort of was wishing she would've done it."

"Why did she come here?" Royale asked again.

"Because I wrote her and asked her to. I knew she was in that prison. I never thought she'd get out before I passed on. But I wanted her to know. I wanted to give her that money, not that it makes up for what I done. I thought it might go a little ways in balancing the sheets."

"What are you talking about?"

"I'm guessing she didn't tell you?" His face suddenly took on the look of a wary rodent. Just as quickly it was replaced by a look of what could only be called amusement. "My, my. She's holding out on you. Wonder why."

"You want to know why she didn't tell me? Because my sister's dead, That's why. Now you want to tell me what this is about?"

Again, his face revealed a gallery of different reactions; surprise, disbelief and finally what Royale assumed was mere disappointment.

"What happened?' he asked, his voice strained.

"It doesn't matter. She died. We never had a chance to talk," Royal said, her irritation almost getting the best of her.

Eloquin stared at her for a long moment before taking another swallow of his Pepsi. He looked away and sighed. When he looked back at her, his eyes were moist. "I told her about Lana. The kid. I told her she didn't die on that boat like everyone thought she did. Hell, she's still alive. Least ways as far as I know."

14

Quist watched Roy stiffen and then slump.

"What did you say?" she stammered, her face ashen and contorted in a look of disbelief.

Eloquin swiped at his eyes and looked away. Quist, who up until now had hung back, brushed Roy aside and stepped up to the bedside. Leaning over, his face inches from Eloquin's, he said softly, "Listen, Tommy because I'm only going to say this once. From this point on, everything you say better be the truth and nothing but the truth or I'll rip those filthy, diseased lungs right out through your ass. Is that understood?"

Eloquin didn't react for a few seconds before smiling. "You don't scare me. I got lots worse things to be afraid of. So who are you? The boyfriend or just pretty muscle?"

"I'm going to be your goddamn undertaker if you don't tell us what you're talking about," Quist replied, looking back over his shoulder at Roy, who met his gaze with a mixture of confusion and what at first seemed anguish but Quist now sensed was panic.

Eloquin took another swallow of Pepsi, cleared his throat, and took another hit of the oxygen. He stared at each of them in turn before going on.

"I thought your sister oughta know," he said, his voice suddenly stronger. "I can't take back what happened. I couldn't give her back those years she spent locked up. But I couldn't let it go." He fell silent for a long moment. "I couldn't face my maker without least ways telling her."

Roy approached the bed and looked down at him. Quist sensed something welling up inside her that he couldn't decipher: anger, grief, or something that she herself couldn't quite yet claim.

"You goddamn toad," she said, her voice low and venomous.

Eloquin held up his hands and looked at Quist hoping he might restrain her. "Look, I'll tell you everything. Okay?"

Quist took a step back.

"She didn't know I was there. On the boat, I mean. You know. When she killed Bisco. Neither did the cops. You see, I was up on top of the cabin sleeping one off when it all went down. I never heard when your sister first showed up but later I heard the ruckus, the two of 'em arguing. I gotta say that bastard Bisco had it coming. Taking the girl from her mother and all," he said, his eyes fixed on Roy. "I never could figure out why he took the kid. Pure spite is maybe all it was. Taking a child from its mother." After a few beats, Eloquin lowered his gaze and fumbled for the oxygen mask. He took a couple of deep breaths before going on.

"I heard that first shot. Heard Bisco yelling. And then two more. By then I'm wondering what the hell. All I could hear was your sister calling for the kid. Next thing I know there's this explosion and my ass is out in the water. Fire everywhere. I read in the newspaper what they figured happened. How one of them bullets went right through the cabin floor and into the engine compartment. The cops said from what they figured the bullet nicked a fuel line and that's what started the fire. Tanks were full, too. I topped 'em off myself."

He paused as if replaying something in his mind. "This dinghy," he said after a moment. "The one your sister used to come out to the boat was blown clear somehow. Anyway, I got in it and that's when I heard the kid screaming her head off. She'd been blown clear, too. Her hair and clothes were almost burned off, half-drowned, but other than that she was okay. I hauled her in. I don't recall a lot of things. It all happened so fast. I just remember the boat being on fire and it sinking right fast. I never saw Charly. You have to believe me. Things might've been different if I would've known she made it."

"Where is she?" Roy asked evenly, her voice without emotion."What did you do with Lana?"

For the first time, Eloquin seemed overcome with what Quist guessed might be a measure of remorse for he let out a sudden sob and raised his hand to his face. His body shook as he quietly cried. He started to cough, prompting another choking fit. Quist thrust the box of Kleenex in Eloquin's other hand. He spit a mouthful of phlegm into his hand and turned away as if embarrassed. No one said anything for perhaps a minute.

"What did you do with her?" Roy asked again, her voice now filled with anger.

Eloquin took a deep breath and looked at his hands, unwilling to meet Roy's gaze. "I sold her."

Before Quist could react, Roy leaped onto the bed and began pummeling Eloquin with first her fists and then with the television remote. It took all of his Quist's strength to pull her away. She swung at Quist, grazing his cheek with the remote. Her screams had alerted the staff for within seconds a pair of nursing aides, one of them a burly young man with a tear drop tattoo below one eye, burst into the room.

"Don't worry, guys," Quist said, trying to defuse the situation. "You know how families get sometimes," he said, still struggling to subdue Roy.

"Are you okay, Tommy?" the young man asked, nudging Quist aside.

Eloquin flopped back onto his pillow and held up his hand. His mouth had been bloodied and there was a bright purple welt on the side of his forehead. "Like the man said," he wheezed. "Family shit. Get out of here. Go on now. I'm okay." He looked at Roy, his eyes revealing a sudden defiance. "Yeah, I sold her. Had to. I needed money, too. I wasn't long for New Orleans, not with those bookies on my ass."

"You fucking sold her?" Roy wailed. "Where is she, goddammit?" She pulled free and Quist caught her just before she was about to launch another onslaught. "Let me go," she yelled, kicking at Quist's shins.

"Ease up and let him talk," he said, jerking her away. He

looked at Eloquin. "You better be giving us some answers or I let her go."

Eloquin wiped the blood from his mouth. "You gotta understand. I'm not proud of what I done. She promised me she'd take good care of Lana. She said she took good care of all her girls. I tell you. If I would've a known Charly didn't die it would've been different."

Roy let out a sob. "Lana had family, goddammit. She had me."

Eloquin glared at her. "You weren't fit to be no mother. I heard Charly talk about you. I heard stories. You weren't no better than one of those Canal Street hookers."

Roy slumped as if deflated by these words. "She was mine. You had no right."

Quist half-carried her to the chair and deposited her there, still wary of what she might do. "You said she," he said, turning back to Eloquin. "Who did you sell her to?"

Eloquin took a hit of oxygen and looked up at him. "A woman by the name of Mercedes Schoenfeld. Least that's what she called herself, but I wouldn't put much stock in that. I told your sister where she could probably find her though. The last I heard she moved her operation down to Old Mexico."

"Where in Mexico?"

"A place called San Miguel de Allende. Maybe you heard of it? Lots of Americans down there."

Quist glanced back at Roy who sat there quietly as if in a stupor.

"What else? There must be something else you can tell us about this Schoenfeld woman."

Eloquin shook his head in resignation. "She was into horses. Race horses and such. She had her fingers in lots of pies. That's how I met her. Through Bisco."

The word Bisco seemed to stir Roy from her fugue. She stood as if to leave. "How much? How much did you sell her for? At least tell me that," she said, her voice again curiously devoid of emotion.

Eloquin looked at her. "Five thousand and change, sorry to

say."

Roy nodded as if in a daze and stalked out of the room. Quist shook his head in disgust and looked down at Eloquin. "That's all?"

"Shit, man. That was all fifteen years ago."

Quist walked over to the door and quietly closed it. He then picked up the TV remote and turned up the volume.

"What are you doing?" Eloquin asked.

Quist picked up a clipboard from the end of the bed and removed the ballpoint pen attached to it. "I was in the Army. A MP. You know. Military Police. Anyway, back in basic training they taught us this little trick. The 'come along' was what they called it. They said you could get anybody to come along with you. Get it?" he said, holding up the pencil before Eloquin's face. "If we found some GI in a drunken stupor. Or a guy high on speed and itching for a fight. The generally non-complaint. They could all be brought around with just a pen. The come along. I have to say it usually worked pretty good."

Quist reached for Eloquin's hand who tried to pull free, but he was no match for Quist who quickly jammed the pen between two of Eloquin's fingers.

"It's pretty simple," Quist said, grasping Eloquin's hand tightly. "You put this between a guy's fingers, right up here in the web, high up. I'm guessing there's a nerve there. As bony as your hand is, it should work pretty good."

Quist squeezed and Eloquin gasped in pain. He squeezed harder and Eloquin started to scream but Quist quickly placed his hand over his mouth.

"Sshhhh. Sshhhh. Are you ready to tell me some more?"

Eloquin, his eyes watering, nodded. Quist eased up on his hand, but left the ball point in place.

"This Schoenfeld woman. She bought these girls," he said, the words tumbling out. "Trained 'em herself is what I heard. To her standards, she liked to say. That way she could get more money for 'em."

"Who'd she sell them to?"

"How should I know? No wait. Shit!" he yelped as Quist

gave his hand a squeeze. "Alright, alright. She sold them to guys like the Marcello's. Mobbed up guys. Guys looking for high class cooze. I know what you're gonna ask," he whispered, anticipating the squeeze. "I got no idea where they went from there."

"So why send Charly to Mexico? That was fifteen years ago. Even if Schoenfeld's there, why did you think she'd know where Lana is?"

Eloquin looked away. Quist started to squeeze his hand.

"Stop it, please. Goddammit! I'll tell you. I sold her other girls. Quite a few of 'em. Runaways and such. Girls with nothing to lose."

"You fucking asshole."

"Thing is, I sold her a couple a girls not even a year or so ago. Not any teenage runaways either. Fine Ukrainian cooze right off the boat. I met up with Mercedes at one of those whadda you call 'em? Boutique hotels, right? Somewhere down in the French Quarter. She had these two young gals with her. A nigger and white girl. Both of 'em around twenty I'd guess. And both of 'em acting like Mercedes was their mama or something. Anyway, Mercedes asks me if I remember who the one of 'em was. The white girl. She called her Luna. She said I sold her this girl fifteen years back. Told me I shouldn't feel too sorry for selling her these girls. Said she treats 'em like they're her daughters."

He looked up at Quist. "It was her alright. Charly's kid. I swear to it. I saw this scar she had on the back of her hand. You know. From the fire."

"And this Schoenfeld woman is in San Miguel? You're sure about that?"

"She let slip that's where she was living. That's all I know. I swear."

"Any ideas how I'd find her?"

"She said she still was breeding race horses. I guess you could ask around and... Goddammit! Please. Stop," he squawked as Quist squeezed his hand. "That's all I know, I swear," he sobbed.

Quist let go of his hand and leaned down until his face was

inches from Eloquin's.

"Jesus, you smell bad. You smell like something dead," Quist said, pulling away. He glanced up at the television screen. Some cooking show was on. The chef, an overweight guy in an Aloha shirt, was sautéing something that looked like a heart attack. Quist turned back and hurled the TV remote at Eloquin's head, barely missing him.

"Have a nice life, Tommy," he said and walked out.

15

Quist caught up with her at the car. She was leaning over with her hands on her thighs, her breakfast at her feet. She gave him a sidelong glance as she wiped the slobber from her mouth.

"You okay?"

She straightened, and without meeting his eyes, got into the car.

He gave her a moment before joining her. She turned away, her face against the window. He waited, torn between the awkwardness of the moment and his uncertainty over how much to reveal to her of what Eloquin had told him. Opting for nondisclosure, he started up the car and began to back up.

"What else did he tell you?" she asked without turning.

He thought for a moment before slipping the car into neutral. "He told me he saw her. Lana. A year or so ago. She was with this Schoenfeld woman."

Royale sat mutely for a moment before reaching beneath the seat for the bundle of money. She started to reach for the door handle.

"Whoa, whoa. What are you doing?" he said, grasping her arm.

"I want to talk to him. And give him his goddamn blood money back."

"Trust me. I got it all out of him," Quist said, snatching the bundle of money from her hands. "And the chances are we might need that money."

"We?"

"I told you I'm in this, like it or not. Bottom line, you'll need me if you expect to get any answers. You forget I've dealt with these sort of people."

"These sort of people? Fuck you, Quist."

"Harlan. Fuck you, Harlan."

"You may have dealt with bad guys, but every day I deal with their leftovers. What they do to women. So don't tell me..."

"Hold on. I was just saying Eloquin saw her and she looked okay. He said that it seemed the woman was taking care of her. Like Lana was her daughter was how he put it. And yeah that was a year ago, but it means if Lana's not in San Miguel, then this Schoenfeld ought to at least know where might be. Maybe she can be persuaded to tell us where she is. Maybe I can do that."

Roy didn't say anything for a moment. "Okay. So now what?"

"Well, if we're going to Mexico you're going to need a passport. And that may take..."

"I have one," she said, cutting him off. "It's back in my bag at your hotel."

Quist shook his head. "Why do I hear alarm bells ringing? I mean, why do you carry a passport to come to New Mexico? Or are you one of those people who don't realize it's part of the US?"

"It's my ID. I don't have a driver's license."

"Now I'm really suspicious. No driver's license. Tell me something. Does that passport have the name Royale Aucoin on it?"

"You're paranoid. I just don't drive. I haven't for years."

"I take it you don't have a hotel room. I'll get you one later. Meantime, I'll drop you off at the La Fonda." He reached into his shirt pocket as he slipped the car back into reverse. "Here's my key card. Go up to my room, clean up and get some rest."

"And what are you going to do?"

"I think I'll see what I can find out about this Schoenfeld woman."

An hour later, he sat sipping an Americano on the patio of a Starbucks in a shopping mall on the city's north side. Finding a parking spot had been hellish, the parking lot filled with cars circling in pursuit of a space. Meanwhile, hordes of pedestrians hauling rolled up blankets and folding beach chairs streamed through the lot. They resembled a throng of oddly equipped refugees all fleeing in one direction. He was contemplating getting a refill of his coffee when CdeBaca strolled up and dropped heavily into the opposite chair.

"I sort of thought I'd be hearing from you," CdeBaca said in lieu of a greeting. He appeared to be wearing the same suit he wore that night in the hospital, only this time he wore a bright red polyester shirt, and instead of a bolo, a thin blue tie splattered with a pattern of what looked like tiny howling coyotes. Quist wondered if the put upon look of fatigue on the detective's face was practiced or real.

"Like I told you on the phone, I need a favor."

CdeBaca shifted his chair so as to better view the parking lot before replying. "We should've met somewhere else. Traffic is gonna really suck in another half hour."

"Is this all about the Zozobra thing?"

"Yep, sorry to say. At least most of the bars around here are closing early. Too bad about the Aucoin woman. The one nurse at the hospital told me you seemed to care about the lady. Is that a fair assumption? If so, then I'm guessing this has something to do with her. Or maybe her sister. What kind of favor are you looking for?"

Quist started at the beginning. Against his better judgment he told CdeBaca about the money he found in Charly's room and why he had kept it. This elicited the slightest twitch of CdeBaca's eyebrows, but no comment. He told her about how he met up with Royale, the Placita de Vida and Tommy Eloquin's story. Only once did CdeBaca motion for him stop while he reached into his coat pocket to retrieve a small notepad and a pen. When Quist was finished, the detective flipped through his notes before tossing the notepad on the table.

"So I'm guessing you want to know about this Schoenfeld woman."

"That and the real story behind what happened on that boat."

"From what I've been led to believe, what happened on that boat is likely to be a hodgepodge of bullshit and conjecture. But I'll try. As far as Schoenfeld's sheet goes, I might be able to help you there. I can access NCIC's data base, and if that doesn't turn up anything, I've got a brother in law who's a computer jockey at the FBI in D.C. If there's anything at all, the Feds are likely to have it."

"How soon can you find out? The sister is biting on the bit."

"So what's your take on her? She seemed a bit   How can I put this? High strung? Maybe it was just the shock of her sister dying. I used to think I could read people, but something about her seemed off."

"From what I gather they used to be close, until they weren't. They didn't talk for ten years."

"Bad blood?"

"Not exactly."

CdeBaca shook his head. "It's funny. When I told her the circumstances. About the two of you together in that hotel room. I know," he said in response to Quist's look of annoyance. "I felt she deserved to know is all. Anyway, all she said was 'well that would be just like her' or something to that effect. Seemed odd is all."

"Here's my cell number. In case you forgot, I'm staying at the La Fonda. Anything you find would be greatly appreciated," Quist said, pushing back his chair.

"What about this Eloquin guy? What with the statute of limitations, him being the only witness, and what I know about the Louisiana judicial system, I can't see there being much point in rousting him. I'll pay him a visit though. If nothing else but to just verify his account."

"I wouldn't expect anything less. I tell you what," Quist said, reaching into his wallet and pulling out a twenty. He laid it on the table. "Why don't you buy him a couple cartons of cigarettes?"

16

Housekeeping had cleared Quist's room of the litter of takeout food cartons and used towels. Other than the nearly empty bottle of Gray Goose sitting undisturbed on the table, the room appeared unoccupied. Royale stood there a moment surveying the room before tossing her suitcase onto the carefully turned back bed. Part of her wanted to take a shower, pop a sleeping pill and pass out in the hope when she awoke all of this might simply be a bad dream.

When the police had called to notify her about Charly it seemed all too unreal. On the one hand, Charly hadn't been part of her life for almost ten years. On the other, the specter of Charly's upcoming release and possible reentry into Royale's life haunted her every waking moment. It went beyond guilt. Royale's life was different now, and any reminder of the past, any accusation and admonition threatened to upend the equilibrium it had taken a decade for her to attain. And now she felt as if that bastard Eloquin had kicked the chair out from beneath her.

She worried at what Quist might have learned from Eloquin after she left. If Quist knew something he wasn't telling her, he didn't let on. And what if she allowed him to tag along with her to Mexico? She would most likely have to reveal things at some point.

She thought back to what Eloquin had told them about Lana. Never in a million years had she expected that kind of revelation. Lana was dead; to her, to everybody. The past was dead. Charly was dead. Why couldn't it all just stay that way? She cursed herself for thinking that Lana was better off if she had died. Maybe I'm still the same selfish bitch I was twenty years ago, she thought as she opened her suitcase.

And now Quist, a man she knew virtually nothing about might become privy to all those secrets. She still didn't know if she fully trusted him. First, there was the matter of the money. She cursed herself for not asking Eloquin how much money he had given Charly. Who knows? Quist could have easily taken the lion's share of it. It would've been easy enough to do. Perhaps the only reason Quist might be willing to accompany her to Mexico was the chance there might be more money involved. Everything about him seemed mercenary.

She glanced around the room and wondered if he might be hiding more cash somewhere. She got up and went to the closet. A small safe sat on the floor. It was locked of course. Who knows what he had secreted there. She flipped through the few clothes hanging there and then ran her hand along the shelf above her head. Nothing. She pulled out his suitcase and opened it. It contained an extra set of underwear and some shirts, a couple of paperbacks, and a map of Santa Fe. She quickly rummaged through the pile of dirty laundry tucked in the corner of the closet, but again found nothing.

She glanced back at the bed. Some instinct caused her to get down on her knees and look beneath the bed. There was something there, a briefcase from the looks of it. As she began to drag it out she noticed a second smaller case. She retrieved them both and deposited them on the bed. Opening the smaller of the two, she realized at once what it was. A gun case, the empty shape of an automatic molded into the foam. Maybe that was in the safe. Along with the money.

She nudged it aside and opened the larger briefcase. It held a sheaf of papers that proved to be nothing more than some bank statements, a few blank copies of what appeared to be a contract for his services, some travel brochures for various places in the Caribbean, and an IPod. She started to close the case when she noticed something else; a small white sliver of something protruding from the lining at the bottom of the case. She picked at it with her fingernail. It was something plastic. She realized there was another compartment artfully concealed beneath the lining.

She gave the lining a cursory tug, and when it didn't give, she worked a finger under the corner until she found the metal snap hidden there.

It took a moment of vigorous prying before she was able to lift it up. Sure enough, it was a clear plastic sleeve of the kind one used to protect paper. She could see it contained a folded, somewhat yellowed newspaper. Slipping it from the sleeve, she unfolded it. Tucked inside the pages was a 4x6 color photograph of an attractive young blonde woman wearing a military dress uniform. She turned it over. Scribbled in red ink was the single word Nell. She laid it aside and looked at the newspaper. It was a copy of the 'Stars and Stripes'. If she remembered correctly, it was an Army newspaper. She had seen one once at a bar outside of Fort Polk. Studying it more closely, she saw it was the Baghdad edition and was dated November 13th 2007.

She quickly scanned the front page for anything that might have mentioned Quist. Seeing nothing, she looked at the second page. Nothing. She went back to the front page and began to study each article. At the bottom, a small caption read "Ambush Outside of the Green Zone Kills Five Military Police." The short article detailed how a convoy of two Military Police vehicles had been ambushed outside of the Palestine Hotel just outside of the Green Zone. A rocket propelled grenade had destroyed a HumVee carrying three of the soldiers. An Army sedan carrying a driver and two MP officers had been attacked by gunfire at the hotel's entrance. Witnesses report both of the officers had been wounded and then taken captive by unknown assailants. A subsequent investigation determined that they were driven to a Baghdad suburb where one of them, later identified as Captain Nell Doyle, died when the car they had been taken in exploded after catching fire. Details of exactly what occurred, the article said, remained under investigation. Two other bodies, presumed to be the kidnappers, also died in the explosion. The sole surviving soldier, identified as Warrant Officer Harlan Quist, suffered injuries in the explosion but was expected to survive. At the time of this publication, few other details were known about the nature of their mission or why they had ventured out of the Green

Zone without sufficient back up.

The second page appeared to be dated two weeks later. Beneath a list of weekly casualties was a short blurb mentioning a court of inquiry had been established to investigate the death of the five military police officers in the ambush outside of the Palestine Hotel. The only available witness to the ambush and subsequent explosion and fire that killed a fellow officer was Warrant Office Harlan Quist of the Criminal Investigation Division. He was expected to be released from the hospital and testify the following day.

Royale inserted the clippings and the photograph back into the sleeve and carefully slipped them into the hidden compartment before sliding both the cases back under the bed. All of us with our goddamn secrets, she thought going over to the table and picking up the bottle of Gray Goose. She took a long swallow and then removed her toiletry bag and a change of underwear and clothes and went to take a shower.

When she came out of the bathroom twenty minutes later still drying her hair, Quist was sitting on the bed. She glanced at her open suitcase and guessed he had gone through her things also. Trust or the lack of it was obviously a two-way street.

"You clean up nice," he commented.

She had stuffed herself into a pair of jeans she hadn't worn in a couple of years and a light cashmere sweater she hadn't worn in at least fifteen years.

"Did you sleep?"

"What do you think?"

Glancing out the window, she could see the low hills to the west had turned purple in the approaching dusk.

"Are you hungry?" he asked.

"Not particularly."

"Then let's walk. They're burning Old Man Gloom tonight. Sounds like just what we need."

17

As they walked across the Plaza and down the crowded streets that led to the park, Quist told Roy what he had learned about the celebration from the bartender at his hotel. The bartender, an elderly Cuban gentleman, related how the word Zozobra was an old timey Spanish term for anxiety, or sometimes sadness. He went on to describe how the Burning of Zozobra or Old Man Gloom had been a yearly tradition and part of Fiestas de Santa Fe since the early twenties. From its humble beginnings, it had grown to a fête attended by upwards of fifty thousand people who would show up to chant 'burn baby, burn' in an almost pagan orgy of music and dance.

Needless to say, the burning of the fifty foot tall papiermâché marionette was a much anticipated event by the locals, providing them the chance to discard their troubles before winter set in, and sometimes discard things more material; photos of unfaithful or spurned lovers, divorce papers, pathology reports, bankruptcy notices and the like, all of which were stuffed into the effigy the week before the burning. The bartender revealed he had once slipped a bundle of papers beneath Zozobra's robe; a yellowed packet of love letters from a woman in Havana he had once wooed before the Revolution. It gave him great relief, he said, for it had freed him to pursue a widow woman that lived down the street.

"And did it work out? With the widow woman?" Quist had asked.

The old Cuban smiled and shrugged. "In some ways."

"Maybe we should burn the money," Roy said as they waded through a crowd of people watching a passing parade of a children's dance troupe dressed in Spanish colonial costume. "As far as I'm concerned it's blood money. Maybe it would do us all some good to come clean. Burn up things that remind us of the past." She gave him an odd look.

"Then burn it. It's only money. Your money. But like I said, it might come in handy."

They passed El Meson, the tapas bar where Quist had met Charly. What had it been? It seemed longer ago than two days. He briefly contemplated pointing it out to Roy but changed his mind, for he had still not processed in his own mind how he felt about that evening. Telling her would only lead to questions he wasn't prepared to answer.

They walked in silence through the gathering dusk, the crowds denser now as they approached the imposing pink façade of the Scottish Rite Temple. Quist sensed an almost palpable aura of anxiety in Roy. Her head began to swivel from side to side and over her shoulder as if she was looking for an escape route.

"Is there something wrong?" he asked.

She looked at him, her eyes revealing mild angst. "You mind if we stop for a minute?" she asked. "I'm not much for crowds."

"How about over there," he said, pointing to a manicured, park-like enclosure across the street. Quist picked a spot on a low stone wall where they could watch the passersby from the relative safety of a gigantic pine tree. He retrieved a flask of vodka from his jacket and offered it to her. She stared at it as if it were some wholly foreign object before plucking it from his fingers and bringing it to her lips. Her eyes fixed on his, she tilted it and drank what he guessed was most of its contents.

"I had you pegged as the type that ascribed to the notion that the body is your temple."

She gave him a cold, hard glance and took another pull from the flask.

"I myself always considered my body an amusement park," he said, observing with dismay as she appeared to empty the flask. "Although lately it seems I'm spending too much time in the House of Horrors."

The remark earned from her a semblance of a smile. She handed him back the empty flask. They waited in silence as the darkness fell and the crowds had thinned to the point Quist figured they were safe to walk again. She didn't resist him taking her hand and leading her back into the street.

"Thanks," she said. "The vodka helped. Where are we going?"

"The other day I saw some houses up this street. Maybe we can see something from there."

Halfway down the street, they encountered a barricade manned by a couple of uniformed cops and a sign stating the road was closed except for residents. Quist approached the older of the two cops, a rangy looking sunburned guy who already looked prepared to turn them away. Quist reached inside his coat pocket and pulled out his wallet which he held up for the cop to see. The cop shined his flashlight at it and studied it for a moment before waving them on.

"What did you show him?"

"My old ATF ID card. When they shit canned me, I had to turn in my shield but I told them I lost my ID in Africa. It comes in handy now and then."

They walked a couple of blocks up the street, the few passersby obviously residents of the neighborhood gauging from their lack of blankets or picnic items. "See that house up there?" He pointed to an adobe structure further up the street that sat perched on a terrace overlooking the street. "I bet if we sat on those steps we could see something."

Sure enough, the narrow stone stairway afforded an unobstructed view of the park and the gigantic, white robed marionette, its puppet-like arms flailing stiffly to the beat of Santana's Black Magic Woman. In some ways, it resembled some crude doll from a child's playhouse, its oversize head crowned with coarse yellow curls, its facial features a crude caricature. No sooner had they settled onto the steps when a woman's voice called to them from the balustrade above them.

"You're more than welcome to come up here and watch," she said. "We've got some wine."

Quist looked at Roy who merely shrugged in acceptance. They joined the woman, a rotund Hispanic in perhaps her sixties and a short balding younger guy wearing motorcycle leathers and sporting enough silver on his wrists and neck to drown a mule. The woman poured them each a full paper cup of red wine from a cardboard carton resting at her feet. They all sipped the wine and made casual conversation for perhaps fifteen minutes before the couple excused themselves and went inside. Several minutes later, Quist caught the unmistakable scent of marijuana wafting through the open windows.

As Quist refilled their cups, the effigy of Old Man Gloom began bawling mournfully as a group of white robed dancers wearing peaked hats reminiscent of those worn by the KKK gyrated at its feet in an ever increasing frenzy. The crowd had meanwhile grown more boisterous, their anticipation palpable in the still, cooling air. In the time they were watching, the sky had become clotted with thick gray clouds, shutting out any appreciation of the stars. In the closeness of the lowering sky and the spectacle before them, it felt like they were standing in the wings of a stage as the curtain was about to go up.

"Who was Nell?" Roy asked abruptly.

Quist turned and looked at her, momentarily taken aback by this unexpected mention of Nell's name. It took him a few seconds to sort out her query.

"Let me guess. You were looking for money. Did you think to check behind the toilet tank or maybe peel back the goddamn carpet?"

She looked at him. In the dim light he could see her face registering a look of both embarrassment and dismay. She started to say something but instead looked away.

Quist finished his wine and then crumpled the cup and tossed it on the ground. "I knew this guy once. Everett was his name. He was like a fucking cat. In the sense he had nine lives. When he was just a kid he almost drowned in a stock tank. When he was nineteen he survived a car wreck that killed his best friend. And I was right behind him when this IED in Baghdad blew his HumVee to hell. He only lost an arm. Six years later he got diagnosed with stage four colon cancer. The point of this story is I went to visit him once at the VA, and he's sitting there in his hospital bed hopped up on pain pills and these Jim Beam popsicles his girlfriend was bringing him. He had tubes everywhere. IVs, piss tubes, tubes draining his bowels. And he says to me 'Don't bother looking for signs of life, asshole. You're wasting your time.'

"You see, back when I was an Army cop we had to write up after action reports on roadside bombings and such. By the time we'd show up everything was cordoned off, the fires put out. But the bodies would sometimes still be there. Everett always got irritated when I wanted to examine the bodies. I'm just looking for signs of life, I would tell him. Maybe they're not dead. I'd tell him that it's been known to happen. I always thought just once I'd find somebody still alive and I would save somebody. I used to always dream about it. Still do from time to time."

He paused for a moment as the crowd in the park momentarily fell silent. Someone was making some kind of speech over the PA system. He looked at Roy. She was watching him not the crowd.

"Some years back I started to see this lady shrink. She surmised I had spent a good part of my life trying to make things right. Trying to save people. Looking for signs of life metaphorically speaking." He looked away, unable to go on with what he was about to say and still be able to look at Royale straight on. "I couldn't save Nell. No signs of life. That's all you need to know."

"She meant something to you though, right? I mean…"

"Drop it. Okay?"

He looked back at the crowd who renewed their pleas. Burn him, burn him, they chanted. Something about their fervor stirred some inchoate dread.

"I'm sorry. I didn't mean to snoop. I guess I had to know if I could trust you."

"I can understand that. In the future, just ask. So how about in this newfound climate of trust, you unburden yourself and tell me about your sister and what happened on that boat?"

She didn't reply at first but instead sipped at her wine as if buying time. He could tell when someone was editing a story in their mind. What to leave in, what to leave out. He had done it himself often enough. In the ensuing silence, he studied her profile in the reflected light. He could see now the resemblance between her and Charly. The line of the jaw, the deep set eyes that he knew to be the exact honey color as her sisters'. Royale's nose was finer, long and slender. And then there was their shape; the full breasts, the loose-hipped gait. He sensed there was something else similar; a vulnerability thinly concealed by a projection of toughness. He wondered how much of her bravado might be mere pretense.

She stared down at the street below for a long moment before speaking. "This Bisco guy that Charly shot," she finally said. "Her so called husband. He had this big fishing boat he kept out on Lake Pontchartrain. It's where he did most of his business. If that's what you'd call it. He dealt drugs and guns mostly. Whatever scraps the Marcellos left on the table. You know, the local Mafia family.

"He was a low life living the high life is how Charly used to always put it. And Charly sure did like the high life. It's what first attracted her to Bisco, and it's why she was willing to look the other way. He was a charmer. I'll grant him that, and in the beginning, he treated her really nice. Bought her things, helped out my dad. Helped me," she added so softly he barely heard her over the crowd's chanting.

"But one thing I've learned is that men are all dogs. Sooner or later they all bark. Just took a little time. First, came the verbal abuse. Then the controlling. The threats. And finally, he started knocking her around. Never bad enough that makeup couldn't hide the bruises. And then he tried to take Lana away from her. You see, Lana wasn't Bisco's kid. Then again, she really wasn't Charly's either." She looked at him. "Lana was my daughter."

18

But I'm guessing you already figured that out. I'm sure Eloquin told you."

"He didn't have to. I suspected something like that. If you recall you said something about her belonging to you."

"She never belonged to me. I was her mother but she never belonged to me. I was…" she mumbled, her voice trailing off.

The crowd below erupted in a cheer. Someone carrying a torch had sprinted up to the feet of the now wildly gyrating effigy and tossed the torch at its long white flowing robe. It took a moment for the flames to catch, but suddenly the robe ignited. In the same instant, a cascade of fireworks erupted from behind the effigy's head, inciting a new round of baleful moaning and spastic swinging of its arms. The crowd cheered even louder. They watched in fascination for a minute or so as the figure became engulfed in flames, revealing in its fatal glow the thousands of upturned faces of the celebrants.

"I was fifteen." She had to shout in order to be heard over the roar of the crowd and the fireworks. "I got pregnant by this boy who I thought at the time walked on water. But he was just treading it, just like me. It was about then that Charly took up with Bisco. She saved me. She saved Lana. She knew I wasn't capable of being a mother. Charly adopted her, raised her as her own. And I just…slipped away. No other way to put it."

"Did Lana ever know?"

"No. She was too young to understand, and Charly wouldn't hear of telling her."

Some of the lights in the park below had been switched on

and he could now see her face. He sensed some immense regret reflected in her eyes.

"You have to realize I was not a nice person back then. And I was only getting worse. There's a line in some song about too busy being free. Maybe I wasn't free, but I was for sure cheap." She shook her head and looked at him. "You want the God's honest truth? There's no nice way of saying this, but I was a skanky drug whore. What? Does that shock you?"

He didn't say anything.

She shook her head. "Would you believe me if I told you I held up a liquor store once? A bit of a cliché, right? An addict holding up a liquor store," she said, laughing softly. "The owner was this old black Dominican guy. Years later, I went back there to give him back the money I stole. But he was dead."

"My mama used to say it's the thought that counts."

Neither of them spoke for a moment as they watched Zozobra collapse on itself in a rain of sparks.

"Charly kept bailing me out. Every time I'd screw up, she'd be there. When the thing on the boat went down I was living with a no account long haul trucker in Mobile. You must think I was pretty awful. Well, I was."

"It's not my place to judge. Besides, if you want to compare sins, I've got you beat hands down."

In the space of five minutes, Zozobra had burned down to its skeletal frame, and some of the celebrants appeared to be streaming to the exits while others continued to cheer.

"I did go to her birthdays," she said with a ghost of a smile. "All except her last one when she turned five. That bastard Bisco made Charly tell me I couldn't come. That was right before it happened."

"So what happened on the boat?"

"Bisco took off with Lana. It was another one of his manipulative power plays. He said he was going to give her to some people. Sell her. He was probably bullshitting as usual but by then Charly was pretty much done with him. She was determined to end it. To take Lana and run away. I'm sure you heard most of what happened. They argued. He hit her and she shot him. It would've been self defense if it would've happened anywhere but god forsaken Louisiana. One of the bullets hit something, a fuel tank they think, and the boat blew up."

She downed the last of her wine and crumpled the cup with both hands before dropping it at her feet. "We didn't know." Her voice caught and she looked away. "If Lana was alive, it would've changed everything. My life. Charly's life. I might've still had a sister," she said, the bitterness in her voice obvious.

"What happened between you and Charly?"

She didn't reply for a half minute or so. "I always guessed it was the guilt she most likely felt," she said finally. "Maybe she thought her life was over. Maybe she wanted to make it all easier on me. I don't know. Whatever it was, she finally refused to see me. It was like she died. I lost her. Her and Lana both. The only good thing that came of it was after she started refusing to see me, I got clean. I joined..." She paused as if she had lost her train of thought. "Later, I went to college. I got a master's degree in social work. I needed to help people. Maybe you and I aren't all that different. You know, looking for signs of life." She looked at him. "Well, I guess we found a sign."

She snorted in what started out as amusement but turned into a choking sob. Unsure how she might respond to any attempt to comfort her, Quist simply waited in silence. He could only imagine what was going through her mind. The shock of losing her sister coupled with the uncertainty of knowing Lana's fate was no doubt overpowering. He felt a brief pang of guilt as he entertained what might have happened if he wouldn't have gone with Charly up to her room. The nurse had said Charly was a walking time bomb; that the aneurysm could've easily happened at any time. Still, what if she would've never walked into that bar?

After a long moment, she took a deep breath and wiped her eyes with the heel of her hand. "So I guess I'll go to Mexico and see."

"I'm going with you."

She looked at him for a moment before nodding. "You have your own money, don't you?"

He laughed and shook his head. "Lady, you just don't let up, do you? Yeah, I have my own money. Now let's go find you your own room. That way we can trust each other not to be poking around each other's things while the other one of us is sleeping. "

She shrugged. "Fair enough. But I don't need to poke around anymore. I think I trust you."

"What? Until I bark? And what if once we're down there I tell you to drop the whole thing? To stop looking for her. Do you trust me that much? To listen to my wise counsel?"

She stared silently at the embers of Old Man Gloom for a moment before turning and starting for the stairs. "You can leave anytime," she said over her shoulder.

Quist glanced once more at the embers of Zozobra and started after her.

PART THREE

San Miguel De Allende, Mexico

"When that rough god goes riding on in, there'll be nobody hiding. There'll be no more heroes." -Van Morrison

19

Two days Later

The taxi driver told them the drive from the Del Bajio International Airport in Leon to San Miguel de Allende would take an hour and a half, but an accident involving an overturned cattle truck blocked the highway for almost two hours. Quist watched with ebbing patience as a pair of policeman strolled among the injured cattle administering the coup de grace while several of their partners struggled to herd the survivors off the roadway. Consequently, it was dusk when they approached the outskirts of the city.

Roy had said little since leaving the hotel in Santa Fe earlier that morning, Quist's attempts at conversation eliciting only nods and monosyllabic replies. The day before she had isolated herself in her hotel room, ignoring Quist's knocks and phone calls. Worried that she might have left, he checked with the registration who confirmed she hadn't checked out. A couple of empty food trays outside her door were the only other evidence of her habitation. It wasn't until eight that evening when he tried to call her one last time that she answered and reassured him she would be ready to leave in the morning.

Earlier that day, CdeBaca had dropped off Mercedes Schoenfeld's dossier. Quist had been surprised at the amount of information, the bulk of which came from a FBI data base. But the file also contained entries from the local law enforcement agencies in New Orleans and Miami, a brief mention in an Interpol report, and a ten page intelligence report from the DEA that seemed more conjecture than any real evidence, although it did indicate Schoenfeld was believed to be currently residing in San Miguel. The report had even provided an address, albeit two years old.

Against Quist's better judgment, he had slipped the bulk of the file page by page beneath Roy's door. The next morning, she appeared in the lobby wearing the same plain- looking outfit she wore when they first met. Her attitude seemed no less lackluster for she acknowledged Quist with a simple good morning and a minimum of eye contact. As they made their way to the parking garage, Quist asked if she had read the Schoenfeld file. Again he was rewarded with a curt yes and nothing more.

Quist assumed the file's contents might have been overly disconcerting when one considered Lana's possible fate. That or she felt some embarrassment over what she had disclosed to Quist the night of the Zozobra burning. He resigned himself to her silence, figuring she might need time to digest what the file had revealed about the woman they hoped to confront.

It turned out that Mercedes Schoenfeld wasn't her real name. She was born Marja Symanski in 1945 in Warsaw. She had entered the US in the company of her mother at Ellis Island in 1954. The only way the FBI discovered this was through an interview with her first husband who ironically was also her first pimp. Shortly after arriving in New York, her mother promptly sold her to a man who wholesaled child labor to the garment industry. Little is known about her until at age fifteen she met Leo Baransky, a smalltime procurer of young girls for the Gambino crime family. Whether out of pity or infatuation, Baransky took Marja in, eventually pimping her himself, and then, after a couple of years, inexplicably marrying her. The sum of her history from 1960 until she appears on the New Orleans Vice

Squad's radar as Mercedes Schoenfeld in 1975 comes from a confession Baransky made to the NYPD in which he names her as an accomplice in the murder of a bar owner. By then she had already taken her new name and disappeared. When she surfaced in New Orleans, she was the madam of a string of low end houses of prostitution posing as Asian massage parlors.

The first of two photos in the file was a mug shot that portrayed a somewhat attractive blonde with bad teeth, staring defiantly at the camera. Her makeup appears too heavy, her rouge suggesting she hadn't quite made it. The second photo, a surveillance shot taken in Miami in 2000, revealed an entirely different persona. It shows her on the arm of a handsome younger Latin man. She was wearing what appeared to be an expensive evening gown exposing sufficient décolletage to distract ones attention from the equally expensive looking jewelry around her neck. It also appeared she had undergone dental work and even some plastic surgery. But it was her. The accompanying caption simply stated the name of her companion, a reputed money launderer for the Sinaloa drug cartel. Her name was scribbled off to the side in parentheses with a series of question marks below it.

Quist was able to determine from the various records that she had been arrested a dozen or so times on charges of engaging in prostitution, receiving stolen goods, and various drug possession charges. None of the charges ever resulted in a conviction. The New Orleans police intelligence unit maintained sufficient interest in her to compile a report linking her to various human trafficking rings, a gun running operation, and a local syndicate that smuggled stolen cars into Mexico. On one occasion she had been arrested in a sting involving the doping of race horses. The arrest sheet mentioned she owned a stable of race horses which she transported across several states, raising speculation that her race track interest was a front for her other enterprises.

After 2007, Schoenfeld suddenly disappeared from the radar, at least domestically. The Interpol report included a brief mention of her name in relation to an undercover operation involving a human trafficking cartel smuggling young girls from Eastern Europe into Mexico. The informant in that case wasn't able to provide anything more substantial than an eavesdropped mention of her name. Later, she appeared on the DEA's radar due to her association with a Mexican politician and fellow horse breeder with ties to the Sinaloa drug cartel. Again, the DEA's surveillance provided little if any concrete evidence of drug involvement other than a close social relationship with the politician. For several years, she consorted with a reputed former Texas drug smuggler. There was no mention of any girls living with her. The report did provide the location of a house in San Miguel de Allende.

It wasn't until the flight from Houston to Leon that Roy broke her silence. And even then, the context in which she brought up the file led Quist to question whether the details of Schoenfeld's enterprises had elicited in her an even greater dread and anxiety about the task they were about to embark on.

"I had this client once," she said, her voice catching. "She crossed into Mexico from El Salvador on foot with her younger brother. They rode on the roof of a train to Chihuahua and then paid a coyote to bring them across. She only had the clothes on her back. The coyotes sold her to this biker gang in San Antonio. She was only fourteen at the time. By the time she was eighteen, she was hooked on meth and looked thirty. A priest rescued her and brought her to New Orleans. You talked about wanting to save people. Well, as hard as I tried I couldn't save her. One night she told me every horrible thing that ever happened to her. She left my office and drowned herself in the bayou. She tied a concrete block to her foot." Royale paused for a moment before going on. "She had my card in a paper sack she left on the dock. My card and a picture of her mother. That's all she had."

Quist waited a moment before saying anything. "I think you're getting ahead of yourself. Remember what Eloquin said? Schoenfeld was treating Lana like she was her daughter. Those were his exact words."

"And I'm not as naïve as you think I am. Did you forget what I do for a living? I know what happens to these girls. If we find her she won't be some innocent. All I'm saying is I know what that kind of experience does to people. Do I sound cynical? I'm being realistic. I know what I might find. I might find my daughter. But she really won't be my daughter. That's all I'm saying. " She looked away.

"You won't know that until you know it. Let's find her first."

Roy said next to nothing for the remainder of the flight. Once, while she was napping, Quist glanced down at the tattoos on her wrist. If all that she had related about herself was true, her past was likely feeding her imagination with the worst possible scenarios for her daughter. To be fair, Quist also felt apprehensive about what kind of damaged goods they would likely find; that is if they even found her.

The taxi driver they had enlisted at the airport was a neatly dressed man in his mid-thirties who spoke English with an accent Quist couldn't readily identify. When asked where he had learned English, the driver replied at a school run by an Irish priest. At times, the mish mash of Spanish with a bit of an Irish brogue made for some difficulty in understanding him.

Once they were on the outskirts of San Miguel, the driver, Jorge was his name, asked where they were staying. When Quist replied that they hadn't yet made any arrangements, Jorge offered to call his cousin who had several houses he rented to mostly well to do tourists. Two phone calls later, Jorge was driving them through the choked streets of the old town.

It was early evening and many of the streets near the city center were filled with people, most of who seemed to be young people cruising the many bars and restaurants. From what Quist had read in a tourist book, San Miguel was a tourist destination with a large and lively community of expatriates and young artists and entrepreneurs. Occasionally, they caught a view down a side street of the illuminated, Neo-Gothic steeple of the cathedral that rose above the town plaza, or the El Jardin as the locals called it.

"This place reminds me a little of the French Quarter," Roy commented, breaking her silence. Sure enough, she seemed enthralled and revitalized by the feel of the street life. "Even smells like it," she added, at one point hanging her head out the open window.

"We will go to the Atascadero," Jorge said. "A very nice neighborhood. *Muy elegante. Tranquilo.* My cousin will give you a good deal."

They climbed through the narrow cobble-stoned streets onto a hillside overlooking the town. Even in the dark, it was obvious the district appeared to be a sedate and seemingly up-scale neighborhood of walled compounds, the parapets draped in bougainvillea. The walls concealed any appreciation of the houses themselves except for the softly illuminated windows of the second stories.

"Tell me, Jorge," Quist said over the drumming of taxi's tires on the cobblestoned streets. "Does your cousin know many Americans living down here?"

Jorge laughed. "There are many living here. Fifteen thousand maybe. Too many to know."

"We are looking for a woman. Maybe you or your cousin have heard her name."

"Por supuesto. What is her name?"

"Mercedes Schoenfeld. She raises race horses."

Jorge nodded and seemed to ponder this for a moment before turning up the volume of the radio. When after a moment he still hadn't replied, Quist glanced at Royale who raised her eyebrows.

"We are here," Jorge said after a few moments, slowing as they approached an open wrought iron gate. A man dressed in what appeared to be motorcycle leathers stood leaning against a canary yellow Suzuki racing motorcycle. "My cousin," he said, easing the taxi through the narrow gate.

The interior of the compound couldn't be immediately appreciated due to the overhanging boughs of a gigantic tree and the heavy shroud of vegetation on either side of the courtyard. A solitary light illuminated the small portal. As Quist started to open the car door, Jorge turned.

"Espere! Un momento. Wait and I will get the keys."

They watched as Jorge walked over to confer with his cousin. The two men spoke for perhaps a minute, all the while the cousin kept stealing glances at the taxi. Finally, the cousin strolled over to the taxi alone, opened the rear door and slid into the back seat beside Roy. He made no effort to close the door, and in the sudden glare of the dome light studied both of them in turn. His hooded eyes, shaved head and narrow, pock-marked face lent him a reptilian appearance. His mouth, thin lipped and small, did little to dispel the impression. He regarded them silently and without expression for a long moment before speaking.

"*¿Hablas Español?*" he asked.

"*Un poco,*" Quist replied. "You speak English?"

The man didn't answer at first but merely stared at Quist with his direct, open gaze.

"You ask about a certain woman. An American. I must ask why it is you look for her?"

He and his cousin must have attended the same school for his accent was identical.

"I want to buy a horse. I hear this woman has wonderful horses."

Several seconds went by before the man closed the car door, enveloping them in darkness. In the ensuing silence, Quist could hear the man breathing through his nose as he considered Quist's response.

"This woman," he said after a moment. "She raises horses. Yes. Among other things. There is a reason I wish to know what it is you want of her. Once, another man, also an American. He comes to look for this woman. He stay at one of my houses. He made many problems for me. Problems I do not need."

"So what kind of problems did this man give you?"

The cousin shrugged and looked out the window. "He die in my house. Not this one. A different place. *La policia* asked many questions." He looked at Royale and then back at Quist. "You say you want to buy a horse, Señor. I can find you a horse to buy."

Quist nodded with his chin at the house. "How much?"

"For a horse?"

"No. For the house. For one week."

He sucked a breath through his teeth, and then muttered

something unintelligible. "Two thousand dollars," he said. "But you cannot die here."

"Who said anything about dying? I just want a horse."

The man looked at him, his eyes indiscernible in the darkness. "I think you do not want a horse, my friend. I think you will find only *problemas*. Do not bring them to my house," he said, nodding with his chin.

"If you tell us where we can find this woman I'll give you three thousand," Roy said.

He turned and looked at her. In the dim light, Quist could see him smile. *"Ambos son loco. Pero.."* He shrugged. "If you want a horse, maybe you will find a horse. Who am I to say?" He opened the door and crawled out without giving them another glance. He exchanged words with Jorge and then got on his motorcycle and drove away, his noisy departure heralded by the barking of a dozen or so neighbors' dogs.

Jorge came back and opened Roy's door and then went to open the trunk. After he had deposited their bags on the portal, he stood and waited.

"Pay him," Quist said.

"He didn't tell us anything," Roy replied.

"The woman. Where do we find her?" Quist asked.

"She has a rancho. It is on the road to Guanajuato. I will not drive you."

"So then tell me how to find her rancho."

"Maybe ten kilometers from here. It has *una puerta grande*. A big gate, yes? And a horse on the top. *Una statua de un caballa.* Statue, you call it. Yes?"

Roy reached into the waistband of her skirt and pulled out a money belt. She turned away from them and appeared to count out the money and then handed Jorge a sheaf of bills. He made a cursory effort to count it and then handed Quist a key.

"It is not a good place. *Este rancho.*"

"¿Por qué?"

"You should be careful," Jorge said, stuffing the money into his pocket and walking back to his taxi.

"I hope you have enough left over for a horse," Quist said to Roy, unlocking the door.

20

Royale stood waiting in the darkened entranceway as Quist searched for light switches. She sniffed the air in an attempt to get a sense of the place. It was a habit of sorts in which she had indulged since she was a small child when her father, a beer deliveryman at the time, would drag her with him on his rounds at the various bars and restaurants in Galveston. Each place had a distinctive bouquet. The seedy sailor bars along the harbor reeked of sweat and menace. Then there was the no less heady aroma of affluence and crab-stuffed flounder at Gaido's Restaurant on the seawall. And their house? Of beer, certainly, and moldy carpet and a different kind of menace. She was certain her sense of smell revealed far more than her other senses. This place smelled of mildew, disinfectant, and burnt tortillas.

A light went on somewhere in the back of the house, and then another. A chair lamp flicked on revealing what appeared to be the living room. She made her way down the narrow hallway, her hands absently sweeping the cool stone wall of either side. A slant of light appeared in a room just to her right and she saw Quist staring inside an open refrigerator.

"I put your bag in the bedroom of the right. It might have a view," he said, checking the freezer. He grunted and then began opening cabinets.

She could see the living room was sparsely furnished with an outsized colonial style wooden cabinet and an equally massive sofa of dark leather, in front of which sat a low wood plank coffee table. In the dim light, the walls seemed to be painted in something close to puce. A pair of heavy, shroud-like curtains concealed what she guessed might be a glass sliding door. The only attempt at décor seemed to be a large, unframed canvas reproduction of Diego Rivera's depiction of a woman kneeling before a bouquet of calla lilies.

She turned and saw that Quist had moved on from the cabinets and was now opening drawers.

"Ah," he said, retrieving a pair of large knives.

"What are you doing?" she asked.

"Just indulging in my fascination for cutlery," he said, stabbing the cutting board with a large butcher knife.

"I take it there's no food," she asked, making her way to the sofa.

"Just these," he replied, holding up a pair of small brown globes that may have once been limes. He joined her on the sofa carrying a pair of shot glasses and two of the knives. He placed the glasses and the knives on the coffee table, and reached into his bag and pulled out the bottle of tequila he had purchased at the airport in Leon. He cracked the seal and poured them each a couple of fingers worth.

"*Salud,*" he said, handing her a glass. When she hesitated taking it, he set it on the table and then proceeded to down his shot.

She started to reach for the glass but instead picked up one of the knives. It looked more like a stiletto than a kitchen knife.

"What is this one for?"

He took the knife from her and slipped it between the sofa cushion and the arm. "Saves me the trouble of looking for it," he explained in response to her look of befuddlement. He poured himself another shot and downed it just as quickly as the first. "I hate to ruin the ambience but we need to talk about what you're going to do if we find her," he said, smacking his lips.

She had asked herself that very question over and over for two days, and still wasn't any closer to an answer. The prospect of coming face to face with Lana, or at least some version of her daughter, filled her with nauseating dread. At the same time, and much to her surprise, allowing Quist to tag along was more reassuring than she cared to admit.

"If we find her," he went on, "it's not going to be as easy as just asking her to come along with us. I mean there's way of knowing how she'll react when you tell her you're her long lost mama."

"I know that," she said, picking up the glass and taking a sip. It tasted surprisingly smooth, nothing like the rotgut tequila she drank in her youth. Neither of them said anything for a moment.

"If we try to persuade her and she's not buying it, then things might get messy," Quist said, downing his third shot.

"You mean if we try to abduct her."

"Is that you want?"

She took another sip of tequila, unsure herself of what she wanted.

"Bottom line is we don't know what we're going to find. Say she wants to leave. Getting her out of Mexico will be a problem. I doubt she's carrying a passport. That and I have a feeling Schoenfeld won't let her go willingly. I don't suppose we could buy her."

"You don't have any kind of plan, do you?"

He stared at his empty glass. "I think I can get us into see Schoenfeld, but after that..." He shrugged. "I'm thinking we use Tommy Eloquin's name. Pose as buyers. Of girls, not horses." He looked at her as if measuring her response.

"And who am I supposed to be?"

"I don't know. My paramour, maybe."

She snorted in derision and downed her tequila. "Do I look like a paramour?"

"It's just an idea. But for that to work we're going to have to do something about your appearance," he said with obvious sarcasm. "The nun look will have to go."

"Well, too bad because that's what I am. A nun, I mean," she added in response to his look of confusion.

"You're shitting me. Aren't you?" He grinned and shook his head. "God, I should've guessed."

She poured herself another shot of tequila. "The last of my secrets." She turned and looked at him. "I joined a convent after

Charly went to prison. The nuns helped me get clean. And they sent me to college. They still carry me on their rolls although I pretty much do my own thing. At least as far as it goes."

Quist shook his head in amusement. "A stealth nun. Isn't that what they call your kind? Sensible shoes and civilian clothes. Sneaking up on the unsuspecting heathens. Lord, to think I'm going to the gates of hell with a freaking nun. You and Charly..." He let what he was about to say slip away.

"What were you going to say?"

"Just that I must be losing my touch. You know, reading people."

"I guess I should've told you right from the start."

"It wouldn't have mattered. But you're still going to have to change your looks if this is going to work. Tomorrow, I'm going to rent us a car. You go into town and buy some different clothes. Change your hair maybe. We're looking for alluring. Think you can do that?" he asked, turning towards her.

She nearly smiled. "I know what you're doing," she said, noticing his look of appraisal. "If you're trying to picture me being alluring, forget it. I doubt I was ever alluring."

She started to reach for the bottle again but stopped herself. "What do you think Charly was planning on doing? I mean, once she was down here. She probably wouldn't have any idea what she was getting into."

Quist shrugged. "For that matter, neither do we."

"Why are you doing this?" she asked after a moment had passed. When he didn't reply, she leaned over and looked in his face. "I know people. God knows I've had plenty of experience sorting out what people aren't telling me. What they're hiding. And my gut says the only reason you're here is out of some misplaced guilt. You feel guilty about Charly, don't you?"

"I don't feel guilty about Charly."

"Then what? Are you trying to prove something to yourself?"

"That sounds like psychobabble. I'm not your goddamn patient."

"Client. We don't call them patients."

"Whatever."

"Is this something to do with… What was her name? Nell?"

"You shouldn't have gone through my things," he said, cutting her off.

"That's a bit ironic since if you hadn't have gone through Charly's things you wouldn't have stolen that money and you most likely wouldn't be here."

"I didn't steal that money and stop reading into things. I'm here because I don't have anything better to do."

"I'm supposed to believe that?"

He stood up and started to walk away.

"What really happened in Baghdad?"

He turned and looked at her. "You read about it. There's nothing else to tell."

"There's more to it than what was in that newspaper. There always is."

He sat back down and started to reach for the bottle and then changed his mind. "I keep that newspaper clipping to remind me how easy it is to lose something. And how I'm not inclined to ever put myself in that position again."

"But you have put yourself in that position again."

"And beginning to regret it."

Neither of them said anything for a moment. "There was this dirt bag," he said, finally. "A State Department official. I got a tip that he and this Iraqi general were skimming aid money. I was going to play them and be the hot shot investigator who caught them with their hands in the cookie jar. Make my reputation. Nell tried to talk me out of it. I didn't listen." He shook his head. "She wouldn't let me do it alone, and so in the end I let her come along."

He took a deep breath almost as if he were coming up for air. She could see that whatever it was that he was reliving was costing him. Everything in her fiber wanted him to stop, to have him step back from the brink, to tell him he didn't need to go there. But she felt frozen by a communion of pain she felt helpless to rebuff.

"You read what happened. We got ambushed. They killed

four of our guys. Nell got shot and was wounded pretty bad. And then they took us. Nell and I." He said this as if he were reciting from some rote memory, reading from something on the far wall of his mind. "They... they fucking threw her into the trunk like she was a dead animal or something. Except she wasn't dead."

"Harlan."

"I don't know where they were taking us, what they were going to do to us. Kill us. I don't know." He shook his head. "They drove into this mob. There had been a car bombing. And there were all these pissed off, scared people. They stopped the car. Started beating on the car. They dragged me out. And then they set the car on fire."

He fell silent, obviously lost in that moment. Perhaps a minute passed with neither of them speaking. "Nell died. People died. All because I was reckless and arrogant. I don't want that to happen again." He stood, picked up the bottle and started to walk away.

"Harlan."

He turned and looked at her.

"You don't owe Charly or me or Lana anything."

"You're right. I don't. I'll see you in the morning," he said and left the room.

She sat there a moment, numbed by Quist's admission. After a minute, she turned off the lamp, retreating into the darkness. The rawness she felt after all that had transpired - Charly, the realization Lana was alive, and then Quist's tragedy - it threatened to crumble the last vestige of her fortifications. She had learned to rely on faith, on prayer, on her so-called therapeutic skills, but now it all seemed woefully inadequate. She suddenly found herself wishing Quist hadn't taken the bottle with him.

And there was still Lana. No sooner had the shock of Eloquin's confession wore off, before she began rehearsing in her mind what she might say to Lana. But she soon realized that whatever version of explanation and justification she came up with would sound pathetic and self-serving. She didn't even want to consider the possibility that Lana wouldn't even give her the chance to explain. And if that proved to be the case, then what?

For the hundredth time, she asked herself why she was really doing this? It wasn't for Charly. Was it to save Lana? Someone Royale no longer knew, someone that experience told her had probably been living a life of gray moral ambiguity, oblivious to any life before this Schoenfeld woman abducted her. She feared this pursuit would prove to be nothing more than an ill- thought out attempt to save someone that didn't want to be saved. And how often had she failed in that very endeavor? Or was this perhaps a mere attempt to appease her guilt over abandoning Lana? She sat in the darkness for a long time sifting through the swirl of these emotions before finally getting up and going to her bedroom.

21

Quist parked the Jeep on a side street near the Biblioteca Publico in the sparse shade of a huge jacaranda tree. They had agreed to meet at the library because it was an easily found landmark and the crowds would be sparser than around the plaza. Besides, Quist had also wanted to see if the library had a more detailed map of the area surrounding Schoenfeld's ranch. One of the librarians, an elderly woman who fortunately spoke excellent English, had shown him where to search, but he found nothing that might prove useful.

Earlier that afternoon, Quist had driven on the road to Guanajuato in an effort to scope out the ranch's front gate and determine what they might expect if they drove up unannounced. There was no way anyone could miss the entry gate. Jorge had been right about the ostentatious size of the gate and the statue of the horse that crowned the thirty-foot-high stone portal. The horse, slightly larger than life and constructed of overlapping rusted metal plating, rose on its hind legs, its hooves pawing the air. A pair of heavy, metal-grated gates sealed the portal from the highway. A small prefab gate shack stood to one side. Quist had slowed just enough to see that at least two men sat inside the shack while another man stood guard just inside the gate armed with what appeared to be an Uzi draped around his neck.

He drove a couple of miles past the gate in search of any adjoining roads, but finding none, he stopped and parked atop an escarpment where he could just make out through the trees the ranch's main compound. He got out and stood for a moment to appreciate the lay of the land around the cluster of buildings. The surrounding countryside was mostly flinty hillsides covered with some kind of low growing evergreen and dry grass. A long open stretch of graveled drive led from the gate to the compound. The drive skirted a large high-walled corral and what appeared to be a row of stables, both of which sat beneath a low hillock on top of which perched a rambling hacienda-like building. He reached into the Jeep and retrieved the cheap binoculars he had purchased at a department store earlier that morning and tried to make out more detail.

A clutch of pickup trucks and what looked to be a pair of BMW sedans lined the drive in front of the house. Quist scanned the landscape on either side but saw nothing that might indicate another exit or roadway. From what he could tell, a tall barbed wire fence enclosed most of the property. He returned his gaze to the house and fixed in his mind what he could about the layout that was visible. He stood there a few minutes more playing out in his mind various scenarios before getting back into the Jeep and driving off.

Confronting Schoenfeld in her lair would most likely accomplish nothing more than perhaps getting a sense of her and what they might be up against. Actually encountering Lana would be a bonus. Beyond that, he had no plan. Taking Lana against her will would prove difficult for he saw no opportunity to easily make an escape from the ranch. They would have to find another way, which meant either luring her away or waiting for some other opportunity away from the confines of the ranch. The wild card was Lana herself. Would she let herself be taken? The other unknowable factor was the dubious connection between her and Royale.

After his fruitless search at the library, he crossed the street and sat at a small outdoor café and sipped an espresso and watched the passersby, a large number of which appeared to be either tourists or at the least, expatriates from the sound of the conversations; a lot of English mixed with various European dialects. It seemed the kind of town where an outsider wouldn't stand out, in other words, a perfect place to hide in plain sight, especially if one had influential friends. From what he surmised of Mercedes Schoenfeld, someone like her would undoubtedly thrive here.

Just as he ordered his second espresso, he caught sight of a woman standing on the opposite side of the street. Like many of the other pedestrians, she appeared fashionably if not casually dressed. She wore a tan leather skirt, an ox blood colored serape-like tunic and a straw fedora. She glanced in his direction and then began to pick her away across the busy street. It took a second or two for Quist to realize it was Royale, her stride giving her away. As she approached his table, she lowered her large designer sunglasses and cocked her head. Quist, taken aback by her appearance, stumbled awkwardly to his feet.

"Will this do?" she asked, dropping her bags beside the table. She pivoted from side to side to give him a better look.

He whistled in admiration and laughed. "Sister Aucoin. I do believe you've changed orders. What is it now? The Sisters of Vogue?"

She removed the fedora, revealing a modish, asymmetrical, layered haircut that had been dyed a coppery auburn. Something about her eyes seemed different, too. He leaned closer and saw their green tint. It left him momentarily speechless. She had yet to smile, and in fact seemed a bit forlorn. He sensed her transformation had required some unnatural effort on her part.

"You look amazing. What did you do to your eyes?"

"Contacts. There was an optical shop next to the hair salon. You like them?"

He shook his head in amusement. "I just wasn't expecting...this much, I guess. Sit and let's have a coffee. We need to talk," he said, allowing himself an appreciation of her shapely legs as she dropped into the chair.

He proceeded to give her his impressions of Schoenfeld's ranch, concluding with his reservations of the likelihood of them leaving there with Lana in tow. She took this in with the same somber expression she had presented since leaving Santa Fe, all the while fingering the small crucifix she still wore around her neck. When he was finished, she shook her head.

"Please tell me this makeover wasn't for nothing," she said, gesturing at her outfit with her hands.

"I'd say it was worth it no matter what we do. Tell me something. How do you feel right now? I mean about the way you look? The hair, the makeup?"

"I'm not sure. It's been a while since I felt attractive. I am attractive, aren't I?"

"Yeah. I'd say so. I guess what I'm wondering is there any going back?"

"You mean going back to being a nun?" She shrugged. "Depends. I don't know. But I'd rather not talk about it right now."

He nodded and watched a gaggle of uniformed school girls passing by on the sidewalk. "We'll go out there tomorrow and see what pops. If nothing else, we might get a look at Lana. It may all come down to intuition and gut sense. Are you ready for that?"

"I've come this far."

"How about I buy you dinner and we talk about something else?"

"Isn't that how this all started? Over dinner?"

"I thought you said it all started when I stole Charly's money. Have I told you yet about my raccoon?" he asked before she could reply.

"Your what?"

"Believe it not, you've now heard my best pick up line. Let's go. I'm hungry and in need of something Mexican."

22

Royale flipped open the compact mirror for perhaps the third time and looked at herself, tilting her face back and forth. Her eye makeup seemed too heavy, the rouge a bit overdone. She snapped the compact shut and tossed it back in the glove compartment.

"You're sure this is the look you wanted? I mean, it's been ages since I even wore any lip gloss much less all this stuff. You mind turning the heater back on? I'm cold," she said, rubbing her bare knees. He had overruled her request to wear jeans, assuring her the short skirt would be more in character.

Quist glanced at her briefly before turning his attention back to the road. It had rained during the night and for most of the morning, and now the dark precipitous skies threatened another storm.

"I told you. We have to play a part here."

"You mean I have to look like I used to be a whore."

"Not a whore. Let's just say experienced. Like you've been around. By the way, I hope you remembered to leave your passport behind."

"You told me to hide it in my room where no one can find it. It's taped to the top of the toilet tank. Satisfied?"

"What did you tape it with?"

"Duct tape. I never travel without it."

"Serious?"

"No. I found some in the closet." She twisted the heater control knob and looked out the window. The bleak light leaking from the clouds had turned the countryside a monotone fish gray. Here and there a brief shaft of sunlight dappled the crowns of the low corrugated tree line.

"We stick to our story that Eloquin gave us her name. We're just down here looking for a connection to procure some merchandise."

"Merchandise? That's how we're going to refer to these poor women?"

"Listen, if you can't do this, let me know now."

"I don't know why we can't just say we're looking to buy a horse. That way we get in without the pretense that we're a couple of low lifes." She pulled down the hem of her skirt and rubbed her hands over her bare arms.

"Because only a low life can relate to another low life. It's how we're going to get her to open up a little."

She sunk lower in her seat. "It still doesn't seem like much of a plan."

"Please enlighten me if you have a better idea."

"How about I tell her the truth? I just want to meet my daughter."

"Sure. You could try that. One, I doubt it would get us through the front door, and two, you're forgetting she may consider herself Lana's mother. She's got home field advantage and we've got squat except our line of bullshit," he said almost too gleefully.

"You're not carrying a gun, are you?"

"Hell, no. Believe it or not it's illegal to bring a gun into Mexico. All I've got is this," he said, lifting his pants leg and showing her what appeared to be a switchblade poking out of his sock.

"You have a thing for knives, don't you? That usually has something to say about your childhood."

"No doubt."

"Maybe you get off to all this subterfuge stuff, but I like to be more up front about things."

"You could've fooled me. Do me a favor Roy and shed the nun bit for now and let me lead."

It was the first time he called her by her nickname. She glanced at him out of the corner of her eye. He seemed too re-

106

laxed, almost as if duplicity was his second nature. That and he seemed to be enjoying himself entirely too much. Their dinner the previous night had revealed a side to him that in retrospect didn't surprise her. Three shots of tequila had loosened his tongue to the point where he briefly alluded to doing undercover while with ATF. That meant he was a practiced liar, which led her to wonder how much of anything he said she could believe. Little wonder that being upfront didn't compute with him.

They had found a restaurant in a hotel a block from the plaza. It was an intimate open air affair just off the lobby and surrounded by balustrades covered by bougainvillea. The night was still and warm although there was a distant rumble announcing the coming storm. They shared a salad, a few plates of appetizers and a fish stew along with a bottle of Chilean wine, most of which Quist drank.

As the night wore on, Quist became overly loquacious, rambling on about his childhood in West Virginia. He glossed over large portions of his adult life, a sentiment that Royale could easily forgive. She felt she had already revealed too much of her own sordid past. The tequila and the wine did lead to a long, colorful soliloquy of the misadventure in Sierra Leone that led up to his termination from ATF, the details growing sketchier as he related how he had been shot and ended up recovering in a jungle hospital. As for herself, she sidestepped any further details of her life other than a few innocent tales of her childhood in Galveston.

As they waited for the waiter to bring their dessert and coffee, Quist's demeanor abruptly turned sober. She could tell from his frown that he was worried about something.

"What's wrong?" she asked.

"I'm just second guessing myself."

"About us going to the ranch?"

"About all this, but mostly about getting you involved."

"What do you mean? I am involved. This is my thing. I told you before, this isn't any of your business."

"Your thing? This isn't your thing. You're a social worker for chrisssakes . You're a nun. You're out of place in this world.

My world. You're not even an accomplished liar. Tomorrow we're going to come face to face with some very amoral people. Dangerous people. People who aren't going to just take you at face value."

"I told you about my past. I'm hardly an innocent."

"It's not the same. You weren't a player. At least not like this."

"Then teach me. Teach me how to be a player."

Quist regarded her silently for a moment before picking up his napkin and almost daintily wiping his mouth, his eyes never leaving hers. He pushed back his chair, rose to his feet and came to her side of the table. Before she could react, he leaned down and took her face in both hands and kissed her; a slow, deep kiss that forced her to tug at the table cloth, almost spilling her water glass. At first, she resisted, trying her best to pull away, but he only held her tighter. Much to her surprise, she gave in. It was only when she reached up and touched his hands that he pulled back. She quickly looked around to see if any of the other diners had noticed, but no one gave them a second glance.

"What do you think you're doing?" she asked.

Quist grinned. "So tell me," he said, settling into his chair. "Was that last part an act? If so, maybe I've misjudged you. Tomorrow you're going to have to do something out of character. Out of character for Sister Royale Aucoin, but in character for…" He glanced at her water glass. "Ronnie Waters."

"Who?"

"Ronnie Waters. She's this East Texas girl. Her parents were Papists passing for bed rock Baptists. Her Daddy was a logger, her Mama a waitress. Ronnie did her share of waitressing, too before she fell for the first smooth talker to put his hand up her skirt. She bartended, was a stripper once. She tried to go straight and went to cosmetology school, but that didn't take. Was married once, no kids. The problem was she couldn't give up the party life." He studied her for a moment.

"And that's where I met you, Ronnie. At this bachelor party for a friend of mine. You and a couple of your friends had been paid to be there. The two of us hit it off and we've been together ever since. Ten years now. Ronnie Waters, you are my partner in crime."

Something like amusement passed behind his eyes. But there was something else, too; a calculated hardness that almost made her shudder.

"You think you can carry that off?" he asked. "Being Ronnie Waters?"

"You mean lie as well as you can?"

"I'll tell you something. Back when I started training to do undercover work with ATF, the first day this one instructor told us the trick was to avoid a defensive lie. You know, one where you're denying something you did or said. Instead, you learn to lie offensively. That way you control the story. Does it always work? No, but you'll be ahead of the game if you get to tell your story first."

"You really think you can teach me to lie?"

"To be honest, I'm not sure."

"Try me."

He drained the last of his wine and regarded her silently for a moment. "So, Ronnie," he said, leaning across the table. "Tell me something about yourself I don't already know."

Royale shook her head and allowed herself a smile. She thought for a moment. "You know that party? The one where we met? I only went home with you because you promised to pay me. I bet you don't remember that. And because you were cute. See, I can lie."

Quist laughed. "That's a start. Let's get out of here and I'll tell you what I do remember about Ronnie Waters."

Later, they walked the dark narrow streets while he spun his fictions. When they finally returned to the casita, it seemed she knew less about him than before, perhaps less about herself. His unforeseen kiss awakened something carnal and forgotten, the fleeting intensity of which led her to begin questioning her identity. Her counseling profession, her closeted life in New Orleans, be that what it may, had provided a much-needed cocoon, a shelter from memory and pain. Now this quest to find Lana had reopened a wound. She wondered how much she would bleed.

"Here we are," he said, interrupting her thoughts. He nodded with his chin. The huge horse-topped edifice suddenly loomed over them on their right. "The gateway to the netherworld. Better make your sign of the cross now."

Quist slowed and pulled in front of the metal gate. A few moments passed before a young Mestizo dressed in tiger-striped fatigues emerged from the gate shack. He carried what appeared to be a shotgun in one hand, a cell phone in the other. He came to a halt several meters away and then circled their Jeep before cautiously approaching Quist's window.

"¿Cuál es su negocio aquí?"

"Let's see. Uh...*Que...Queremos...ver* a Señora Schoenfeld. Did I say that right?"

"¿Americanos?"

"Si. You speak English, yeah? We just want to speak to Señora Schoenfeld."

"You have *nombramiento?*"

"Nombra what?"

"¿Cómo se dice? Appointmente?"

"No appointment, but she wants to see us."

"Lo siento. No es posible."

"I promise. *Prometo.* You call and tell her we are friends of Señor Eloquin. Eloquin. You got that? She will see us. *Prometo.* ¿*Si?* Tommy Eloquin."

The guard stepped away from the jeep and lifted the cell phone to his ear, spoke something quickly in Spanish and then walked back to the gate shack. They waited in silence for a minute before a Ford Expedition appeared on the other side of the gate. A tall, lanky man in a wide straw sombrero got out and walked to the gate shack to confer with the guard. They spoke briefly and then the man began to make us way to the Jeep. Even from a distance, Royale could make out the sun ravaged skin; his complexion only a shade darker than albino. As he turned to glance down the road, she saw him in profile. Something about him tugged at some nascent thread of memory. It came to her in a rush of foreboding.

Quist, perhaps sensing her discomfort, glanced at her. "What's wrong?"

She quickly slipped on her sunglasses. "I think I know him."

Quist stared at her a second before rolling down the window. Royale brought her hand to her mouth in the hope of concealing anything of her face the sun glasses didn't hide. The man approached Quist's window and leaned over to inspect them. A pair of dark RayBans concealed his eyes.

"Good morning. Are you acquainted with Miss Schoenfeld?" he asked.

She remembered his voice. It was that distinct. Twenty years and the cadence of his accent and the tone, gravely and deep, left no doubt in her mind. For the life of her, she couldn't recall his name, only the sole circumstance in which she had encountered him. It was in a dank holding tank in Metairie, Louisiana. She had been scooped up in a raid on a party in a half-star motel. They had her for possession of a gram of coke and what she assumed might be prostitution; inaccurate but not too far off. This guy was the one that sprung her. She could still remember his leering grin as he opened the cell door. She took him for a narc. Sharkskin and knitted Polo. A Miami Vice wannabe. She remembered the last thing he said to her.

"So, hon. You're free to go. Just remember your old daddy Manny next time we meet out on the street," he had said in his Brooklynese New Orleans accent.

Manny. That was it. Bisco had called him that when he later told her he had reached out to one of his cop friends. "A favor to your sister," Bisco had told her. The way he said it made it seem she now owed him something in turn. It was shortly after that she left town with the long haul trucker.

"Did your guy here tell you we're friends with Tommy Eloquin?" Quist asked.

"Eloquin, you say? I don't recall that name."

"He said he used to do business with Miss Schoenfeld. We did some business with him a couple of three times. Tampa. Miami. Once in Biloxi. Wasn't it Biloxi, babe?" Quist said, turning to Royale.

"Muscle Shoals, honey. Not Biloxi. You're confusing Tommy with that other peckerwood that sorta looked like him. Tampa and Miami I do recall though." She did her best to approximate an accent that came out sounding vaguely East Texas.

"Is that so?" Manny said, leaning on the window with one

111

arm. "What did he look like? Maybe I can place him."

Quist laughed. "Ugly little fucker. Bred and born that way and he never got prettier. Reliable dude though. I'll grant him that. Why don't you ask the lady of the house if she remembers him?"

Manny lowered his glasses with one bony finger and looked at them each in turn. She remembered the eyes: deep set and pale blue. She maybe only imagined that his pupils dilated as they met hers. He gave her a broad open smile revealing a mouth crammed with gold crowns.

"Hang on," he said and walked back halfway to the gate shack. He retrieved a cell phone from his jeans, spoke briefly to someone on the other end, and then waited for perhaps a half minute before resuming a conversation that lasted almost a minute more. He slipped the phone back into his jeans and strolled back to the Jeep.

"What did you say your name was?"

"I didn't. It's Quinton. My friend here's Ronnie," he said, tilting his head at Royale.

"You happen to have some ID?"

"Sure." Quist leaned to the side and pulled out his wallet and took out what appeared to be a driver's license which Manny plucked from his grasp. He studied it for a few seconds and handed it back.

"Atlanta, huh? How about a passport?"

"Locked up in the safe back in the room."

Manny straightened up and glanced up and down the highway for a moment before leaning back down. "This is your lucky day. She said she'll see you. As a favor to this Eloquin guy. Follow me," he said and made his way back to the Expedition.

"You say you know him?" Quist asked, cranking the ignition.

"From a life time ago. His name is Manny and he used to be a New Orleans cop and a dirty one at that."

"You think he made you?"

"I doubt it. It was just that one time and I looked a lot different."

"Still, better mind your Ps and Qs. It's show time."

23

The gravel road wound for perhaps a quarter mile through prickly pear cactus and scrub oak. Quist noticed twice what appeared to be surveillance cameras concealed along the roadway. There would be no sneaking up on the house, at least not from the road. The grounds surrounding the house would no doubt also have its share of surveillance. Manny led them through a large wooden gate and into a cobblestoned courtyard. As they crawled out of the Jeep, Quist made a mental note of how many vehicles were parked there; a BMW, a Mercedes SUV, and two pickups. He also allowed himself another quick glance to see if there might be any guards, but he saw no one.

Manny stepped from the Expedition and retrieved a shotgun from behind the front seat before motioning for them to follow him. Quist noticed the butt of an automatic protruding from Manny's waistband, and concluded the show of force was just that – a display intended to make an impression.

Manny deposited the shotgun and his sombrero on a small table just inside the archway and proceeded to lead them down a long, Saltillo-tiled portal that was bordered on one side by an open garden dense with tropical foliage. Several bird cages containing parrots and toucans hung from the trees. Manny paused about halfway down the portal and turned around.

"You don't mind if I pat you down, do you?"

"Not at all," Quist said, raising his hands.

It was obvious Manny was a professional. He found the switchblade in a matter of seconds.

"A blade man, huh? I like that."

"Habit," Quist replied. "I've carried one since first grade."

Manny nodded in appreciation. "I suppose you don't mind if I hang on to it. Miss," he said, turning to Royale.

Royale lifted her hands, and he gave her the same brisk, professional frisking, lingering for an extra second or two on her bra. He reached up and took her handbag and opened it.

"No ID?" he asked, rifling through the contents.

"What? And take the chance some Mex boosts my purse?" she said, smiling and arching her eyebrows. Manny studied her for a moment and handed back her purse.

"Why don't you take off the sunglasses, Ronnie? That was what your friend called you, right? Ronnie?"

Quist tensed in anticipation, his mind quickly shuffling through options if things suddenly went south. The last thing he wanted to do was to have to try for the automatic in Manny's belt. Better to come up with some lie.

Without a moment's hesitation, Royale slipped off her glasses and offered Manny a smile. Manny held her gaze for a long moment before dropping his gaze to the cleavage showing from her low cut peasant blouse.

"Seen enough?" she asked, the challenge in her voice a bit overdone.

Manny shot her a hard glance. "Something wrong?"

"I just don't like people fucking me with their eyes."

He laughed and looked at Quist. "This girl's a firecracker. Bet you feel like a rodeo rider most times." He gave Royale another look and shook his head. "Best not keep the boss waiting," he said and turned abruptly and walked off.

Quist looked at Royale and nodded in admiration. She shrugged and allowed herself another smile. He didn't know what kind of well she was drawing from, but she was playing the role much better than he expected.

Manny led them down another hallway that opened onto a massive multi-level living area, the far wall of which was entirely glass, offering an expansive view of the muddy corral below and the distant, rain-shrouded hills. A granite fireplace large enough to easily hold a small car anchored another wall, the source no doubt for the pervasive ashy smell. The room was tastefully decorated with finely carved modern colonial furniture, the sofas bound in cowhide. Most of the tiled flooring was covered with Oriental carpets the size of Quist's last apartment. A pair of chandeliers fashioned from deer antlers hung from the fiftee- foot ceiling. It reminded Quist of the lobby of a hotel he used to frequent in San Antonio.

"Make yourself at home," Manny said. "There's a bar over there. Just don't touch her things." He shook his head in what seemed amusement and exited the room.

"You think he recognized you?" Quist said softly, edging up to Royale's side.

"I doubt it. The last time he saw me I probably looked like I crawled out of a gutter."

He leaned over and kissed her on the cheek. "You're doing great, but be careful. There're cameras everywhere," he whispered in her ear.

She smiled and looked around the room. Her eyes suddenly widened as she peered over Quist's shoulder. He turned and followed her gaze to see what she had noticed. He watched as she made her way slowly over to the fireplace, her eyes seemingly fixed on the large painting above the heavy stone mantle.

The size of the painting alone was sufficient to draw anyone's attention, but it was the subject matter that immediately enlisted the urge for closer inspection. It was a portrait of a young woman standing in profile. She wore a floor length brocaded skirt, but was nude from the waist up, her small breasts glistening as if wet. Her thick black hair was piled atop her head and adorned with small seashells in a style that called to mind the image of a Mayan princess. A thin thread of gold looped from her nostril to her earlobe from which dangled a large disc of emerald-encrusted gold. In the background, a gibbous, bone -colored moon broke through a bank of wispy clouds. Shards of lightning on the far horizon completed the depiction. All in all it seemed overdone, its impact suggesting more spectacle than art. Still, the young woman's obvious beauty and the almost theatrical setting left one awestruck.

115

Quist stood there a moment, struggling with the notion that he had seen the young woman somewhere before. He began to lean closer in an effort to assemble in his mind what he was seeing when the realization struck him like a bolt. He turned and glanced at Roy. It was the same profile he had seen just several nights ago in the glow of Zozobra.

"Do you like the painting?" a woman's voice asked from behind them. "It's a portrait of my daughter, Luna."

24

Royale spun around at the sound of the voice. It took a second or two for her to locate the source of the voice. Mercedes Schoenfeld shuffled awkwardly from behind a large potted ficus. It took a moment for Royale to realize the bundle Schoenfeld held closely against her chest was a small dog: a Chihuahua wearing a sweater of sorts. She clung one-handed to a walker as she scuttled into the room. Still, something about her relatively unencumbered gait led Royale to briefly consider the walker might be more theatrical than functional.

Schoenfeld wore a pair of form fitting leather trousers and a wine colored cashmere sweater. Her long blonde hair was pulled back into a chignon so severe it seemed to pinch her face. Something about the face seemed off. It was tight and heart-shaped, almost cat-like. Her violet eyes, curious and furtive, did little to dispel the effect. Her face seemed remarkably wrinkle free, considering the fact Schoenfeld had to be at least seventy. Only the shots of gray in her honey-blond hair betrayed her age.

"Come sit," she barked, gesturing at one of the cowhide sofas. "I'm told you are friends of Tommy Eloquin."

Royale detected a lingering hint of Eastern Europe in the accent, her voice brassy and hoarse. She guessed it had taken a lot of cigarettes to earn that voice.

"Tommy was an asshole," she added as she dropped stiffly into a simple wooden chair beside the gargantuan fireplace. She gingerly set the oddly silent Chihuahua on the table beside her. The dog stood there on its thin spindly legs sniffing the air, its rheumy, marble-sized eyes listlessly gazing around the room in

117

a way that suggested the dog might be blind.

"There's no disputing that," Quist replied, sauntering up to the woman. "He still is. Ma'm, my lady friend here is Ronnie and I'm Henry Quinton," he said, extending his hand.

Mercedes Schoenfeld glanced briefly at his hand but didn't accept it. Quist shrugged and dropped onto the sofa across from her.

"I'll grant him this though," Quist said. "Tommy did have an eye for merchandise."

She studied Quist for a moment before glancing up at Royale who returned her gaze and forced a smile in response to the woman's withering look of appraisal. With a tilt of her head, Schoenfeld indicated that Royale should join Quist on the sofa.

Royale sat and stared at Schoenfeld for a long uncomfortable moment before turning and raising her hand to point at the painting. Quist quickly reached to lower her hand.

"I'll get right to the point," Quist said. "I don't believe in wasting anyone's time, especially since you've been so kind to see us. Tommy told me the two of you used to do business."

"Horses? The closest Tommy ever got to a horse was a betting card. Is he still behind with the bookies? He never did have any luck at the track."

"Not horses. He said you might have some contacts. Labor representatives, if you catch my drift. Someone that might help me find some workers."

"How is Tommy?" she asked, ignoring Quist's remark.

"Last we saw him he was on the down and out. I guess he's got some kinda cancer. He didn't seem like he had long, I'm sorry to say. He said…"

"You need laborers?" she asked, cutting him off. "Mexico's full of them. But you needn't come all the way down here. Just stand out in front of the Wal-Mart in Brownsville and you'll get all the labor you need."

Quist looked at her and sucked his teeth. "You see, Miss Schoenfeld. I own a string of establishments throughout the South. Florida and Mississippi, mostly. Restaurants, bars. Some back room gambling. And I provide entertainment, if you know what I mean. Now Tommy told me you used to be in that same line of work. Providing entertainment, that is."

She laughed, a hard, truncated snort and reached for a pack of cigarettes on the table at her side. She directed the pack to her mouth and then changed her mind.

"Light or dark?" she asked.

"What?"

"Light or dark skinned? Or the Asian variety?" She smiled but only her mouth moved. "You see, Mr. Quinton. I knew a woman once who provided that sort of entertainment. Young Ukrainian women without the benefit of visas. Those pretty little Thai girls. But I also know for a fact this woman is no longer in the entertainment business. Perhaps, Tommy confused me with her."

She lifted the cigarette pack to her mouth, extracted one with her lips. As she bent her head to the side Royale saw what appeared to be a linear scar on her throat; a crudely performed surgical procedure perhaps. Her mind hurriedly discarded something more sinister.

"Yeah, I guess Tommy could've got it wrong," Quist said, nodding. "I've heard that chemotherapy can mess up your mind some." He shot Schoenfeld a smile. "Unfortunately, we're not in the market for any of your fine horses. Hell, it's hard enough keeping a dog. Isn't that right, Ronnie? It's just such a shame we came all this way for nothing. I guess we can always do some shopping. I'm sure that wouldn't bother Ronnie here none."

"I just love all your furniture and stuff," Royale said, taking her cue. "I bet this kinda furniture would cost a small fortune to ship back to Atlanta. I may have to just settle for glassware and jewelry. I would like to get a painting though. I've always liked art." Royale turned and pointed at the portrait above the fireplace. "I just love that one. You said it's a picture of your daughter?"

Schoenfeld regarded her silently for a moment before lighting her cigarette with a silver lighter she retrieved from her lap. "Yes, that's my daughter," she said after taking a violent suck on her cigarette.

Royale sensed more bitterness than pride in her reply.

"Gosh. She's beautiful. I bet she's gorgeous in real life, too. I mean, you know, not all dressed like that and posing. I'd love to meet her, you know, in person."

Schoenfeld smiled and patted the motionless Chihuahua. "I'm so sorry but that wouldn't be possible. You see, she is away at school. In the States."

"Oh, really where at?"

Schoenfeld looked at her with what seemed amusement for a few beats before answering.

"Houston."

"Where at? Rice University, maybe? I hear that's becoming a real good school."

Schoenfeld looked at her with a mixture of condescension and irritation, but didn't reply. Instead, she looked over at Quist. "I don't wish to be rude, Mr. Quinton. But I feel our business here is done. I am sorry you came all this way." She shrugged and waved the smoke away from her face. "Please give Mr. Eloquin my best wishes. Manert will show you out."

She picked up the dog and pushed herself up onto the walker with one hand and shuffled out of the room with what again seemed minimal effort. Royale looked at Quist who flexed his shoulders in an eloquent shrug. She stood up and walked back over to the painting. She felt an involuntary shudder as she more closely studied the young woman's image. At first, the likeness in her face suggested nothing. Not hope, not love. Not even regret, her face inscrutable except for perhaps the faintest intimation of defiance, a sort of tension that might be mistaken for vulnerability. And something else; something that made Royale feel as if she were seeing herself in a mirror.

On closer examination, there was the subtle projection of curiosity; detached, yet searching, the eyes casting about for the tiniest clue that might account for one's life, or at the least, some indication that all this would one day be the past, and the past could always be recast as fiction. That idea always appealed to Royale; the convenience of erasing the past; erasing regret.

She stepped back and tilted her head to study the image

from a different angle. No there wasn't the slightest hint of regret on her daughter's face. That'll come in time, Royale thought and wondered if she might tell Lana that when they met. She flinched when she sensed Quist moving up beside her.

"Nice painting. Maybe we can find you one like that back in San Miguel. It would look great in the TV room, wouldn't it?" he said loud enough for the benefit of Manny who approached them from the portal.

"I guess it's time to go," Manny said, gesturing with his arm.

"Manert. Is that what she called you? Sounds sorta...I don't know. Foreign, maybe. Or like something out of some old movie. Like someone might call the butler. Manert. "

He looked at Quist coldly and then smiled. "Manert's my given."

"Odd is all. Lead on, Manert."

Instead of leading them, he slipped in behind them. "I take it your meeting went well?" he asked.

Quist looked back at him over his shoulder. "You could say. At least I call it even anytime I walk out with my spending money still in my ass pocket."

"You two enjoy the rest of your time in San Miguel, you hear?" Manny said, and started to close the door behind them. "Oh, I almost forgot this." He reached into his pocket and pulled out Quist's switchblade and tossed it to him. "You never know. You might need this. Mexico can be a might dangerous."

"I'll try to remember that," Quist said and took Royale's arm.

"What do you think?" she asked as they climbed into the Jeep.

He turned on the ignition and hesitated a moment before driving off. "I can't really say. Maybe she's here, maybe she's not. Tell me. What did you think of the painting?"

Royale looked out the window, reluctant to meet his gaze. She didn't know what to make of the painting. It was Lana. Or was it Luna? Or both? She didn't reply until Quist slipped the Jeep into gear.

"So now what?" she asked.

"It is her though, right?"

"Yes, it's her," she muttered.

"I'm sorry," he said, sensing the defeat in her voice.

"What are you sorry for? I've told you, she's not your problem. "

Quist kept silent until they reached the gate. "We can go into town and ask around. Keep our eyes out. I guess I could watch the highway but they'd most likely spot me. Truth be told, I have this gut sense that says they'll come to us. If so, we better have a story. Better yet, a plan B. I'll work on it. By the way, you did real well. I didn't think you had it in you."

"What? Making things up? Outright lying? You must not be Catholic. You see, I learned from an early age what to admit to in the confessional, and what I needed to make up. Because you always had to come up with some kind of sinning or it didn't count. You made things up, and the priest believed you. It was a big thing when you're a kid and you know you can lie and get away with it. This guy Laing. You ever heard of R.D. Laing, the Scottish psychiatrist? No? He called it the territory of ourselves. The world we create out of our lies. That kind of innocent lying was sort of like a gateway drug. It made it so much easier to tell the whoppers later. Don't look at me like that. I may be a nun, but I'm not perfect."

"Best you keep that in mind for when we find your girl."

"If we find her."

"We'll find her," he said, waving graciously at the gate guard. "Let's just hope she didn't learn too much at her mother's knee."

25

Bless me father for I have sinned. My last confession was…" Royale fumbled to recall. "My last confession was two…or maybe three years ago."

The priest's head jerked up as if he had been sleeping. He turned and peered at her through the wooden grating separating them.

"Lo siento, señora. No hablo Inglés," he muttered.

From what she could see of him, the priest looked young. She thought it odd someone of his age didn't speak at least some English. Perhaps he didn't want to hear a tourist's sins, his experience telling him their sins were too foreign in too many ways.

"No problema," she replied, using up the extent of her Spanish. "I guess it doesn't matter." She paused for a moment before going on. "My sins. I'll spill the venial ones first. Since my last confession I haven't taken any drugs. I'm clean and sober except for some wine every now and then," she said, discounting the tequila Quist had plied her with. "I drink it sometimes so I can sleep. Not that I ever really sleep. Shutting my mind down isn't all that easy. It's hard to forget the things I have to listen to all day. I'm betting you can relate." She paused again as someone entered the adjoining confessional. "I've been celibate, too," she went on. "Not that I haven't had impure thoughts. I only touch…."

The priest tilted his head in such a way to convince Royale he spoke English after all. She smiled in amusement.

"Let's see. That about covers gluttony and lust. Pride? I obviously have none. Despair? Is that one of the original sins? If not, it should be." She paused, unsure how to go on. The shadows rendered the priest's face undecipherable. "Maybe that's my big one though. It's probably why I'm here. I came to confess I'm not sure I believe in anything anymore. I don't.... I can't believe. Not in any of it. Not this," she said, tilting her face upwards. "None of it. You see, I can't believe if I don't understand. And I don't understand." She leaned closer to the grate. "How about you? Do you understand what I'm saying?"

The priest cocked his head in vague acknowledgment.

"I've been doing God's work. Or so I've been told. You see, I sit all day and listen to people's shitty lives and it really makes me wonder about God's work. Do you ever feel like that?" The priest only looked at her. "And I ask myself if the awful stuff that happens to people is God's work. And am I doing it or undoing it? It's probably why I can't sleep."

She fell silent and after a moment, the priest gestured with his hand for her to go on.

"I'm here to look for someone. And I'm not even sure why. Here's something to confess. Part of me doesn't want to find her. That's probably my biggest sin. I'm afraid if I find her she'll reject me. Or maybe worse, I'll reject her. And then there's this man I'm with. I don't know if I trust him. There's something dark about him. As if that ever mattered," she added.

The priest started to fidget, obviously impatient for her to get on with it.

"I remember when I was kid, what it was like to walk out of confession. How light I'd feel. To go out into the world and feel clean." She paused and allowed herself a smile. "I can't remember the last time I felt like I was clean. Maybe I'm wondering whether anyone can really forgive me. Okay, okay," she said, sensing the priest's annoyance. "For these sins I'm heartily sorry. Now do your thing and I promise I'll leave."

The priest hurriedly began mumbling the absolution in what sounded like Latin. Raising his hand as if he were about to make the sign of the Cross, he hesitated. "I absolve thee in the name of the Father, and of the Son, and of the Hoy Ghost," he said in accented English. He waved his hand in blessing and turned away.

She remained kneeling for a moment and listened as the next penitent began their litany. It was only when the priest glanced at her over his shoulder that she rose and slipped out into the hushed silence of the cathedral. The expanse of pews was mostly empty of worshippers. Instead throngs of camera-toting tourists meandered through the aisles, their heads craned upwards at the stained-glass windows and pink-bricked vaulted ceilings. She stood there, self-consciously aware of the three elderly Mexican women kneeling just outside the confessional, their eyes downcast, their thoughts unknowable. She wondered as to the nature of their sins; surely nothing more than the sloth of old age.

She started down the side aisle and then paused beneath a painting of the Madonna and the infant Jesus, Mary's luminous gaze fixed on the baby cradled in her arms. Was there ever even a shred of that kind of bond between her and Lana? She stared at it a moment longer then slipped through a group of teenagers feigning interest in their guide's monologue.

She exited through the massive front doors, blinking at the sudden transformation from the dim interior to the late afternoon sunlight. It had still been cloudy when Quist had deposited her on the plaza. He told her he intended to check out some of the high-end boutiques in the off chance one of the clerks might know his friend Señorita Luna Schoenfeld. His ruse would be that he wanted to buy her a gift as a surprise. And would they maybe call the señorita and tell her to drop by the store and pick up the anonymous gift. For some reason, he told Royale he would do better finding something out if she wasn't along, his rather lame explanation being that she might prove to be a distraction to the shop clerks. It was more likely he didn't want a critical audience for his display of fawning duplicity.

She sat on the cathedral's wide stone steps and leaned back, stretching her bare legs. She couldn't recall the last time she had basked in the sun, at least not like this, her legs bare to mid-thigh. The sense of lightness she had felt a moment before gave way to fascination as she gazed at the spectacle of the various passersby. Besides the ubiquitous tourists, there were buskers hawking everything from trinkets and straw hats to trays of street food. A pair of young men, hipster types gauging from their skinny jeans and modish, quasi-athletic footgear, were attempting to enlist a gaggle of uniformed school children to pose with them for a selfie. All in all, the procession reminded her of a parade of exotic, mismatched circus animals like the ones she had once seen at a Ringling Brothers performance in the Astrodome in Houston.

It had been the occasion of her tenth birthday, one of the rare occurrences when their father had taken her and Charly on an out of town trip. It hadn't ended well. Her father had sat out in parking lot and drank himself into a stupor. Consequently, they slept in the car that night, serenaded by elephant trumpeting.

Royale treated herself to ten minutes of mindless observation before she spotted Quist at the edge of the crowd. She waved to get his attention and then waited as he made his way towards her. It took a second or so to realize someone was with him; a young woman, Hispanic and dressed in black jeans and a stylish purple smock. Her long black tresses were done up ala Frieda Kahlo. They both appeared to be eating something wrapped in a cone of newspaper.

"Hey," he said in greeting. He showed her the contents of the grease-stained packet; some kind of roasted meat from the looks of it. *"Churrasco de cabra,"* he said in explanation. "Barbecued goat. I would've gotten you some if I'd known I'd find you so soon. Want a bite?"

"No thanks," she said, glancing at the young woman.

"This is Fortuna," Quist said thickly through a mouthful of goat.

Fortuna dabbed her mouth with a paper napkin and smiled.

"She knows Luna. They used to hang together. Isn't that right, Fortuna?"

"Hang together? *No entiendo.* My English is not so good," she said.

"It means you two used to spend time together," Royale said. She waited for Quist's lead.

"She and Luna were friends. They went to school together."

Fortuna wadded up the cone of grilled meat and held it, uncertain what to do with it. She looked nervous.

"Fortuna works at a dress shop where Luna used to come into. She hasn't seen her though in a month or so."

"You were friends? Friends that would talk to each other?"

Royale asked.

Fortuna glanced at Quist. "Go on. Tell her what you told me," Quist said.

"Si, we speak *muchas veces*. Many times. She tells me things. About her *madre*. Bad things. Luna, she tells me she wishes to go away. Run away is how you say, Yes? She had a boyfriend. They both go away."

"Fortuna says the last time they spoke is the day Luna said she was leaving. But she doesn't know where her and her boyfriend were planning on going."

"So she's in the wind, and we don't know where." Royale looked up at Fortuna. "Tell me about her. About Luna. What kind of girl was she?"

Fortuna looked at Quist as if unsure of what Royale had asked.

"*Creo*...I think I know what you mean," Fortuna said. "*Luna fue amable.*"

"*Amable. ¿Qué es eso?*" Quist asked.

Fortuna shrugged. "*Amable*. Kind, I think is how you say. Yes? *Pero muy agitada. Luna a veces...*" She looked again at Quist. "She does drugs. Many times. *Ella se turbó. ¿Entiendo?*"

"And you don't know where she went?" Royale asked.

Fortuna shook her head and looked at Quist. "I must go back now."

Quist touched her shoulder. "*Muchas gracias,* Fortuna."

"Why did you bring her? You could've just told me what she said," Royale said.

Quist picked a morsel of meat from the edge of the cone and tossed it into his mouth. "I thought it might help to meet someone that knew her. Maybe make Lana seem more real to you."

"Gee thanks. Now I know she does drugs and she's *agitada*. Yeah, I caught that." She got to her feet and looked around. "So now what?"

"It looks like we've gotten someone's attention." He nodded with his head to a clutch of people gathered around a street musician. "See the guy with the baseball cap? Not the skinny one. The guy who looks like a weight lifter. He's been following me around all afternoon. I'm pretty sure he picked us up when we drove into town from Schoenfeld's place. The first time I really got a good look at him though was when I parked the Jeep."

"Let's quit with these games," she said. "We should've just come right out and told Schoenfeld why we're here. There's no good reason we have to be as duplicitous as that old witch."

"Oh, you think? Listen, Roy. I don't think Schoenfeld 's going to get warm and fuzzy over your maternal yearnings. Somebody like her has got too many secrets. She'll be paranoid no matter what. So we might as well approach on the sly."

"This is being sly? When she probably knows we're going around town asking about Lana?"

"It's their move now. It's the only way we'll know something."

"You weren't very successful as an ATF agent, were you?"

Quist stifled a laugh, his mouth full of goat. He chewed for a couple of seconds and swallowed. "Truth be told, I guess I wasn't. Least ways in the narrow confines of what they referred to as protocol. Like they say in the movies, I always got my man though. Well, maybe not always. Whoa," he said, almost choking on another bite of goat. "We got a strike," he said gesturing with his chin. "Looks like she sent her erstwhile minion to feel us out."

Through the crowd of people listening to the street musician, Royale saw that Manny had joined the beefy guy in the baseball cap. She felt herself shudder. What if he had finally placed where he knew her from? And so what if he did? The worst that could happen was the truth would come out about why they had come. No, perhaps worse than that would be finding out the truth about Lana, she reminded herself.

Quist finished his goat and wadded up the greasy wrapping. "Come, Sister Aucoin. I say we get a beer. That place over there looks promising." He made a point of extending his arm in the direction of an open-air bar on the edge of the plaza. The sign above the portico announced El Centro Bar. "It should be easy for him to find us there."

26

Quist led her to a table on the edge of the portal that provided a view of the garden in the center of the plaza and the front of the cathedral. Placing their chairs so they could see the entirety of the plaza, they waited. Sure enough, no sooner had the waiter taken their order then Royale spotted Manny making his way towards them, a cell phone to his ear.

"*¿Qué pasa, amigo?*" Quist asked as Manny drew up next to their table. "Hell of a coincidence. We were just talking about you and Miss Schoenfeld. I was just telling Ronnie here how nice you all seemed. Gracious in fact, considering we might've been way off base in asking what we did. Don't you agree, Manert?" he asked, offering a grin. "About us being off base?"

Manny slipped the phone into his shirt pocket. He wore the same wide-brimmed straw hat as the day before. He looked at them each in turn, his face expressionless, then paused to light a cigarette before pulling up a chair. He took a deep puff, exhaled and rotated the cigarette back and forth between his fingers for a moment, examining the end from every angle.

"I called around. Tommy Eloquin is dead," he said, looking up at Quist.

"That's news to us. Too bad. He was still alive when we spoke with him not three days ago. He was in a nursing home in Santa Fe. Hon, remind me that we should send some flowers or something. You still have that number of that place, don't you Ronnie?

"Indeed I do. Tommy might've looked dead but he still had a pulse last we saw him.'

Royale could see the glimmer of uncertainty on Manny's face. He took a puff of his cigarette, as if buying some time for

129

his comeback. "Okay," he said finally. "Say that half-wit is still alive. I still don't buy he would tell you to come down here asking around for a line on some whores."

"Well, I beg to disagree. It's...." Quist paused as he scooted his chair forward to allow a tourist couple to edge past them to an adjoining table. The female, a pale, slim woman in a sundress and a long beaked cap thanked Quist and settled into the chair behind him. Her partner, his face partially hidden by an over-sized pair of sunglasses and a Stetson pulled low nodded at Quist and fell heavily into the chair facing their table. From what Quist could see it appeared the man had been out too long in the sun, his face puffy and boiled. His black T-shirt, the short sleeves rolled up to show flabby biceps, heralded a country western concert in Bakersfield that advertised Merle Haggard and Rosanne Cash as the headliners.

"I told him I needed some labor help," Quist resumed. "The fleshy kind. He suggested we look up Miss Schoenfeld. If I was out of line, please extend her our sincere apologies. You can do that, can't you, Manert?" Quist shook his head in amusement. "That name. Manert. I can't get it out of my head. You said it was your given? Let me guess. Your mama would call you that when she was pissed. Manert," Quist barked in exaggerated annoyance.

Manny smiled. Before he could reply, the waiter brought their beers. After the waiter left, Manny took a long draw on his cigarette. "I'm laying odds you're not who you say you are. Maybe you are just some two-bit grifters. Although you don't seem quite slick enough. Your pitch is a little too weak." He took another drag on his cigarette, blowing the smoke across the table in Royale's direction.

"And you," he said, nodding at her. "You don't come across as a whore. Even though you want me to think you used to be one. So that leaves the possibility you're law dogs. But I don't think you're one of them either. So there's gotta be some other con you're playing that I just haven't quite figured out yet. But I guarantee you I will. Until then I'll put you two down as just stupid. And if that's the case, you need to wise up, drop this bullshit and cut your losses."

The guy in the T-shirt with Haggard's image on the front cursed aloud as he fumbled with his camera. He grimaced as he made an adjustment then said," Smile, darling," as he took a shot of his partner.

Royale leaned forward across the table. "Look here, you coon ass. I'll tell you what we want." She sensed Quist stiffen beside her. "Don't make the mistake of taking us for a pair of redneck rubes just because my friend here likes to chew his way around things. We didn't come down here blind. We checked your boss out. All we want is a line on some girls. That painting she's got hanging on that wall. That's the kind we're looking for. Something exotic looking. Any chance that girl's in the business?"

Manny stared at her, obviously taken aback by her directness, or possibly her indiscreet stupidity.

"Why are you so damned interested in Ms. Schoenfeld's daughter?"

"I told you. She's the kind of girl we're looking for."

Manny smiled and dropped his cigarette in Royale's beer glass. "You really think you can pull the wool over ol' Manny's eyes? I tell you what. I think it best you two call it a day and head north. San Miguel isn't really all that safe of a town no matter what your guidebook says. People breaking into your houses. Stealing things or worse. Think about it," he added, rising to his feet. With that, he turned and left.

"Were you by any chance a grifter in between your skanky whore days and that nunnery?" Quist said, shaking his head in amusement. "Some previous life maybe? I mean to tell, girl. I swear I don't know whether to give you a prize or run for my life."

"I'd say that went rather well," Royale said, picking up Quist's beer and taking a sip. She hoped he didn't see her hand shaking.

"I say let's get out of here," he said, signaling the waiter. He took back his glass and downed half of it in one swallow. As they waited for the check, the guy in the T-shirt at the next table leaned over and asked rather loudly. "Pardon me. But I was wondering if you could take a picture of me and the missus? I'd sure appreciate it."

Before Quist could reply, the man had scooted his chair next to his wife who had turned her chair to face them. She put her arm around her husband's shoulder and offered up a smile as fake as her overdone makeup. Quist smiled back, realizing it was too late to refuse. The man handed Quist the camera.

"You just have to hit this little button. Oh shit, I just took one. I'm sure gonna have a lot of these pictures to delete. Right, hon? Haven't quite got the hang of this new camera is all," he explained.

"Say cheese," Quist said and shot two quick photos and handed the man back his camera.

"Where you folks from?" the man asked. "The missus and I are down here from Dallas."

Quist grinned but didn't reply. Instead, he fished a few crumpled peso notes from his shirt pocket and dropped them on the table. Without bothering to wait for Royale, he stood and began walking off.

"That was a little rude, don't you think?" she said, catching up with him.

He looked at her but didn't reply. They walked down a side street in the direction of the restaurant they had dined at the night before. "Plan B," he said finally. "We go back out to the ranch in the morning and tell her the truth."

"What? I thought you said..."

"I know what I said, but this isn't going the way I planned. Besides I didn't especially like Manny's tone of voice. It sounded like he might've meant that part about this not being such a safe place."

"And how are we supposed to tell Schoenfeld how we know about her and Lana? After all, she sure didn't adopt her. She bought her for chrissakes. You really think she's going to admit to something like that? Besides that Fortuna girl said she's gone."

"Maybe she's gone. Maybe not. Tell me something. That

painting. That's what's got the bee in your bonnet, isn't it? Well, you shouldn't read too much into it. You don't even know if she even posed for that or somebody just used her likeness."

"You don't get it, Quist. Since she was five years old Lana was raised by an amoral sex trafficker who's probably mixed up with the drug cartels. I can only imagine what Lana's adolescence was like. You saw that painting. As much as I don't want to admit it, that's her. That's Lana."

"So why are we still here?"

She hesitated before answering. "I don't know. Not anymore."

"Well best you figure it out, but you won't forgive yourself if you didn't at least try to find her. And this may be your last shot. I say we just put our cards on the table and see what Schoenfeld knows. Besides, I may have something to trade."

"Trade? What do we have that she might want?"

"I'll tell you when I got it all worked out. Meanwhile, let's eat. You know that place we ate at last night? I saw cazuela de camrónes on the menu. I had that once at this place in Baja. Really liked it."

"God, how can you think about food?" Royale shook her head in amusement. "Okay, as long as you stay in your chair."

"I won't kiss you again if that's what you're referring to. Kissing a nun was on my bucket list, is all. I scratched it off."

"Good, because I've already done enough penance today."

"What does that mean?"

"Nothing." She took his arm. "Eating two nights in a row in a really nice restaurant is on top of my bucket list. Not exciting, but attainable. Now feed me."

27

Quist lifted his bowl and slurped up the last of his soup, the thin broth still rich with the tang of shrimp and garlic and serranos. He shook his head in appreciation and started to reach for Roy's margarita which remained untouched. She intercepted his hand and shot him a look of admonishment.

"You've had enough," she said, handing him her water glass.

He shrugged and gulped the water. She had remained oddly silent through drinks, his drinks that is, and supper. His attempts at small talk elicited only the most perfunctory of responses. He initially sensed her detachment stemmed from an understandable anxiety and ambivalence surrounding finding Lana. Ever since leaving the ranch, Roy seemed more distant than even before. He assumed the cause was the painting. He had to admit it had made an impression on him also. There was something about the young woman in the portrait; a sensuality and enigmatic energy that belied someone Lana's age. Roy seemed convinced it was Lana. Quist still wasn't so sure that it wasn't merely some artist's fanciful portrayal, much like some Renaissance portrait of some burghers' wife or baroness that most likely bore little resemblance to reality.

He leaned over and peered past Roy to the street.

"What do you keep looking at?" she asked with obvious irritation.

"Street life is all." It was the second time Quist noticed the woman from the bar strolling by. This time she was dressed differently and her hair hung loose. "Tell me something. What was

Charly like when she was inside?"

"In the prison? Why do you want to know that?"

"Just curious." He picked up her margarita, this time unimpeded.

She didn't reply right away. "The first few years she was pretty bitter. We both were. I think after a while she gave up. She just couldn't fight anymore. I figured that was about when she stopped seeing me. I heard later she taught reading and writing to the other inmates. But that's all I know. The warden was this tight assed Pentecostal type. Anyway, she said Charly had settled. Those were her exact words. She said it like you might be talking about a dog you had trained. I felt like slapping her. To answer your question, I really didn't know what she was like then. She never let me in, never talked about what it was like."

"Living isn't the same as being alive," he muttered.

"What did you say?"

"Nothing." He finished off the margarita. "We should go."

"No. Not until you tell me what we have to bargain with."

"All right. That couple at the El Centro. The tourists whose picture I took. I'm pretty sure they saw us come in here. The woman has walked by here at least twice. I know a tail when I see one."

"You sure you're not just being paranoid? I've seen the same people all day long. It's a small town."

"Nope. I'm pretty sure she was wearing a wig back at the bar. No wedding ring either. To top it off, her hubby's T-shirt was brand new and too tight."

"That's all? The guy's T-shirt was new and too tight?"

"I know for a fact that concert took place eight years ago. I know because I was near there at the time. And I doubt the guy just happened to pull that heirloom T-shirt out of the bottom of his drawer. I guess maybe he could've gained some weight since then. Just saying."

"Say you're right. Then who are they?"

He shrugged. "All I know is the guy took a picture of us. Look, give me a day to find out about them. Something tells me they're not on Schoenfeld's payroll. In that case, she might like to know about them."

"That's your trade? What if they're just some innocent yokels from Dallas? Then what? You're going to just turn that psychopath Manny on to them?"

"I'm open to other ideas."

She stared down at the table. Quist could tell her confidence that they would ever find out about Lana was flagging. Or was it her confidence in him? Either way, he knew they needed a quick resolution before things got ugly. He knew better than to underestimate the menace of people like Manny.

"Let's go back to the casita and talk about it."

Roy got up from the table and walked out. Quist quickly paid the check and hurried after her. He could tell she was upset, but part of him didn't care. He wasn't prepared for this to end badly, and that's where this whole misadventure seemed to be headed. And he sure a shell wouldn't allow himself to be responsible for something happening to Roy.

"You're sure you don't want to call it quits?" he asked, catching up to her.

"No, I just want… Christ, at this point I just want to know she's alright."

"And what are you going to consider being alright? She's not one of Schoenfeld's prostitutes? Maybe you're just hoping she's just some fucked up twenty-year old airhead. All I'm saying is I doubt we're going to find her. And if we do." He fumbled, unsure whether he was being too crass and cynical. He touched her arm. "That didn't come out right."

"I know what to expect. Have you forgotten what I do for a living? I'm going to recognize her for who she is. I've seen enough of women like that. You can't avoid the damage done to someone brought up with the likes of a mother like Schoenfeld. If that's who she really was to Lana." He reached for her arm but she pulled away. "Yesterday I would've settled for just seeing her, not even up close. Just seeing her. And now all I can think about is I have to save her. And I'm not sure I can even do that. Christ, I don't think I've ever saved any of them. And I'm not so crazy naïve to think this will go any better."

Neither of them said anything as they walked in the direction of where Quist had parked the Jeep. It was late and only a few of the streets were populated by tourists window shopping or trolling for a late night bar. The further they walked from the plaza the more the pedestrians seemed to be locals hurrying home for a late supper. The busier thoroughfares gave way to narrow cobble-stoned streets lined with shuttered shops. As the streets grew darker, Quist glanced over his shoulder to see if they were being followed but so far he saw nothing out of the ordinary. Still, he was starting to regret not taking the time to find a closer parking spot.

It wasn't until they drew near to the Jeep and Quist had removed his keys that he heard an engine roar to life on the street behind them. His instincts heightened, he nudged Royale onto the sidewalk. In his previous life, he would've at least ducked into a doorway and checked out any likely exits. But in retrospect, he realized he had become careless, his edge numbed by assignments that required nothing more disquieting than baby-sitting an inebriated spouse, or nudging away a street hustler or one of the client's disgruntled ex-employees. Back in the day, he would've seen it coming.

He glanced over his shoulder and saw the van speeding down the street towards them, its headlights off. Before he could react, another vehicle, a taxi, pulled out of nowhere, blocking their way forward. Roy, perhaps sensing his sudden apprehension, pulled away. Quist grasped at her arm in an effort to pull her back. If they could run back in the direction they had come the van might not be able to easily follow on the narrow street. Perhaps anticipating he might try this, the van slowed and a figure leapt from the van, cutting them off.

It all happened quickly and with a disquieting precision. The van screeched to a halt next to them, the doors flew open and two men dressed in dark clothing jumped out. One of them carried a large handgun. The man motioned with the gun for Quist to stop.

Another figure wearing a red ski mask emerged from the taxi and started towards them. Quist stumbled back against the grated doorway, momentarily paralyzed by the fleeting memory of that afternoon in Baghdad. He had to do something or it could end the same. He pushed Royale out of the way as he plowed into the man wearing the ski mask.

He yelled at her to run, knowing it was probably useless. The man in the mask grunted as Quist drove him down hard onto the sidewalk. To Quist's surprise, the man offered not even half-hearted resistance. Behind him, Quist could hear Roy struggling with their captors. A man cursed and Roy yelled something. As he started to turn, someone jammed what felt like the barrel of a gun against his head.

"Tómelo con calmo, Pedro," the guy on the ground in the ski mask said and the one with the gun stepped back. "Okay, Harlan. Enough of this," the man said, his voice betraying more amusement than menace.

Quist straightened up and shot a quick glance over his shoulder. Two of their assailants were half-pushing, half-carrying Roy towards the van.

"Relax," the man in the ski mask said, staggering to his feet. "No one's gonna get hurt. We just need to talk. *Hey chicos,"* he yelled at the men. "Easy. *Fácil ir con la mujer.* Alright?"

"We have to hurry," he said, glancing quickly at Quist. "Are you coming?" he asked as he started for the van.

Quist hesitated and then followed him. He heard the taxi speed off behind him. The two men from the van waited on the sidewalk until Quist crawled into the van before slamming the door shut and running back down the street from the direction they had come.

"They need to deal with whoever it is tailing you," the guy in the ski mask said.

"So you know my name. So who the fuck are you?" Quist asked, glancing around to assess their situation. Roy was pressed up tight against his side, snug between Quist and one of their captors. The one wearing the mask sat perched on a fold down bench seat across from them. Counting the driver, only three of them, Quist thought. Not the greatest odds, but not the worst either. But something told him it wasn't going to come to that.

The guy in the ski mask rolled the mask up over his forehead. Even in the dim light Quist recognized him as the tourist from El Centro.

"Where's the missus?' Quist asked.

"She's home fixing supper. She hoped you wouldn't keep me long. I assured her our business would be brief."

"You never said your name."

"A name isn't important. At least not now. But heck, if you need to call me something, call me Sam. Just Sam from Tulsa. You know, if you ever need to ask for me."

Tulsa. That explained the flat drawl.

"I guess by now you figured we're not taking you hostage or anything. If we were, I wouldn't have let you keep that knife in your boot. Yeah, I read about that in your profile. That file was pretty detailed, right down to how much gin you drink and your taste in tail. It says you do private work now, whatever that means."

"You guys work pretty fast. It's been what? Three hours since you took my picture? So I'm just guessing here. You have to be government. DEA would be my guess."

"Close enough. You weren't the hit I was expecting when we got your resume back. I was expecting some mid-level hustler. So the question is, what's a former ATF guy doing visiting the Lady McBeth? You're not working a job or they would've told me. So what is it?" he asked when Quist didn't reply.

Quist knew there was no point in not offering up something close to the truth. It was the complications of that truth that might carry ramifications he hadn't yet considered.

"He's working for me," Roy said before Quist could say anything. "The young woman that Schoenfeld claims is her daughter is really my daughter. You don't need to know anything more than that."

"You're talking about Luna? That little hell bitch?" Sam snickered before breaking out into a laugh. "Now if that don't beat all." He shook his head and looked at Roy. "Your passport says Royale Aucoin. Only person with that name and New Orleans address is supposedly a nun. So are you Sister Aucoin?"

Royale nodded.

"New Orleans. Schoenfeld's got history there. This is beginning to sound like a story I'd like to hear."

"Do you know where my daughter is?" Royale asked.

The van driver had taken them down a stretch of well-lighted boulevard that led past a mall anchored by a modern grocery store and several American chain stores. In the piss yellow light, Sam's sunburned face appeared morbidly pasty. The dim light made it difficult to make out his eyes. He removed the ski mask from his head and tossed it over his shoulder into the front seat. The wet hair plastered to his scalp made him look even more like one of the undead. Turning back to Roy, he said, "And what's mama here wanting to do? Share family photos? Spend some quality time? All I'll say is if you happen to get a line on her, please call me up because I sure would like to hear some of her reminisces about her life with the spider woman."

"She's not here in San Miguel?" Quist asked.

"Hold on," Sam said, glancing at his phone. He read what must've been a text and then leaned over the seat to speak to the driver. *"Volvamos. Todo es claro."*

The driver made a quick U-turn, heading back down the way they had just come.

"Your tail met with an unfortunate accident. Mugged is what I hear," he said, slipping the cell into his shirt pocket. "No, she's not here. At least as far as I can tell she's high-tailed it. And believe me, I've looked for her. I figure only the Schoenfeld woman knows for sure where she is. Or at least where she maybe was. I think at this point she might be looking for her, too."

"What do you mean?"

"The girl skedaddled right about after Schoenfeld broke her hip and ended up in that walker. She must've seen her chance. We've got a friend of the housekeeper on the payroll. Apparently, the housekeeper hasn't seen Luna since the day the old lady took the fall.

"We tapped a phone belongs to a friend of Luna's here in town. Seems Luna's in Mexico City. And not too happy about it either. Sounded sorta desperate actually, but she was too cagey to offer any details over the phone. Then, two days ago, a contact of ours with the Mexican task force say Luna pulled twenty grand from an account she kept at a bank there."

"The Mexican police are looking for her, too?"

"We're not the only ones wanting to know Schoenfeld's business dealings."

"So you're sweating us because we might know something," Quist said.

"No, I just saw you two with Manny Fontenot and I had to know what your game was. I figured you must be dirty. Then I pull up your resume and I get to thinking there's gotta be more. Now that I know, well, it gets me to thinking. I'm assuming you're not being straight with Schoenfeld. So maybe you two should keep up that ruse of yours. See what you can find out. Maybe help us find the girl."

"And you really think Schoenfeld would tell us anything? Besides, you said she most likely doesn't know where she is either."

"What I meant to say was she isn't saying. Maybe she knows, maybe she doesn't. I want you to find out. You see, Luna knows a lot about the old gal's business. Shit, I'd wager at one time she was being groomed to take over. But maybe now, that ship has sailed and she can be persuaded to talk to us. Savvy?"

Quist looked at Roy, her face unreadable in the dim light. She looked out the window for a moment before looking back. "And what happens to her?" she asked.

"WITSEC, maybe."

"Wit what?"

"He means Witness Protection," Quist said.

"And I never see her again." Roy looked back out the window.

"We've got a problem," Quist said. "This Manny wants us out of town on the next train."

Sam pondered this for a moment before leaning forward. "Let me see if I can neutralize Manny. At least hobble him a little. That might give you a clear angle at working Schoenfeld. How you do it is up to you."

"Thanks for the vote of confidence, but this isn't going to be as easy as you're making it out to be."

Sam shrugged. "Apparently, you've done undercover. You must know how to work these things. We just need a line on Luna."

"Lana," Roy murmured.

"Lana. Luna." He looked at Quist. "So? What do you think?"

Quist thought for a moment, all the time realizing any ideas were merely grandiose bullshit. If there was anything solid in the way of a plan, it had yet to occur to him. All he knew for sure was that Roy couldn't be a part of it.

"Sure. But I'll need some things from you," Quist said. "A bankroll to flash around for one. And some help."

"Money's no problem. What kind of help you have in mind?"

"Another partner."

Roy turned and looked at him. He couldn't decipher her expression, but sensed something more than confusion. Disappointment? Anger?

Sam nodded at Roy. "You're saying she won't do?"

"No."

"Too bad. Seemed like a fit. No matter. I'll see what I can do. Meanwhile, here's your ride," he said as they pulled up next to his Jeep. "You should be fine tonight. I'll put some eyes on the casita." He tossed Quist a small cell phone he dug out of his jeans. "My number's programmed in there. Call me in the morning when you've got some ideas," he said, sliding open the van door.

Quist tried to take Roy's arm as she crawled from the van but she jerked away.

"I'm not getting you involved," he said after the van pulled away.

"A little too late for that, don't you think?"

"Wait, goddammit," he said pulling her back onto the sidewalk. "I'm not going to get someone killed again because I might've half-ass thought I knew what I was doing."

"You said it right. You don't know what you're doing. Or even why. This isn't for Charly. It's not for me. Or is it?" She turned and looked at him. "Is this just that bull shit knight in shining armor complex guys like you want to pull? I would've thought what happened in Iraq cured you of that."

Quist stared at her, unsure where to direct his anger. He turned finally and started to walk to the Jeep. "You coming?" he yelled. He crawled in and sat there for the minute or so it took for her to decide to get in

"Nell. That was her name, wasn't it?" Roy said, sliding into her seat. "You say she trusted you. It was her decision to go along with you. Then it wasn't on you. And this isn't on you either. I've come this far. I'm doing this," she said.

He nodded and started the Jeep.

28

They pulled up to the casita, but neither of them made an effort to get out. Nor had either of them said anything on the drive back. Therapeutic silence is what Royale had been trained to think of this dead space. Just wait for something, a thought, some emotion, to break out.

"I think we both owe each other an apology," she said, finally.

"Accepted."

"You're an asshole. You wanted to cut me out. You said you wanted another partner. One, I'm not your partner. And even if..."

"Hold on, Sister. Hear me out. This isn't going to work, no matter what that Sam guy thinks. The odds of us convincing Schoenfeld to tell us anything are slim to none. It can't be done, at least not without a lot of planning and prep. I know how these things work."

"So why did you tell the Sam guy you'd do it?"

"I told him I'd think about it. And I have. They can find Lana. We can't. Simple as that."

"I'm not ready to give up yet."

"Are you ready to end up in a hole in the desert? Because that's how these things usually end. Come on, let's sleep on it. Maybe something will come to me. Light's burned out," he said as he started to open the Jeep's door.

"What?"

"The porch light's out. Isn't that how it always goes in those scary picture shows? And there's always some idiot decides to check it out. You stay here. I'll check it out."

She watched Quist slowly approach the porch in the darkness. A moment later, she saw a brief slant of light as he opened the door. Maybe he was right. She had no experience in this kind of subterfuge. Let Sam's people, whoever they were, let them find Lana. She waited another minute and when Quist didn't appear, she opened her door and stepped out.

A hand suddenly clamped over her mouth and someone twisted her left arm roughly behind her mouth. *"Silencio, chica."* a voice hissed in her ear.

She could smell onions on his breath. The man pushed her forward. She had a flash of memory from something she had learned in a self-defense class. It was best to act right away. Don't hesitate. And give no quarter. Stomp on his instep. Go for his eyes. His nuts. She stomped with her foot but missed. As she tried to twist away, she felt something in her arm pop. The pain blinded her. Still, she reached back and tried to swipe at his eyes with her fingers. Before she knew it, she was on her knees and her assailant's knee was in her back.

"Pinche puta! No me jodas," he said, jerking her back to her feet.

She stifled a sob, the pain in her elbow all she could focus on.

The man pushed her forward, kicking open the front door which stood slightly ajar. The first thing she saw was Quist on his knees in the living room, his hands folded behind his head. He looked up at her as she was shoved forward. The regret in his eyes made her own regret loom even larger.

From what she could see, there were just two of them; the man behind her and a big, barrel-chested Mexican with a large hand gun in one hand and what most likely was Quist's switchblade in the other. The man smiled at her approach.

The man behind her laughed and said something that ended with the word *puta*. On the floor behind Quist, she could see what looked like a large wad of crumpled up plastic sheeting like the kind painters used. She almost stumbled as the man behind her nudged her forward. And so this was it, she thought. Quist was right about how things like this usually ended. She was shoved on to the sofa. She stifled a moan as she gripped her left elbow.

"I'm supposing Manny would like to know what exactly my lady friend and I are doing down here," Quist said. "Why don't you call him up and tell him to come on down and we'll talk."

"*No necessario*. Manny say it make no difference. We are not here to listen to you talk." The man looked at his partner and smiled. "*Te gusta su culo?*" He nodded at Royale and then tilted his head toward the bedroom.

"Hold on, *amigos*," Quist said, staring at Royale. "I just want to give *mi esposa un...* embrace. *Un abrazo*. Yeah? Say goodbye? *¿Comprendes?*" He nodded at Royale, his eyes dropping to the sofa. "*Sólo un momento, por favor.*"

Quist rose cautiously to his feet and made his way to the sofa. The big Mexican stepped back, as if unsure of how to respond. The other Mexican, a younger, muscle bound guy dressed in camouflage pants and a T-shirt snickered, but made no effort to stop Quist. He instead moved behind the sofa. Royale noticed he was carrying a roll of twine.

Quist knelt in front of Royale and leaned over, his face inches from hers. "I'm real sorry," he whispered, and then placed his arms around her shoulders. She felt his right arm drop to her side onto the cushion. She remembered then; the other knife hidden in the fold of the cushion.

He kissed her gently on the cheek and brushed her hair with his left hand, and looked in her eyes before glancing up at the young Mexican behind her.

"*Suficiente*. Stand up, *pendejo*," the big Mexican said, grabbing Quist by the collar.

As Quist pushed to his feet, he pivoted and swung before the man could react. In her mind's eye Royale saw the slice, heard the hiss, the guttural scream. The big Mexican dropped his gun and staggered back, his hands on his throat. His partner, momentarily too stunned to react, uttered a curse, and then leapt over the sofa, knocking Royale aside.

The big Mexican grasped Quist's shirt collar with one

bloodied hand as he stumbled backwards over the coffee table, dragging Quist with him. His partner landed on top of them both, straddling Quist, who swiped at him blindly with the knife, all the while still trying to escape the grasp of the wounded man, whose desperate, foundering efforts were more than Quist could deal with.

The younger Mexican proved too fast and too powerful for Quist, and before Quist could act, the man had looped several strands of twine around Quist's neck, jerking Quist back and onto his knees. The wounded man on the floor attempted a feeble kick that served nothing more than to throw Quist off balance. Quist tried to struggle to his feet, forcing his assailant behind him up against the sofa, almost pinning Royale. As she tried to wriggle free, Quist swung his arm back, stabbing the knife into the Mexican's thigh. This seemed to do nothing more than enrage him, as he jerked the twine tighter around Quist's neck.

For a long time afterwards, she would awaken in a cold sweat, the memory of what happened next all too real. It was as if she were watching someone else in one of those jerky, old time movies. She saw herself pummeling her fists against the Mexican's head; Quist grunting as he dug at the ever-tightening twine around his neck. And then the surreal image of herself grabbing the table lamp and swinging it at the Mexican's head over and over again.

It was the pain in her arm that seemed to bring her back. She became dimly aware of Quist on all fours, coughing and vomiting. At her feet, the young Mexican was sprawled on the floor, his legs kicking spasmodically, his battered head lying in an eve-widening pool of blood. She stared at him for what seemed an interminable amount of time before she fell back onto the sofa.

"Are you okay?" she thought she heard Quist ask. After a moment, she looked over at him. He swayed unsteadily on his knees as he swiped at his face with a blood-soaked hand. When she didn't reply, he clambered over the crumpled body of the big Mexican to where she cowered on the sofa. He knelt in front of her, his face inches from hers.

She could see the thin lines of blood on his neck where the rough twine had bitten into it. The wild look in his eyes made her pull back in alarm. He sat back on his heels and gazed down at the young Mexican who was convulsing and making small gasping sounds as if he were choking. Quist turned him onto his side and leaned over to inspect the man's head wound.

"Did I kill him?" she heard herself ask.

"No. At least not yet," he said, glancing up at her. "What's wrong with your arm?"

"I can't move it. My elbow hurts like hell."

Before she could react, he took her arm, and in one quick motion, flexed and wrenched it.

"Shit! What are you doing," she yelled, pulling away.

"It's better. Right?" He dug into his blood-soaked jeans without waiting for her reply and retrieved the cell phone Sam had given him.

Royale flexed her arm. It still hurt but she could at least bend it.

"You said you were putting eyes on us," Quist said into the phone, his voice betraying his anger. "Yeah, well, too fucking late for that." He listened for a few seconds as he reached down and retrieved his knife from the Mexican's leg. "Two of them. One dead, the other will be soon enough. I'd suggest you get your cleaning crew in here right away." Another pause as he listened. "No, we're done." Another pause as he listened. "Maybe I'll call, maybe I won't," he said turning off the phone and stuffing it in his jeans.

"We need to go. Clean yourself up and then get your things together. "Did you hear me, Roy?" he said when she failed to respond. "We need to go."

"He's still alive," she said, staring down at the young Mexican.

"Don't worry about him. Sam will take care of him. Now go get cleaned up."

29

The sun was just beginning to bleed through the smog that hung like a poisonous brown cloak over the Valle de México when they reached the outskirts of Mexico City. They had driven all night, stopping only once to fill gas and use the restrooms. Quist had also bought a map and asked directions for the easiest route to the airport. He didn't want to gamble trying to fly out of the airport at Leon or Quere- taro in the off-chance Manny might have someone watching for them. Nor did he want to take the chance Sam's people might try to intercept them. The burner phone Sam had given him had chirped incessantly, but Quist ignored it, his reticence born both of his mistrust and the desire to forget the calamity from which they had narrowly escaped.

Roy had remained silent for the entire trip, undoubtedly in shock but also most likely in grief over their failure to find Lana. Or so he assumed. He could only speculate whether her somber mood stemmed from despair or ambivalence. Either way, his queries about her arm or her state of mind were met with stony silence.

She held to this silence throughout the lengthy ordeal of turning in the rented Jeep and the protracted explanations of why they had neglected to turn the vehicle in at San Miguel. It was only when they tried to find the earliest possible flight to the U.S. that she vehemently made her opinion known that she wanted a direct flight to New Orleans. When nothing was avail- able until afternoon, she conceded to Quist's suggestion they take a 9AM flight to Houston.

No sooner had they found their way to the departure lounge

when Roy grabbed her overnight bag and wandered off. Quist sensed her remoteness might be in part some unspoken anger with him. At this point, he didn't care. He just wanted out of Mexico.

He surveyed the departure lounge, scrutinizing the fellow passengers for anyone that might look suspicious. To his satisfaction, everyone either looked like a businessman or families returning to the States. The only person that drew his attention, a young man with tattoos and not carrying any luggage, he dismissed when a young woman and a child joined him. He counted on having at least a three hour or more head start before anyone in San Miguel knew they had escaped; anyone that is except maybe Sam.

He must've nodded off, awakened only by Roy dropping into the seat beside him. He could see that she had changed clothes, exchanging the designer jeans and soiled silk blouse she had been wearing for the same drab skirt and blouse she had worn when they first met. The only reminder of her previous persona was her haircut. She shot him a look of what could only be construed as defiance and then began fiddling with her bag.

He couldn't resist offering her his hand. "Harlan Quist. And who might you be?"

She looked up at him and gave him cold, hard glance. Before she could say anything, the burner phone in Quist's his pocket chirped. He gave it a few seconds before retrieving it from his pocket. He clicked it on and waited.

"Quist? You there?" Sam sounded like he had a cold, his voice raw and strained.

"Speaking."

"Where are you?"

"Doesn't matter."

"Okay, as long as you're somewhere a good ways from here. I thought you might want to know the shit's hit the fan. A couple of hours ago the Federales informed me somebody iced Schoenfeld. They're putting it down as a cartel hit, something I'm inclined to agree with. Turns out last night a business partner of hers in Matamoros also got whacked. And if you catch the news, a banker and his wife in Mexico City had their throats slit. It seems the banker was Shoenfeld's money man. Someone's cleaning house. And those two guys back at the casita. Well, their fingerprints point to the Sinaloa cartel. Which begs the question of how you two fit into the blood letting. Maybe you two were just bonus points. Manny's idea would be my guess. He probably was beginning to think you were maybe one of ours."

"What about him?"

"Who knows? He's in the wind for now. It wouldn't surprise me if he's changed teams."

Quist glanced at Roy. "What about the girl?"

Sam hesitated before replying. "Still nothing, but I'd guess they'll find her and take care of her, too. Tell your friend I'm sorry but that's the way things work out in these matters." Neither of them said anything for a moment. "I hope you two are safe and are heading home."

Quist didn't reply. He clicked the phone off, thought for a moment, and then rose and walked over to a nearby trash bin. He tossed the phone into the bin and then returned to his seat.

"Our friend Sam," he said. "Seems Schoenfeld's dead. He thinks it was a cartel hit. Those two assholes from last night probably had something to do with it."

Roy looked at him, her face impassive. "That means they'll be looking for Lana, doesn't it?"

He didn't say anything.

She was silent for a long moment. "I keep asking myself if I ever really thought this was going to work out. Part of me had this fantasy where we'd be reunited like in some reality TV show. Be honest with me. Did you ever think we had a chance?"

"Honestly? No."

"So why all this? I almost got you killed."

He shrugged. "It seemed like a good idea at the time. But if you're asking me if I would do it again, knowing how it turned out." He laughed. "Shit. Probably so."

She worked up a meager smile and started to reach for his hand and then stopped herself.

"Have you ever killed someone before?" she asked.

151

Her question caught him off guard. Killed someone? Or was just responsible for their deaths, Quist asked himself. The shading of the latter made him shake his head. "Two guys in Africa. It was one of the reasons I was fired. Not that it wasn't a good shooting. My boss was more pissed about me getting shot and laid up for a month in Sierra Leone. You need to stop dwelling too much on last night. You did what you had to. "

She nodded and looked away. "You know," she said turning back. "I was only her mother for six months. I like to think I took good care of her those six months. And then I left her. Gave her up to Charly. I didn't see her for a year afterwards. I could tell she didn't remember who I was." She held Quist's gaze for a few seconds and shook her head. "So why would I think she'd remember me now?"

Quist wasn't sure what to say. They sat there and waited in silence for the boarding call.

PART THREE

New Orleans

30

A Year Later

He's not really a bad man. It's only when he drinks. He's always been a good provider. I can't deny that. And the kids don't even..." The remainder of what the woman sitting across from Royale was about to say wilted away as she slid her gaze to the window. Royale knew there was nothing to see other than the neighboring building's mossy brick walls and some dead ivy.

Margot Detweiler was the name her client scribbled on the registration sheet that she had filled out two months ago. It was most likely her real name. Royale's clients that paid in cash rarely gave a real name, but Margot Detweiler had insurance coverage. Her listed date of birth made her just shy of thirty-three, but her pale skin and the wrinkles around her eyes made her seem older. Her hair appeared to have been recently styled and dyed. Royale could see the roots were darker than the coppery ringlets that framed a face too thin for the hairstyle. She had a small mouth, the narrow lips creased; a smoker's mouth. From the cant of her angular nose, it appeared it might have been broken more than once. Her eyes, light brown and small, seemed to reflect a perpetual wariness.

"The kids," Royale prompted her.

Margot looked back at Royale and bit her lip. For a brief instant, a weary smile rearranged her face. "You think I should leave him, don't you?" she asked, the resignation in her voice too practiced, like she had tried it out in the mirror too many times to count.

Royale didn't reply for a moment. "I think you need to consider your kids. All they're exposed to. But I can't tell you what to do. If you want to know if I think one of these times he's going to hurt you more than he already has." Royale shrugged and glanced at the clock on the wall behind the woman. "You've gone to the shelter before. You know it's always there. And I'm here, too. I just want you to think about it. I mean really think about it."

"It's a disease, you know. Like the measles or strep throat. My mama used to call it that. A disease. She meant it in the way that all the shit men do to us is an illness they caught somewhere. The lying, the stealing, the fornicating. The meanness. She called it the sin virus. You believe that?"

Royale stared at her, unsure of her reply. Hadn't she wondered that very thing on more than one occasion? Maybe the hurtful things people do to each other were just as communicable and virulent as measles. The size and ugliness of her caseload surely didn't argue against the premise.

"Let's save that for another time," she managed to say.

Margot nodded like she was considering the cost of a box of paper towels. She pushed herself up out of the chair and grabbed her handbag, a faux leather knockoff the size of a carry-on bag. Royale often wondered if she might be packed for a hasty exit.

"If you can't come next week make sure and call me," Royale said as Margot skittered out of the room. She sat there a moment before opening the desk drawer and retrieving the pack of cigarettes crammed behind a sheaf of papers. She had never even broken the seal on the wrapper. Instead, she would finger the pack like someone might a rosary. She sorely wanted one right now. If the truth be told, she wanted a drink even more. Ever since Mexico, she had relapsed, allowing herself a single shot of tequila; one drink, once a week on Friday night from a bottle she kept beneath the sink. Unfortunately, today was only Wednesday.

She had confessed this transgression to Sister Frances, the Mother Superior who had served as her sponsor and confidante for all these years. The Sister was an elderly black woman from the Mississippi Delta who had lived a brutal and secular life before becoming a nun. Royale always assumed her compassion and appreciation for Royale's past had allowed Royale the leeway to live outside many of the constraints of the order. In fact, Royale's revelations about her ill-fated search for Lana elicited the Sister's painful admission of abandoning her own child as a young woman. In a surreal twist of fate, the Mother Superior died in her sleep a week after her confession. It was not long afterwards that Royale decided to renounce her vows.

In the six months that had passed, Royale buried herself in her work, fighting against the undertow of a life without the comforting if not confining structure of her Carmelite sisterhood. The evenings proved the hardest, and all too often she found herself aimlessly wandering the less picturesque side streets of the Quarter, partially out of habit, but also as a test of her own resolve to live a life free of her past.

It was with this intention in mind that she checked her schedule for the following day, gathered her things, and strolled out of her office into the humid New Orleans dusk only to find Quist sitting on her stoop.

She hesitated as she contemplated going back inside since he hadn't yet seen her. Instead, she jangled her keys to alert him. He turned and looked at her and grinned. He looked different since she had last seen him at the Houston airport. What had it been? A year? His head was shaven, accentuating his angular face. The short hair somehow made him look older, wearier. He wore a wrinkled white dress shirt with the sleeves rolled up, the tail stuffed loosely into a pair of faded jeans.

She looked down at him and smiled. "How did you find me?" she asked.

"It wasn't that hard. New Orleans is a small town." To her surprise he pronounced it like a local. New Awlins.

He noticed her scrutinizing his head and absently ran his hand over the shaven crown. "I had this job in Nigeria as a bodyguard for this oil executive. Hair didn't make sense. Ungodly hot and so much humidity you hardly had to drink. I see you kept yours. I mean the way you had your hair in Mexico."

It was the one nod to vanity she had allowed herself after leaving the Carmelites. She still wore the same understated, boring clothes and she didn't wear makeup to speak of, but she had liked the hairdo.

"I left the order."

Quist considered this for a long moment and nodded. "No shit. I imagine that must free up your weekends."

She waited as he rose to his feet. He looked leaner since Mexico; fit and tan. She thought back to that afternoon at the Houston Airport. When he walked her to the departure gate, he seemed more crestfallen than she would've expected. Had it been simply from a sense of failure or had it been something more personal she had no desire to explore? And when the months went by and he made no effort to contact her, she experienced a mixture of both relief and regret.

She started down the sidewalk without waiting for him. When he caught up to her, she gave him a sidelong glance. "I'm sorry about how I left things at the airport," she said. "The simple truth was I couldn't deal with it. It wasn't just what happened that last night. It was Lana. It took me a long time to get over the guilt of giving up on trying to find her. To just walk away. What was even harder was admitting to myself that I maybe didn't really want to find her. To forgive myself for that was difficult." She shook her head. "Does that make sense?"

He shrugged in acknowledgment.

"Why are you here?" she asked when he remained silent. She looked at him and felt an immediate sense of dread. "You heard something, didn't you? About Lana?" she asked, stopping in the middle of the street.

He took her by the arm and led her to the curb. "I'd like some oysters. You know a place?"

"Wrong time of year," she replied, her eyes locked on his.

"Tell me. Don't make me guess."

"Let's go somewhere. You know a good bar?"

She shook her head in annoyance and started down the street with Quist in tow. The place she took him was called 'The Bedouin'. It was a simple, non-assuming storefront kind of place. A chalkboard placard at the front door announced 'Soup of the Day – Bourbon and Branch Water'.

The interior was taken up by a long wooden bar, the stools populated by locals, mostly older black men in short sleeves and straw fedoras. A haphazard assortment of Mardi Gras memorabilia covered the wall behind the bar. A small television perched high in one corner broadcasted a dog race. A lone table sat empty in the back.

Royale slipped past the bar stools, ignoring the inquisitive stares of the denizens. Once she was seated, she glanced at Quist. "If you want something you'll have to go up the bar and get it," she said.

He nodded and started to rise. "Can I get you something?"

She thought for a moment. "Some *añjeo* if they have it. With a lime." She watched him as he ordered. He had inserted himself between a pair of burly men that looked like dockworkers, one of whom with he appeared to start a conversation. It bothered her to no end that she had wanted Quist to look her up, or at the very least call her. Quist and Sister Frances seemed to be the only two people with whom she felt any degree of intimacy. Other than the woman who did her billing and the cashier at the neighborhood grocer, her case load of clients comprised the extent of her human contact. As a result, the prospect of re-engagement with Quist roused a mixture of angst and also something akin to guilty pleasure.

He returned a couple of minutes later with a tumbler of thin brown liquor and a can of Coke.

"I thought you wanted a drink."

"I said a bar. I just happen to like the ambience of a bar. Cheers," he said, raising the can to his lips.

"I'd like to be able to say I don't drink alone, but..." She shrugged and took a swallow of the añjeo, rolling the smoky liquor on her tongue for a few seconds before swallowing. They eyed each other uncomfortably for a moment before Quist reached into his back pocket and retrieved a folded envelope that he tossed on the table.

"Please, don't do this," she said, bowing her head.

"It's not what you think." He took another sip of his Coke and pushed the envelope across the table. "You remember Sam? From San Miguel? He emailed me these last week. They're not the best quality. The printer I used to download them was in the back of a bar in Lagos. If you want I can forward you the originals."

She looked at him for a moment before picking up the envelope and opening the flap. She could see what appeared to be photographs printed on plain paper. She unfolded them and laid them on the table, flattening them with her hand. The first two pages displayed a series of less than optimal black and white shots of the kind taken by a security camera. A young woman with long light-colored hair stood at what appeared to be a counter. Behind her Royale could see a line of people with suitcases. Royale squinted at the image. The woman's face was shown in profile, and thus difficult to recognize.

From the look on the woman's face, the subsequent photos suggested a possible argument had ensued with clerk on the other side of the counter. It had to be airline counter, Royale thought gauging from the look of the two patrons standing at the adjoining check in station. They appeared to be much too well dressed for bus passengers. The last of the series showed the woman gesturing to something she held in her arms. Royale struggled to make out what it was she was carrying. It suddenly dawned on her what she was seeing.

"What is she carrying?" She looked up at Quist. "Is that a baby?"

Quist took another sip of the Coke before carefully placing the can on the table. He picked up the first page and held it up in front of her. "I know it's hard to tell from the photo, but this is Lana. It was taken at the airport in Guadalajara. She had a U.S. passport in the name of Luna Schoenfeld. And yeah, she's carrying a baby. It seems even in Mexico you need a passport for an infant if you're planning to fly international. She didn't even have the kid's birth certificate so even flying domestic was out of the question."

"Maybe somebody was impersonating her. I mean it doesn't look like her."

"Look at the other ones," he said, shuffling the pages.

She picked up the last two pages. Even taking in consideration the poor quality of the printer, the last four photographs revealed the kind of detail and color that suggested they were taken with some kind of high quality surveillance camera. It was Lana. Her hair was blonde and her face appeared fuller, but it was her. She was wearing shorts and a loose-fitting T-shirt. An empty baby carrier sat on a table behind her. The look on her face, pensive and strained, made it appear obvious the camera had caught her unaware. The next two photos showed her speaking with what appeared to be a man in a straw hat, his back to the camera. Again, her body language and facial gestures suggested an argument.

"Look at the last one and tell me who you see," Quist said, tapping the last page with his finger.

Royale stared at the image, not believing what she was seeing. She looked up at Quist. "I don't understand," she said, her voice breaking.

The man in the photo had turned toward the camera. Even with the hat perched low on his head, she recognized Manny Fontenot.

31

Yeah, our old friend from down Mexico way," Quist said, scooping up the photocopies. He hesitated a moment in response to the look of confusion on Royale's face. "The last shots were taken by a Mexican Federale surveillance team. They were taken at a villa Manny keeps outside of Guadalajara. It's private , isolated, and no one gets in or out without Manny's say so. Apparently, when she went to the baby's pediatrician a bodyguard even went with her posing as the father. If she ever had to go somewhere else, they always made her leave the baby behind."

"You're saying she was there against her will?"

"It would appear that way."

Roy stared at the glass in her hand. He assumed she was already unbraiding the possibilities in her mind. She lifted her gaze to meet his and finished her drink.

"How old is the baby? It's hard to tell from this picture."

"From what Sam could find out, six months or so."

"Which means she was pregnant when she ran away in San Miguel. So who's the father?"

"Who knows? Maybe that boyfriend she had down there."

He could see a dark shadow cross her face as she considered another possibility that neither of them seemed inclined to verbalize. Something about her looked different than he remembered. Her gaze appeared less guarded; her facial features seemed softer, especially around her mouth. Her eyes too appeared different, older perhaps, or maybe simply jaded; the fine delta of wrinkles in the corners more pronounced. The overall effect was one of vulnerability, an impression that led him to second guess himself for what he was about to reveal.

"They think that she somehow got away from Manny's people and was running away. She was trying to buy a ticket to Sydney, Australia. When that didn't work, she tried to book a flight to LA. But without that birth certificate she wasn't going anywhere."

Roy slouched back in her chair, her despondency obvious by her body language. Quist had gone and back and forth in his mind if revealing this development was the right thing to do. In the end, he figured she deserved to know. The incident in San Miguel had stirred the all too familiar feelings of guilt and self-doubt to the point he questioned his judgment and skill. And yet here he was again tempting fate, and again possibly putting someone else's life on the line, for he knew what she would do.

He would be lying to himself if he didn't admit he had wanted to see her again, even if Lana hadn't reappeared. The lack of closure after Mexico had nagged at him. That and some vague, unrequited longing for a woman like her. Or at least a woman that resembled her, not so much in appearance but temperament. Or maybe it was just the shared wounds.

"You want another?" he said, nodding at her empty glass.

"No. What I want..." She shook her head. "I don't know what I want. I guess I want her to be safe. Beyond that, I don't know. Manny will be looking for her, won't he?"

"Most likely."

"What about Sam? The DEA?"

"I got the impression their interest in finding her was low priority."

"So why did Sam tell you this?"

"He tracked me down about a month after San Miguel to tell me Lana had completely dropped off the radar. He assumed the cartel had found her. He felt bad about it. Said he wished he would've scooped her up before it all went down. When those Federales that were watching Manny's place ID'd her, they told Sam. He thought you should know."

"How thoughtful," she said with obvious bitterness. "I hate to admit it but part of me wishes you never would've told me any of this. Am I horrible to think that?"

He shrugged.

"I'm guessing you're not telling me everything. You said they wouldn't let her fly with the baby. So where did she go?"

Quist crushed the empty Coke can and brushed it aside. "It seems she rented a car at the airport and then drove to Oaxaca."

"How do you know that?"

"The rental companies have GPS on their cars. Sam's people found it a week ago abandoned in a hotel parking lot in Oaxaca."

"Does anyone…Sam, anybody know why she went there?"

Quist hesitated a beat before replying. "Apparently there's someone in Oaxaca she knows. Some guy. It seems he and Schoenfeld used to be an item in San Miguel. They lived together for about five or six years. This would've been when Lana was maybe eleven until she was seventeen or so. No one's going to say he was a father figure or anything, but he might've been the closest thing to it. It might explain why she ran to him. Maybe she trusts him."

"And I imagine he's dirty, too."

Quist shrugged. "Maybe he is, maybe he isn't."

"You don't live with a woman like Schoenfeld and not get dirty. Christ. Lana had Schoenfeld for a mother and then this guy. What else do you know about him?"

"Not much. Sam won't say."

"Not even a name?"

Quist held to his silence, feeling his way along the truth. "Roy…"

"He told you more, didn't he? He has to know that I'll go down there. So why did he tell you? It can't be out of the goodness of his heart."

Quist took his time answering. "I made a trade. I used to have this client. After I stopped working for him I found out some things about him, things Sam would like to know. If Sam helps us find Lana, I provide him with some information. He's not sure Manny knows yet where Lana went. So who knows how much time we've got. We're supposed to meet Sam down there day after tomorrow. I've already got the plane tickets."

"Aren't you being a bit presumptuous."

"Am I?"

She twirled the empty glass between her hands, her eyes fixed on something over his shoulder. "I asked you once before, but why are you doing this?" she asked, looking back. "And don't give me any crap about not have anything better to do."

"You'll need me. Simple as that. And I owe you. You saved my life. Besides I've always wanted to see Oaxaca. The Day of the Dead's coming up in a few days. Not that I'm taking that as some kind of omen or something."

She shot him an opaque, humorless look. "God, not another festival about doom and gloom."

Quist nodded and grinned. "I guess we're star crossed that way. Now you tell me something. Say we find Lana. Then what? You said once you couldn't save her. That she wouldn't know you from Adam."

She shrugged. "I've had time to think about it. Before, after Charly died, I wanted to find her because I felt guilty. Maybe I thought finding her would somehow wash away all my sins. For abandoning her like I did. I guess I was looking for her for the wrong reasons. Now…" She shook her head and looked away. "All the crap that's happened to her. I mean I know it hasn't been all my fault. But I owe her something." She looked back at Quist. "I'm not going into this with my eyes closed. You said she won't know me. But I'll know her. I know women that have gone through this kind of crap. That's an advantage, isn't it?"

Quist nodded and glanced over his shoulder. "I wonder if that little teacup knows how to make a decent martini?" he asked, nodding with his chin at the petite young black woman behind the bar. "You sure I can't get you something?" he said, rising to his feet.

"No, thanks. No, wait. I've fallen this far. Get me another añejo. Make it a double."

PART FOUR

OAXACA
"Para todo hay mañas, menos para la muerte."
There are tricks for everything – except for death.

32

Royale plucked the thermos from between her feet and poured the last of the coffee into the only cup she had been able to find in the spare kitchen, a chipped and stained ceramic mug adorned with a Happy Face. The rooftop on which she sat consisted of nothing more than a bare concrete slab surrounded by a low parapet studded with a barricade of chest high lengths of rebar, giving one the distinct impression the house had been built to possibly keep guests from leaving as much as preventing intruders from entering. In one corner, four tattered and sun-bleached lawn chairs sat grouped around a rusted café table.

The safe house Sam had arranged, a two-story, semi-finished cinder block affair, sat situated in a low valley a mile or so from the outskirts of Oaxaca City. A dry arroyo meandered along one side of the house; on the other stretched a narrow field of spindly corn stalks surrounded by neat rows of waist- high, spiky vegetation. Agave, she guessed, recalling reading somewhere that Oaxaca was the mezcal capital of Mexico. The low hills on either side obscured the surrounding countryside and any appreciation of the nearby town other than the blocky spires of a small church just visible above the ridgeline.

It had been midnight by the time one of Sam's men dropped

them off, the already long day made longer by bad weather in Houston and a three-hour flight delay. The drive from the airport in Oaxaca City had taken them through seemingly endless and indistinguishable neighborhoods that for the most part appeared more commercial than residential. Some of the structures she recognized as mechanics' garages and grocery stores along with a preponderance of shops proclaiming to be panaderias and muebles. There also seemed an inordinate amount of stores selling cell phones. A few places, bars and small restaurants mostly, appeared to be still open even at this late hour. Most of the structures appeared to be two story affairs, and gauging from the lighted windows, she surmised they might be the residences of the proprietors. The traffic seemed denser than she would've guessed for this late hour; holiday traffic she assumed for she had read in a magazine on the plane that The Day of the Dead, *Dia de los Muertos,* was probably the largest holiday of the year for Oaxacans.

After fifteen or twenty minutes, the city became less compact as they entered a district the highway sign indicated as Sta. Maria Atzompa. Their driver took a partially paved side road lined with rows of cars that soon led past what looked to be an uninhabited parcel of land illuminated by what appeared to be hundreds of candles.

"El cementerio," the driver said, making a furtive sign of the cross.

As they slowed, Royale could make out crowds of people walking amongst what she suddenly realized were graves, their flashlights and lanterns revealing a forest of gravestones. Many of the people seemed to be carrying large bundles of something for which the dim light allowed no appreciation. She rolled down her window and immediately caught a whiff of something that reminded her of the Frankincense used during various Catholic liturgical rites. For a brief second or two she heard what sounded like a trumpet playing and someone singing some baleful melody.

Sam's driver deposited them at a house a mile or so down the road. It stood alone, detached from any adjoining houses.

He accompanied them inside long enough to turn on the lights and the water pump before driving off. Quist chose the bedroom nearest the front door, mumbled good night and disappeared into the room, closing the door behind him.

Too exhausted to sleep, Royale had tossed and turned in the narrow uncomfortable bed, her thoughts an endless loop of the various scenarios detailing the moment when she and Lana would finally meet, none of which seemed even remotely satisfying. In the end, and in spite of her assurances to Quist, she felt her commitment waver. It had only been Quist's silent authority that encouraged her to board the plane in New Orleans in the first place.

And therein lay her other midnight quandary, Quist most notably. It had been a good two decades since she had allowed a man into her world, much less allowed one to influence her. Up to this point, their embryonic relationship had been nothing more than one of expedience. But when he showed up on her office doorstep in New Orleans something changed; something nebulous, dormant, and decidedly uncomfortable. By dawn, she was questioning whether she might've just as readily accompanied him if he asked her to spend the weekend with him in Cancun.

She had stirred from this restless sleep to the first light of dawn and the sound of voices in the street outside. She lay there for a while trying to catch snatches of the conversation before giving up and walking to the window and studying the narrow dusty street. Although she couldn't see anyone, she thought she recognized one of the voices as Quist's.

She peed in the grimy toilet and then made a reasonable attempt to bathe herself in the cold water of the rust-stained sink, drying herself with a piece of stiff fabric that resembled a towel. After changing into fresh jeans and a T-shirt, she made her way to the kitchen in the hope of finding something remotely edible. She was rewarded by an overripe papaya, some rubbery carrots, and a box of stale Ritz crackers. Fortunately, she found a coffee maker and ground beans in the freezer. She made a mental note to complain bitterly to Sam about the accommodations. By the time the coffee had brewed, the voices outside had faded. The door to Quist's room was closed, so thermos in hand, she climbed the crude concrete stairway to the rooftop.

As she gulped the last of the bitter coffee, she strolled over to the parapet. It was only then she noticed the dust-cloaked pickup parked in the rutted track that served as a driveway. She hadn't heard it approach and wondered if it had been there all night. She traced the road with her eyes along the arroyo to the town and the slumping blue gray mountains beyond before turning and surveying the opposite direction to an adjacent road where a faded blue school bus heaved like a boat along the furrowed and uneven surface. She watched for a minute as every few seconds the bus paused to disgorge a clutch of passengers. Only the sound of footsteps scraping up the concrete stairway made her turn away.

Quist and another man emerged through the doorway. Quist wore only a white T-shirt and knee-length pajama bottoms. The other man, taller and stouter than Quist, wore a blue denim work shirt with the shirt tails out atop black stovepipe jeans.

"Roy..." Quist started to say.

"Miss Aucoin," the other man interrupted. "Good to see you again. I'm just sorry about the circumstances," he said, lumbering towards her, his right hand extended.

She recognized the voice but its owner bore little resemblance to the man that had abducted them that night in San Miguel. That night his features had been concealed in the back of the darkened van, and she had admittedly paid him scant attention earlier that day when they first encountered him at the bar. Still, she would've never picked him from a lineup.

His head was shaved, revealing a horseshoe-shaped scar above his left ear. His full, crudely trimmed beard obscured the shape of his face, but gauging from its bulk, she imagined it to be fleshly. The bit of his face that was visible appeared deeply tanned. His one hand still outstretched, he plucked off his sunglasses with his other, and smiled. His stone gray eyes, close set and dime-sized, narrowed in the bright morning sunlight. He stood there still grinning as he waited for Royale to take his hand.

"Fair enough," he said when she made no effort to shake his hand. He turned and glanced at Quist as if questioning Royale's rejection. "I get it," he said, looking back.

His thin, sun-bleached eyebrows arched as if in a constant state of amazement. The whole package - the crinkly eyes, the beard, the solicitous smile and his almost bulbous nose lent him an air of congeniality that she guessed served him well in his line of work.

"I'm sorry if I seem rude, but I'm not in the habit of going out of my way to be courteous to people who use other people," Royale said in the way of an offhanded apology.

"Well, I can't deny we got off on the wrong foot, but I'm trying to make something right here."

"No, you're simply closing a deal. So why don't we dispense with the pleasantries and get down to business?"

Sam glanced at Quist again before retrieving a folded manila envelope from his back pocket and tossing it on the table.

Quist shot her a look as if to say play nice and dropped into one of the chairs. Sam paused to pull a pack of cigarettes from his shirt pocket. As he turned and bent to catch the light from his Bic, Royale noticed the dense web of lurid, overlapping tattoos covering both his bare forearms, a detail she felt she surely would've remembered from the afternoon at the El Centro bar. He sucked violently on his cigarette a couple of times and then plopped into the chair between her and Quist. She picked up on his sour body odor. He smelled like her father.

"So, our man is Mateo Zenner. Age sixty-five. Had a Mexican mother, hence the name. His old man was a third-generation rancher in South Texas. Both of the parents died in an auto accident when Mateo was twenty-five. He inherited the ranch, a thousand acres of prickly pear and mesquite alongside a stretch of the Rio Grande that ran dry for most of the year. The place was mortgaged to the hilt to boot. At the time, Mateo was in graduate school up in Austin studying English Lit, if you can believe. He drops out, moves home and before you know it he's got a landing strip cleared out on the south forty. Mind you, this is the early seventies, back when the drug trade was more like a friendly game of pickup basketball. The War on Drugs was still just a glint in Tricky Dick's eyes. So before you know it he's flying in weekly loads of pot in this second hand Cessna he pretty much taught himself to fly."

He paused to slip a stack of photographs from the envelope. "This was taken about then," he said handing one to Royale.

It was a black and white photo of a lanky young man in reflector sunglasses. His shoulder length black hair was tied back in a bandana. He was leaning against what looked like the wing strut of a small airplane. He wore a broad smile of satisfaction, his gaze and attention directed at someone or something off to the side of the person taking the photo. Painted on the fuselage behind him was the image of a crow landing on a cactus stump along with the block letters spelling out "El Cuervo".

"El Cuervo means the crow. That's what people on both sides of the border called him. Within a year, he paid off the ranch. The economy the way it was back then, the bank didn't ask questions. By 1975, he's got a couple of brand new Cessnas and an old surplus crop duster. He'd never bring in big loads. Bigger planes would've gotten him some attention from somebody is my guess. Border Patrol or maybe competitors. Or maybe he never saw the Big Picture and just wasn't greedy enough. But it does seem he made a handy enough living. By 1980, he's got a shit load of money squirreled away, mostly in Mexico. So he goes legit and starts himself a business importing high end Mexican furniture and art work. Rumor had it though that he continued to finance friends that were still in the business. Maybe laundering their money, too. But he was smart about it because no red flags ever came up." Sam picked up another photo and slid it over to Royale.

"By all accounts, he first met Mercedes Schoenfeld fifteen or so years ago. I'm not sure of the circumstances, but that photo was taken in Mexico City in 2000."

The photo showed a man and a woman sitting in a booth, their tequila shot glasses held up in salute. The woman's right arm was draped around the man's neck. Royale immediately recognized Mercedes Schoenfeld. She appeared quite attractive, alluring in fact, and the man sitting next to her seemed taken in by her attention. He looked equally attractive. He wore his thick black hair stylishly long. His tan, chiseled features and brilliant white teeth made him look like some television actor whose name one could never seem to conjure up. He bore only a slight resemblance to the young man leaning against the Cessna in the earlier photo.

"Zenner shows up next in San Miguel in 2007. Moves in with Schoenfeld and lives with her until 2012. To his credit, he walks out on her. From all accounts it wasn't exactly amicable. There really isn't much decent intel about their relationship as to whether it was business mixed with pleasure or the poor asshole was just stuck in her web. And nobody knows about what kind of relationship he had with Luna. I'm sorry. Lana," he said, correcting himself.

"He lives here now. He's got himself an import business, owns a restaurant and a small hotel. His house is out on the edge of town. I've got someone watching it, but no sign of the girl." He handed Quist a photo of what Royale could see looked to be a large two story stucco and stone structure surrounded by what appeared to be a well tended lawn and gardens.

"I'd say Mateo's done real well for himself," Quist said, nodding in appreciation.

Sam handed Royale the last photograph. She could see it was an older version of Zenner. He was still youthful; tanned and fit looking. He was sitting in a rattan chair holding a cigar in one hand and peering down at a batch of papers on the table in front of him.

"That's him taken two days ago at his restaurant."

"And I suppose you have some kind of plan in mind?" Royale asked, still studying the photo.

"That's what Quist and I were just talking about."

Royale glanced quickly at Quist. Why hadn't Quist included her? Quist turned and looked at her.

"I'm thinking this time we tell the truth," he said. "We tell Zenner exactly why we're looking for Lana. I don't see what we'd have to lose."

"Unless she doesn't want to be found," Royale said.

"If Zenner's her protector, he might not be willing to give her up just on your word," Sam said. "You'll have to somehow convince him."

And I'll still have to convince Lana who I am, Royale reminded herself.

No one said anything for a moment. "I'd go with the direct approach considering we've probably got a time element here," Sam interjected. "The word on Manny is that he's still in Guadalajara. At least he was a couple of days ago. We know he still has ties there to the Sinaloa cartel. I've got no idea if he knows she's here."

"Does he know Zenner?" Royale asked.

"He must. Manny started working for Schoenfeld back in 2000."

"Any reason for Manny to think she'd run to Zenner?" Quist asked.

Sam shrugged. "Who knows? But if not to Zenner, then why come to Oaxaca? I'm figuring it's just a matter of time before Manny shows up."

"So what do we do?" she asked.

"Zenner's usually at his restaurant in the evenings," Sam said, flicking his cigarette over the parapet. "A place called El Cuervo. It's just a block or so off the *zocalo*. He's usually there by nine. I'd say you two show up there tonight and make your play. Trick or treat him. It's Halloween after all. I'll have some of my guys watching his house in case she's there and he tries to tip her off and she decides to run again."

"What about you?" Quist asked.

"I'll be around. You still carry a blade?" he asked Quist. Quist nodded.

"You want something heavier?"

"Not yet. Tell me something. Are your people after Zenner for anything?"

"Nope. As far as I can tell he's clean. That albino cock sucker Manny's a different matter. Sorry," he said, turning to Royale.

"I understand you're a nun."

"Ex-nun."

Sam shot a look at Quist that was hard to decipher, but when he turned back there was a grin on his face. She leaned across the table.

"And you're guaranteeing no harm's going to come to her. You do understand that's part of the deal, right?"

"Yes, ma'am. I do," he said, his eyes holding hers' for a moment before glancing at his watch. "One of my people will be here soon. Her name's Frieda. She's a Mex. Local talent. You can depend on her for anything. She's more than capable. She'll stay with you. She'll drive you into town if you want. Tomorrow's a big feast day. There's bound to be lots of goings on in town this afternoon that you might find interesting. Meanwhile I've got work to do," he said, pushing to his feet, all the while avoiding Royale's gaze.

"I don't like him," Royale said as Sam disappeared down the stairs.

"I gathered that."

"Do you really trust him?"

Quist made a sucking noise with his lips and cocked his head. "I guess we really don't have much choice. If he wants the information I promised he's going to have come through. That was the deal." He scooped up the photographs and stuck them back into the envelope. "It's Manny we really need to worry about."

"What about Zenner?"

"Who knows? I haven't met the man yet. But he's the wild card." He got to his feet, the envelope in hand. "I need coffee. Is there anything here to eat?"

"Are you by any chance vegetarian?"

He pulled a smirk. "So I guess we wait for this Frieda. We can do lunch and maybe practice our lines. As I recall, you're pretty good at that. Role playing," he added in response to her look of confusion. "Isn't that what you therapists like to call it? By the way, did you bring any nice clothes?" he asked, pushing away from the table.

"You're saying these jeans and my Saints T-shirt won't cut it? Don't worry. I bought some more clothes after the last time. Not that I've ever worn them. The opportunity never really came up."

"Well, maybe you need to thank me for providing you the opportunity to wear them. Who knows? You might even develop a social life," he said with a grin and ambled off.

She watched him as he disappeared down the stairwell. Role playing. What role exactly would she be playing? Mother? Savior? And what about Quist, the knight errant with the sketchy motivations? She would have to wait and see. She picked up her cup and the thermos and followed him downstairs.

33

Somos muy fiesteros," Frieda shouted at Quist over the noise of the banging cymbals and drumming.

"What?"

"We Mexicans love our celebrations," she said, leaning towards him. "And this is *la mejor.* The best."

He studied her as she turned and said something in Roy's ear. Quist guessed the young Latina weighed in at no more than a hundred and ten pounds, her head barely reaching to Quist's shoulder. She had one of those rock-hard bodies though, athletic without an ounce of fat on her. He put her age at no more than her late twenties, thirty at the most, for he often found it difficult to assess a Latin women's real age. She wore her thick black hair plaited and piled atop her head which accentuated her high cheekbones and dark eyes. She had a wide, sensual mouth and teeth like ivory. He assumed she was of Zapotec heritage like much of the populace in Oaxaca.

Earlier, when she had climbed into the front seat of the Land Rover, Quist noticed the bulge in the rear waist band of her jeans. Her thigh-length embroidered blouse easily concealed what he assumed was a hand gun. He took Sam at his word that Frieda was capable, sensing from experience that her gracious, ebullient persona disguised a confident vigilance, an impression bolstered by the manner in which she maneuvered the Land Rover though the narrow, crowded streets, her eyes constantly taking in every detail of their surroundings. When she finally located a parking spot on a side street near the *Zocalo,* she asked Quist and Roy to wait before exiting the vehicle until she had surveyed the street.

As they slipped through the crowds of celebrants, Quist glanced at Roy who seemed both enthralled and intimidated by the crush of people. He remembered her agoraphobia and wondered how she was dealing with the bedlam. She seemed to only briefly hesitate as she followed Frieda into a teeming indoor market place. Inside, the various stalls displayed everything from cheap household goods to an array of fruit and vegetables. Other stands were laden with piles of bread loaves of various sizes decorated with the images of small skulls. Another section consisted of butcher shops and booths selling some sort of drink ladled from huge steaming pots, while another sector sold nothing but mounds of marigolds. They passed several vendors offering barrels of dried chili pods and something that upon closer inspection Quist realized were small dried locusts. The thick air smelled of flowers, grilled meat, ripe produce and a resiny incense of some kind.

"It is the copal what you smell," Frieda said when she noticed him sniffing the air. "And yes, those were *chapulines* you see in the barrel. Grasshoppers you call them. *Muy delicioso.*"

They emerged out onto a street lined with more booths that displayed rows of apple-sized sugar candy skulls. Other stalls offered garish carved wood and paper-mache masks of every conceivable size and color. As they made their way along the crowded sidewalk, Quist caught a glance through an open barred window. Inside the small room was an elaborate altar decorated with the small candy skulls, floral arrangements, and assortments of fruits and the round loaves of bread he had seen in the market. Several framed photographs were arranged before a rank of votive candles. As he passed the next window, he shook his head in amazement at the sight of a recumbent statute of the crucified Jesus lying on a narrow cot surrounded by flower vases and more candles.

They feasted on churros, omelets and strong Mexican coffee at a colonnaded open air restaurant alongside the Zocalo as they listened to Frieda provide an animated history of the celebration. It seemed to Quist that the Day of the Dead was nothing more than a morbid family reunion of the living and the dead, the idea of which made him shudder, for he couldn't think of any relative he wished to confront on any voluntary social basis.

No sooner had they left the restaurant when they encountered an impromptu performance of street theater. A crude wooden bed sat in the middle of the narrow, cobblestoned street, its occupant a scrawny, middle aged man dressed in soiled bedclothes. Kneeling beside him was a woman and two small children, their wails almost drowning out the litany of prayers being recited by a priest standing at the foot of the bed. A young man dressed in a white lab coat knelt on the opposite side of the bed, his stethoscope planted on the man's heaving chest. Behind the bed hovered two figures, one of whom obviously represented Satan.

He wore a long flowing robe of red silk, his head adorned with a pair of outsized, paper-mache horns. In one hand he held a bottle of mezcal, in the other what appeared to be a lurid painting of a bosomy, partially dressed woman. Looming behind him stood a tall figure dressed in a frock painted to look like a skeleton. He wore a crown fashioned out of what appeared to be flattened beer cans. In one hand he held a scepter of wood wound with rolls of gold colored paper, in the other a scythe which he waved ominously over the bed. A pair of small children in the crowd screamed in terror while several older children laughed and tossed small pebbles at Satan.

Frieda, ever watchful, shepherded them on through the crowds, pointing out various scenes of interest as if she were a tour guide. Occasionally, Quist hung back to observe Roy who he sensed was becoming increasingly apprehensive, in spite of the otherwise benign nature of the crowd. She had been strangely nonverbal throughout breakfast. At first, he assumed she was merely listening to Frieda's verbose running commentary on the Day of the Dead. By the end of their meal though, he guessed her preoccupation might stem from what they might very well encounter later that evening. They had been strolling through the streets for a couple of hours when he took her aside.

"Are you okay?"

She stared at him for a moment before shaking her head.

176

"It's just a little too much," she said over the din of the street.

"Is something the matter?" Frieda asked in her heavily accented English as she stepped between them, her eyes circling the street behind them.

"I'd like to go somewhere quiet," Roy replied. "I have to think."

"Very well. *Es no problema.* I know just the place. There is a small church not far from here. It is *muy tranquilo.* Come, we will go there," Frieda said, taking Roy's arm.

"You two go," Quist said. "I'll meet you back at the car in an hour or so. Really. I'll be okay," he said in response to the look of hesitation on Frieda's face. "I'll just sit in a bar and have a cerveza."

"Sam say…"

"To hell with Sam. Didn't he tell you I used to be a *policia?*"

"He say you were…*¿Cómo?* How do you say? No *confliables.* Yes? Not to be trusted. *Peligroso,* mebbe also."

"*Exactamente.* So run along."

Frieda shot him a look of skepticism but nevertheless took Roy's arm and led her away. Quist watched them disappear in the crowd before turning and walking in the opposite direction. Earlier in the restaurant, he had studied a tourist map at the cashier and noted the location of Zenner's restaurant. What could it hurt to check it out and at least get a lay of the land?

El Cuervo occupied a corner framed by two improbably narrow streets several blocks off the Zocalo. The building's exterior appeared decidedly unassuming if not somewhat run down. Rustic was the word that came to mind. Cracks lined the blue stucco walls, and here and there the parapets were missing some clay tiles. The unlit neon lighting on the sign above the door spelled out the words El Cuervo. Atop the sign perched a gigantic metal sculpture of a black bird.

Quist paused for a moment at the heavy double wooden doors at the entranceway to study the menu board. A small sign above it announced the restaurant opened for dinner at seven. One of the doors stood slightly ajar and from somewhere deep inside came the clinking clatter of what sounded like someone stacking cases of bottles. He hesitated before slowly opening the door and stepping into the darkened interior.

The austere whitewashed foyer sat empty of any furnishings other than a pair of expensive-looking leather settees and a lectern. A barrel-arched brick-lined corridor led into the dim interior. It took a moment in the muted light to make out the dozens of black and white photographs lining the hallway's walls. Most were shots of various small aircrafts; Cessnas and other assorted single prop planes, a series of World War II vintage fighters, and a few shots of old twin engine DC-3s. Quist recalled that as the demand for marijuana grew the DC-3s had been a favored aircraft among the pilots and the dealers due to its reliability, cargo load, and the fact it required a minimal runway.

Several of the photos depicted nothing more than what appeared to be overhead shots of crude dirt landing strips. A chrome propeller was mounted over the doorway leading into what Quist could see was a large open room and a long varnished wood bar occupying the length of one side. The large skylight above the dining area and a row of dim overhead lamps above the bar provided the only illumination.

Quist allowed a moment for his eyes to adjust to the dimness before he noticed someone sitting in the shadow at the end of the bar. He could see it was a man and he was studying an open laptop. The man, unaware of Quist's presence, seemed engrossed in the screen for perhaps a half a minute before glancing up in Quist's direction.

"Lo siento, pero estamos cerrado," he said, his voice echoing in the empty dining room.

"I'm sorry. I was just checking your place out. I didn't realize you were closed."

The man didn't reply, but instead simply stared at Quist. "I can make y'all a reservation if you'd like," he said finally. "Tonight we're opening the bar a little earlier. At five maybe if my barkeep shows up."

The lack of a Spanish accent gave him away. He obviously wasn't Mexican. And the 'y'all' led Quist to wonder if he had perhaps stumbled onto Mateo Zenner, an assumption Quist was more certain of as he walked up to the bar. The man at the bar wore faded jeans and a plain black T-shirt, but it was definitely the man in the photograph Sam had shown them that morning.

Quist made a show of glancing at his watch. "Any chance I could get a beer and just sit here in the corner? Get out of the sun for a while?"

Before Zenner could reply, a young man dressed in a white smock emerged from a door behind the bar lugging several cases of beer. Zenner said something to him that Quist couldn't catch, and the guy plopped the beer cases on the floor and disappeared down the hallway leading to the entrance.

"I told Jerónimo if he wants his holiday bonus he better lock the front door before some other..." He paused.

"Some other asshole."

"Yeah, before some other asshole wanders in," Zenner said without a trace of amusement. He slapped the laptop shut and stepped behind the bar. "What's your pleasure? I was about to have myself a michelada. I usually add a shot of vodka in mine," he added, his voice a smoky baritone.

Quist nodded. "Sure. I've never had one, but I'll give it a try. I didn't mean to interrupt anything. I just wanted a quiet place to have a beer."

"Where're you from?" Zenner asked, retrieving a couple of Coronas from below the bar.

"West Virginia originally," Quist replied, sidling up to a bar stool. "How about yourself? I'm guessing somewhere west of Louisiana and south of Kansas."

Zenner glanced up at him as he opened a can of Clamato. "You want the vodka, too?" he asked, emptying the can of juice into two tall beer glasses.

Quist nodded. "Sure, no sense being half-ass about drinking in the middle of the afternoon. My name's Quist by the way."

Zenner merely nodded as he measured out a couple of shots of vodka into each glass.

He looked younger than sixty-five. Maybe it was just the light but Mateo Zenner looked like he had been making deals with the devil for a decade or more; that or some Botox and a ton of moisturizer. Quist glanced up and noticed the ragged sheet of aluminum metal mounted on the wall behind the bar. Even though the peeling paint made it almost indecipherable, he could just make out the words El Cuervo. The image of the crow on the cactus appeared faded and sand blasted. "An interesting sign you've got there," he said, gesturing with his chin.

"Part of a plane I used to fly."

"My old man flew. He owned one of those little whatta you call them? Cessnas? He hocked our car once to buy one. My Mom never forgave him, but he just had to have that plane."

Zenner nodded. "I assume you're here for Dia de los Muertos." He divided what looked like a jigger of lime juice into each glass, and then added a shake or two of something unnaturally red and lethal looking. "You know your way around Oaxaca?" he asked, topping off the glasses with the Corona before handing one to Quist.

"Can't say I do. You work here?" Quist asked, sipping the michelada. It tasted better than he expected.

"More than I'd like. I own the place."

"No shit. Good for you. How long have you lived down here?"

"Oh, going on maybe five years," Zenner replied, downing half the glass.

"Let me guess. Some señorita made you an offer you couldn't refuse. You have kids? No? Smart. I have to admit I wouldn't trade this daughter of mine for the world, even though she's been putting me through the ringer. Her boyfriend got her pregnant. They played house for a while, but now she's run off and left him and wants to come home. Expects her old man to save her. My girl friend says I'm...what's the word? Enabling her. But I figure somebody's got to pluck her ass from the coals."

Zenner didn't say anything but instead studied his michelada.

"Let me ask you something. Do you think I'm enabling her? I mean, what would you do if she was ..."

Zenner stopped him with a raised hand. He set down his glass and placed both his hands on the bar, and then looked at

Quist, his gaze level. "I don't want to seem rude, but why don't you finish your drink and be on your way?"

Quist stared at Zenner for a few beats and then smiled. "What do I owe you?"

"On the house," Zenner said, his face still unrevealing.

Quist drank the beer in one long swallow and carefully set down his glass. "See you around," he said and walked out. Jerónimo seemed to appear out of nowhere to unlock the door and let him out.

Quist blinked at the late afternoon sunlight. He could hear the music of a brass band and singing coming from the direction of the Zocalo. He stood there a moment contemplating his conversation with Zenner. He couldn't help but think that his comment about a troublesome daughter had registered with Zenner. Had he perhaps tipped his hand too soon? To live the kind of life he had, Zenner had to be cagey and someone who played things close to the vest. Nor did he seem the type to suffer fools. Quist's instincts told him approaching Zenner head on was their only option. And the sooner the better, for if Manny showed up, things might become more complicated. He took out his cell phone and dialed up Sam as he set out down the empty street.

34

Royale switched on the Land Rover's dome light and flipped down the visor mirror. She hadn't worn this much makeup since the time in San Miguel, and now she questioned whether she had overdone it. The eye shadow, she thought, made her look too spectral. She touched up her lipstick, turned off the light, and climbed out to join Quist and Frieda.

Her red Spandex jeans were decidedly too tight, and the high-heeled sandals much too impractical for the uneven, cobble-stone streets. Quist had whistled his approval when he saw her emerge from her bedroom earlier that evening. Even Frieda seemed impressed by the makeover. Still, Royale had wavered about her choice of clothes. She didn't look exactly maternal if that was the impression she was trying to make with Mateo Zenner. In the end, she decided an attractive woman might prove more persuasive. She also couldn't deny that the way Quist had looked at her gave her a wholly unexpected sense of empowerment.

Quist wore a black leather blazer, white shirt and jeans and black driving moccasins. For someone that appeared to travel light, he always seemed to have an impeccable wardrobe.

Frieda touched the earpiece she had been speaking into and turned to Quist. "We wait for a moment." She nodded at the street. *"Los niños.* They have a parade so we must wait." She looked at each of them in turn. "You both look *muy mota.* Chic, yes?"

"Where's Sam?' Quist asked.

Frieda shrugged. "He says he will be around. I will let him

know if we have trouble. Look. They honor the souls of dead children," she added, pointing down the street.

They watched as several dozen children strolled past. Two young boys dressed in skeleton costumes led the procession while banging randomly on a set of drums, while the other children four abreast marched somberly behind them. Some of the girls wore angel wings, others wore brightly colored skirts, their faces painted like death masks. A few waved purple glow sticks. Bringing up the rear was clutch of boys wearing top hats, ghoulish face paint and playing flutes. Behind them strode another parade of presumably parents keeping a watchful eye on the children.

Quist waited until Frieda gave them a nod of her head. "I will wait here," she said. "Someone inside will watch you."

Royale sought out Quist's hand as they crossed the street and entered the restaurant. They were immediately welcomed by an attractive young Hispanic woman dressed in traditional and elegantly embroidered Zapotec dress.

"You have a reservation?" she asked.

"No, but we're happy sitting at the bar," Quist replied.

The woman smiled and gestured for them to follow her. As they passed through the arched hallway, they heard the sound of a piano and a woman singing in Spanish coming from just inside the dining area. Quist hesitated a second as they approached the bar, his eyes scanning the room. The singer, an attractive, older Latina, wore a tight black body suit embossed with the image of a skeleton, the bones ghoulishly illuminated by a black light above the stage. An elderly couple danced a decidedly out of sync rumba on the postage stamp sized dance floor. Quist could see most of the café tables appeared taken, their occupants visible only as silhouettes in the reflected light from the stage and the smattering of tea candles.

"Do you see him?" Royale asked, climbing onto a barstool.

"Not yet. I guess we wait. In the meantime, what'll you drink?"

"I'm not sure I should drink."

"I'd say a shot of mezcal is in order. Steady the nerves." He leaned over the bar to study the selection of bottles on the shelf behind the bar. "I'll be damned," he said, waving the bartender over. "Del Maguey. Did I ever tell you that was the mezcal Charly was drinking the night I met her?"

"No, I think you failed to mention that detail," she replied, not bothering to hide her irritation. "I'm guessing you got her drunk, didn't you? Right before you took advantage of her."

"More like the other way around. I'd like to think..." The bartender interrupted him. *"Dos Del Maguey, por favor. Con limón.* Your sister..." He paused as if measuring what he was about to say. It seemed he passed through a range of emotions before coming out the other side. "I've contemplated it, and all I ever come up with was that we were both hungry."

"In other words, consenting adults. That's your story?"

"Maybe I was just convenient, crass as that may sound. One always likes to think there's more to it than that. I've learned it's not always easy to read things like that. You know. Falling into bed with someone you hardly know."

Guilty as charged, she thought, avoiding his gaze. She smiled at the bartender as he poured them each a shot of mezcal.

Quist raised his glass and said, "Well, we're all older and wiser. And now that you've renounced the vow of chastity things must be looking up. I mean, there's an outside chance of you having a date on Friday night."

She waited to reply until she had taken a sip of the smoky liquor. "Yeah, about that. I'm not entirely convinced that giving up my vows is a good thing. They always kept things from getting complicated."

Quist sipped his mezcal and smacked his lips. "Yeah, there's that, but I've always felt the more complicated things are, the more interesting things are."

He glanced up at the mirror as the singer launched into a Spanish version of Sinatra's 'My Way.' They both watched in silence for a moment before Royale broke away to eavesdrop on a conversation between two women seated on her right. They were discussing the best place to shop for rugs. She studied some of the other people at the bar before glancing to her left.

"Oh, God," she muttered. "That's him, isn't it?"

Quist turned to look at her, and then followed her gaze. Zenner was leaning on the far end of the bar. He seemed to briefly make eye contact with Quist before gesturing to the bartender.

"Curtain's up. Are you ready?" Quist asked.

Zenner stepped around behind the bar and slowly sauntered towards them.

"Quist, wasn't it? You showing up comes as no surprise. So, let's cut to the chase, why don't we?" He looked at Royale and smiled. "What's your part in this little charade?"

Here goes nothing, she thought, holding his gaze. "I'm her mother."

A look of confusion flickered across Zenner's face. Obviously, this was the last thing he expected as a reply. He recomposed his smile as he attempted to uphold a semblance of equanimity. "I beg your pardon, but I don't think I understand," he said, his eyes circling the room before settling back on Royale.

"I thought you said let's cut to the chase," Quist said.

He considered this for a few seconds before relying. "Well, first I need to know the name of this parlor game you're wanting me to play."

"I think you know," Royale said.

"Okay. Then I guess it comes down to you show me yours and maybe I'll show you mine. Just to see if we're playing the same game."

"I want to see her," Royale said.

Zenner studied her for a moment and smiled. "I have to admit I can see a resemblance."

"So she's here?" Royale asked.

Zenner didn't reply at first. "And if I say she is, then what?"

"I want to see her," Royale said again, struggling to hold back her anger.

"Let's say, hypothetically speaking that is, that Luna's here."

"Lana. Her name's Lana."

He cocked his head in what appeared to be amusement. "So, hypothetically speaking, if I knew where she is, what rea-

185

son would I have to tell you anything?"

"Manny Fontenot for one," Quist interjected. "You're familiar with that prick, aren't you? We're under the impression she's running from him. And he's most likely going to show up in Oaxaca any day now looking for her. But something tells me you might already know that."

"First, why don't you tell me how you knew she was here. I'm assuming someone has their sights on that cockroach Fontenot. DEA would be my guess. Maybe the *Federales.* Which also means you know all there is to know about me. Or think you do."

"I know you're enough of a low life to share a bed with someone who traffics in young girls," Royale said with enough venom in her voice to make Zenner stiffen.

"If you're really her mother then I'm guessing you're no Snow White yourself, so let's dispense with the moral judgments. Look, I always figured Mercedes wasn't really her mother. I even asked her once. She said she adopted her. I dropped it."

"Even though you knew what Schoenfeld did?" Quist asked.

"You mean the sex trafficking? I didn't know about that until later. It was the reason I walked out. One of the reasons at least."

"You're right, Mr. Zenner. I'm no Snow White. And I've associated with my share of low lifes. I know who you are. What you've done. Who knows? Maybe you've put all that behind you. Found God. I don't really care. But just out of curiosity. What was it about Schoenfeld that you found attractive? The sex, the money. What?"

Zenner glanced down at the bar and absently ran his hand over its surface before replying. "It was complicated."

Quist snorted in amusement. "Look, we don't have time for your rationalizations. Are you going to help us or not?"

He looked at each of them in turn. "Depends."

"On?" Royale asked.

Zenner looked at her but said nothing, obviously playing out in his mind what he might be willing to divulge much less how much he was willing to cooperate. He glanced away for a second before turning back.

"She came here because she trusted me. I'm not sure if she'd still trust me if I helped you. You know about the kid?"

Quist nodded.

"Well, it's more than that. She seems pretty fragile. She's been...What do they like to call it these days? Self-medicating? Just pot and tequila as far as I can tell. It seems like she's taking good care of the baby, just not herself. She was like that as a teenager, too. Wilder than wild. She'd come to me whenever she got in trouble. Boyfriends, the Federales, Mercedes. I couldn't count how many times I tried to set her right. But she's headstrong. I'm suspecting she got that from you," he said, looking at Royale. "She says she stopped the drugs and the booze when she found out she was pregnant. And I believe her. But then Manny found her."

"Where is she?" Royale asked for the third time.

"Hold on. The point I'm trying to make here is that I don't think she's in any kind of shape for a family reunion. I mean, does she even know about you? That you even exist?"

"I haven't seen her since she was five. That's when Mercedes Schoenfeld abducted her. Look, I just need to make sure she's safe. That she's alright."

"I can guarantee her safety."

"If we could find her, Manny can, too," Quist said. "You really think you're up to protecting her against someone like him?"

"How did you find her?" Zenner asked, his eyes drifting past them to a couple that had just taken the adjoining bar stools.

Quist hesitated a moment before answering. "Turns out the Federales are watching Manny. She showed up on their surveillance. They knew DEA had been looking for her. They were the ones tracked her to here."

Zenner smiled. "Hell, that's impressive. Back in the day, those federal narcs couldn't find their own ass without a flashlight." He took a sip of something brown from a shot glass the bartender had left at his elbow. "Tell me this. Are they looking to nail me for anything?"

"Not that I'm aware of."

"That's hardly reassuring. Who are you? I mean, where do you fit in here?"

"You don't need…" Royale started to say.

Quist shushed her with his hand. "I used to be a Fed. ATF. Now I free-lance. I'm working for her," he said, nodding at Royale.

Zenner suddenly straightened and reached into his pants pocket and pulled out a cell phone. He squinted at it, and then looked up at them before turning away.

"Hey," Royale heard him murmur. He listened for a second, his body noticeably tensing. .

"Wait! Ximena. *Espere!*"

There was anger in his voice and even from three feet away Royale could hear the voice on the other end of the line shouting.

¿Qué? ¿Cuando? ¿Tamaron el bebe?" Zenner asked as he glanced at them, his face showing obvious alarm. "Shit! *Y Luna. ¿Donde es Luna?* Ximena, where the fuck was she? You were supposed to watch her."

The voice on the other sounded frantic. Zenner turned his back on them and covered his one ear. He shouted something in Spanish into the phone and then hurriedly stuffed the phone back into his pocket. He turned and looked at them, his face cold with anger.

"Mister, what in the hell kind of shit did you bring here?"

"What happened?" Quist asked.

Zenner turned and started to walk away, but Royale leaned over the bar and grabbed his arm.

"I don't have time for this," he said, pulling away.

"Wait. What's wrong?"

"What's wrong is they took the baby. Now get out of my bar."

"Hang on, Zenner," Quist said. "What do you mean someone took the baby?"

"I mean somebody came looking for Luna and when they didn't find her they took the kid."

"Who's with Lana?"

Zenner hesitated. "A friend."

"No security?"

"Sure. I've got a guard, but Ximena said he's gone."

"One guard?"

"Look, I need to get there. Luna's out of her head."

"We're going with you. We've got a car right out front and backup. Just in case," Quist added.

"Backup? Who are you people?" Zenner considered this for a few seconds and then nodded. "Okay, let's go."

35

Turn here. It's shorter," Zenner shouted at Frieda from the back seat.

"No, señor. There are many celebrations on Independencia. We go on Miguel Hidalgo," she said, slowing to allow a group of pedestrians to cross the street. She glanced at him in the rear view mirror. "I know the way to your house, señor," she added in a way that sounded more menacing than reassuring.

Zenner leaned over the seat and grabbed Quist's arm. "You've been watching my house? Then why the fuck didn't you stop this?"

Quist didn't reply, but instead looked at Frieda. "Try him again."

Frieda retrieved her cell phone from the console and punched in a number. She listened for perhaps a minute before dropping it back in the console. "Sam, he does not answer."

Roy started to lean forward just as Frieda hit the accelerator and swerved around a corner, flinging her against Zenner who shoved her aside with more force than seemed necessary. She shot him a look before leaning across the front seat, her hand on Frieda's shoulder.

"He said he had someone watching the house," Roy said.

Frieda shrugged. *"No sé,"* she muttered under her breath as she blew through a red light.

Quist turned to look at Zenner. "Tell me again exactly what your friend said."

"I already told you. Ximena was feeding the baby when these three guys came in the back door. The door was locked so

190

they must have had a key. Maybe they took it from the guard. They wore ski masks. They asked where Luna was."

"Did she say anything about these guys? Anything else about their appearance?"

"Shit, you heard me. I spoke with her for what? Ten seconds? All she said was they couldn't find Luna so they took the baby."

"Lana. Her name is Lana. Where was she?"

Zenner shrugged. "I don't know, but Ximena said she's there now."

Frieda slowed at what appeared to be a police checkpoint. As she approached, she rolled down her window. As one of the policeman started to lean into the window, she held up what appeared to be an ID of some sort. The policeman glanced at it briefly before waving her through.

Quist picked up Frieda's cell phone and held it out to her. She sighed as she took it from him and punched in a number. Quist took it from her and held it to his ear. He let it ring for a good minute before hanging up. No one spoke as Frieda barreled through what appeared to be the same part of town they had driven through the previous night, only this time they turned onto a road leading into the hills. The highway sign indicated it was the route to Monte Alban, the Zapotec ruins located in the hills on the outskirts of the city. They drove up a winding road notable for its lack of any structures. Thick stands of what looked like some sort of scrub oak lined either side. After a minute or so, Frieda turned down a crudely paved road marked by a faded sign that read Los Ibanos. Only once did they pass another car, otherwise the road was empty save for a pair of older women ambling through the darkness, each lugging a clutch of bulging plastic shopping bags in each hand.

At the bottom of a hill, Frieda suddenly slowed as they approached another vehicle parked along the roadway and facing towards them. It looked like another Land Rover, black like the one they were in. The passenger side door hung open. Frieda stopped a good thirty feet away and flicked her high beams on and off several times. When there was no response, she slipped the SUV into park.

"You wait," she said, retrieving a flashlight from the console.

She stepped out and made her way forward in the shadows just beyond the periphery of their headlights. Quist could see she had taken the automatic from her waistband and now held it half-raised in front of her. She disappeared in the border of darkness for a brief moment before the interior of the other Land Rover was suddenly illuminated by what Quist realized was the beam of Frieda's flashlight. Even from this distance, Quist could see a figure slumped sideways in the driver's seat. The light went out as quickly and abruptly as it had come on. A moment later, they saw Frieda jogging back towards them. Something in her face telegraphed both wariness and what Quist guessed might be anger. She swung back into the driver's seat and slammed the door. Quist heard her breathing; short controlled breaths and then a long sigh as she slammed the gear into drive and started back up the road past the other SUV.

"What's going on?" Zenner asked.

Frieda didn't reply as she braked and swung the Land Rover through a large stone gate. A winding driveway led through stands of thick shrubbery before opening up to a cobblestoned courtyard beyond which loomed a large two story house with every window illuminated. Before the Land Rover had even to come to a stop, Zenner flung open the door and began sprinting up the stone stairway. Roy wasted no time in following him. Frieda cut the engine and sat there staring straight ahead.

"Who was that back there?" Quist asked.

She looked at him. "One of Sam's men. Henry. A *guero*. A *Tejano*. Someone shot him in the head."

"He was the only one watching the house?"

She shrugged. "I am not certain. There was no sign of someone else. But Henry had...how do you say? A partner?"

"Do you have another flashlight? And how about a piece? Another *pistola*," he asked.

She handed him her flashlight and then reached across him and opened the glove compartment and handed him what felt

192

like a Glock.

"I say we take a look around. I'll take the back," he said, climbing out just as Frieda's cell chirped. She glanced at it and motioned with her hand for Quist to wait.

"*Si.¿Qué ha sucedido?*" she asked, the irritation obvious in her voice. "*Henry está muerto. Tamaron al bebé. Si,* she is here." She listened for a few seconds. "*No sé. Si. Claro. A sus ordenes.* Okay."

She slipped the cell in the pocket of her jeans. "Sam say he will be here in fifteen minutes."

"That's all he said?"

She stalked off without replying.

36

Royale hesitated at the top of the stairs, overcome by a swirl of emotions. The drive to Zenner's house had provided just enough time for her to fully realize the irony of what was happening. Everything seemed to be coming full circle, and the looming tragedy left her nauseous and uncertain. She stood there a moment and took a deep breath in an attempt to compose herself, unbraiding the scenarios, what to expect, and not expect, what to say and not to say. The sound of the Land Rover's doors slamming stirred her from her thoughts. She shrugged off her angst and stepped through the open doorway.

A formal foyer, its floor covered with expensive looking native rugs, led to a large atrium courtyard open to the dark night sky two stories above. She paused at the sound of voices arguing from somewhere across the courtyard; a woman's voice mostly, the other she recognized as Zenner's. She cautiously made her way to the open doorway that was the source of the disturbance. Peering around the doorway, she saw Zenner and a woman standing on opposite sides of a kitchen island. The woman pressed a towel to the left side of her head. In the other hand she brandished a long fork which she waved in Zenner's face with each strident outburst. She was tall with waist-length salt and pepper hair and wore a loose fitting shift that at first Royale thought was long-sleeved before realizing the woman's arms were covered in tattoos.

"*Puede ver,*" she said, jabbing the fork to within inches of Zenner's face. "You bring this girl into our home. I tell you. Not good. You no listen. *Puede ver lo que ocurre.* They could have killed me. *Bastardos. No mas.* You hear me? *¿Entiende?* "

"Get that goddamn fork out of my face. Remember, you were the one who wouldn't let me turn her away. You said yourself she needed our help."

The woman must have caught sight of Royale out of the corner of her eye for she abruptly turned and gazed at Royale in direct and open appraisal, the towel still pressed to her head.

"¿Quién es esta mujer?" she asked without taking her eyes off Royale.

"Es su madre," Zenner said after a moment's hesitation.

Royale walked into the kitchen and stopped well out of reach of the fork. She could now see the woman more clearly. She could've been anywhere from forty to fifty years of age, her smooth unlined face the color of latte. It was a face that could only be described as exotic in its misalignment; fine boned with angular cheekbones, full lips and a too large mouth, and emerald green, deep set eyes, the right orbit noticeably larger than the left. Her head somehow seemed too large for her graceful, elongated neck. Still, the discordant elements did little to dispel her allure.

"Where is she?" Royale asked.

The woman offered a wintry smile and walked over to Royale. *"Su madre.* And where has this mother been hiding?"

"Where is she?" Royale asked again, turning to Zenner who gave her a hard stare before gesturing with his head to the upstairs.

"If you are really her mother," the woman said as Royale turned away, "Take her. She is no good. Even much better, take her baby."

Royale stopped and looked at her, but said nothing. What could she say? She turned and left them to their recriminations. A stairway at the end of the courtyard led to a second story landing lined with several rooms, the doors of which were all closed. She stood there a moment listening. The only sound, a muted keening seemed to come from the room at the end of the hallway. She made her way to the door, hesitated a second and opened it.

Something blocked the door, a piece of furniture from the

screeching sound it made when Royale forced it open.

"Get out! *Ir lejos!*" a voice screamed from inside.

Royale pushed the door open enough to squeeze through and immediately faced a barrage of hurled shoes, an empty bottle and what could've been a jewelry box, none of which found their mark. A table lamp, knocked on its side and without a shade, provided the room's only light. The room stank of dirty laundry and the skunky bouquet of pot. It took Royale a moment to see Lana crouched against the far wall like a cornered animal. She appeared to be wearing nothing more than a pair of panties and a T-shirt. Even in the muted light, Royale could see Lana's red-rimmed, puffy eyes, the rest of her face obscured by her lanky, unkempt hair. Royale remembered Lana's lustrous black hair in the painting at Schoenfeld's home. Now her dirty blonde hair looked dull and in bad need of a trim.

"It's okay," Royale said, holding out her hands in an effort to reassure her. "I'm your..." She couldn't say it. "I'm a friend," was all she could muster.

"Go away. I don't have any fucking friends," Lana muttered, her voice throaty and dry.

"I'm Mateo's friend. I just want to make sure you're okay."

Lana swiped at her hair and looked up at Royale. "Why in the hell do you think I'd be okay?" she asked, her voice cracking with tension. "How could I be fucking okay? They took my baby. They took Bella."

"Bella?"

Royale flinched, for the first time aware of the baby's name much less its gender. The hysteria in Lana's voice, the tenseness in her posture, triggered a forgotten memory of her own panic when the cop told her they weren't able to find Lana's body. She had been sitting in Charly's jail cell when the cop told them. She could still remember Charly's cry of anguish, and her own sense of guilt at not being able to match her sister's pain.

Royale stood there a moment before edging closer. Lana retreated, scooting until her back was against the wall. A half-empty bottle of what appeared to be tequila sat on the floor beside her along with an ash tray containing a roach clip and what

Royale guessed was a partially smoked joint.

"We'll find her. I promise."

Lana turned her face aside as if in disbelief, pushing her hair back with both her hands. When she looked back, there was mild curiosity reflected there, and something else, something amorphous and fleeting. Regret, perhaps. And still the gleam of defiance. The image of the young woman in the painting suddenly came to mind. Still, it was difficult to reconcile the girl in the painting and the defeated young woman huddled at her feet

"Manny took her. Because he couldn't have me," she said. "I should've been here," she said, reaching for the bottle of tequila.

Royale knelt before her and gently removed the bottle from her grasp. It was only then Royale saw the scars on her hand. She took Lana's hand and held it to the light. An angry web of scar tissue ran from her right hand down the length of her arm.

"Do you remember how you got this scar?" Royale asked, doing her best to conceal the trepidation in her voice.

Lana regarded her silently for a long moment before she broke away and looked back down at the bottle. The silence built, the only sound a dog barking somewhere in the distance.

"Lana. Has anyone ever called you that? Lana?"

When Lana looked up her eyes were moist. Royale leaned forward and put her arms around Lana. She felt the girl tense for just a second before allowing herself to collapse in Royale's embrace. Royale stroked her hair and rocked her. There would be no telling her the truth. Not yet. She held her like this for a long time until she seemed to settle.

"Is there any more of this?" Royale said, releasing her and picking the joint from the ashtray.

"Why? You want a hit?" Lana asked with a ghost of a smile.

"If you want Bella back, you're going to have to be strong. And sober. You don't need any of this right now," she said, picking up the ashtray and the bottle of tequila and getting to her feet. "I'll be back in a little while. Clean yourself up and we'll talk some more."

"Why did you call me Lana?"

"Because that's your name. Your real name. Now clean up."

197

37

Quist found Zenner's security guard hog-tied and rolled beneath a stand of stunted pine trees. A somewhat antiquated looking shotgun lay broken open beneath a nearby shrub. The guard looked to be in his sixties, and most assuredly not menacing enough for the task at hand. It made him question how seriously Zenner took the possibility of Manny showing up. After cutting the guard loose, Quist questioned him to no avail in his broken Spanish for any information on his assailants before sending him back to the house. By the time, Quist circled back to the front of the house, Sam had arrived and stood talking with Frieda. He wore dress slacks and a crisp white guayabera. He had also shaved off his beard.

"You find anything?" Sam asked.

"Just Zenner's half-ass security detail. They tied him up but he's okay. I doubt he saw much of anything. Frieda says you're maybe missing one of your men."

Sam glanced at Frieda before replying. "He'll turn up. Come daylight I'll look for him."

Quist noted the obvious lack of concern in his voice.

"Why not call for some help?"

"Calling in the local *policia* or the *Federales* is the last thing I'll do. Not yet at least. There's no way I want them sticking their nose in this."

"I thought they wanted Manny."

"Where's the girl?" he asked, changing the subject.

Frieda cocked her head towards the house.

"You stay here," Sam said to her, turning for the steps. He glanced at Quist who was right on his heels. "A royal clusterfuck. Now we have to go looking for the kid."

"You sound like you wished they would've nabbed the girl instead."

"It sure would've made things less complicated," Sam said without breaking stride.

They found Zenner and a tall woman with long silvery hair seated at a table in the kitchen along with the guard. The woman, Ximena was the name Zenner had used, held a dish towel to the side of her head. Sam grabbed a nearby chair and spun it around and straddled it.

"So. What happened?" he asked, his gaze directed at the woman.

*"¿Quién es este hombre rudo?"*she asked Zenner.

Zenner looked at Quist before turning to Sam. "Let me guess. DEA, right? It seems you guys never change. You always feel you can just barge into someone's house all attitude and a shit load of questions."

"Escuche, señora," Sam said, ignoring Zenner. "Just tell me what the fuck happened."

Ximena offered him a spiteful glance before tossing the washcloth on the table. Quist could see the beginnings of an angry bruise on her temple. She shot Zenner a questioning look who nodded for her to go on.

"These men. They come through the back door. I was here, at this table, feeding Bella. The men, they say they want Luna. I tell them nothing. They threaten me. They say they will beat me. I still say nothing. So they hit me," she said, gesturing to the bruise on the side of her forehead. "I still say nothing. They look for her and they cannot find her so they take *la enfanta*. From my arms, they take her."

The calm manner in which she told this story led Quist to wonder if she was somehow involved. That or she wasn't the type to be easily intimidated. Something about her bearing, an almost fierce defiance, led him to settle on the latter.

Sam stared her down for a moment before asking, "So where was the girl?"

Ximena shrugged. "Who knows? She goes outside many

times to smoke marijuana."

"This old geezer didn't see her?" he asked, gesturing at the guard who stood silently in the corner rubbing his wrists.

"They jumped him before he knew what was happening," Zenner explained.

"These guys were Mexican?"

"*No sé.* Only one man say anything. He speak in Spanish but he was not from here. His accent, no? A *Chilango*, maybe. From the city."

"Mexico City, huh? What did they look like?"

"Nobody big. One man was very small. They wore... *¿Cómo se dice?* The ski mask, yes? One man he had very nice boots. Iguana, I think."

Sam thought for a moment. "Get the girl down here. I'm taking her."

"She stays," Zenner said.

"I take her into protective custody until we get the baby back."

"I doubt they'll come back here," Quist offered. "Maybe she's better off here. I'll stay. Give me Frieda. You find the baby."

Sam shook his head in annoyance. "Shit. Do you really think you're gonna find the baby? This is Mexico for chrissakes. Besides Manny doesn't want the baby. He wants her."

"Then negotiate," Quist said. "There must be something he wants."

"Yeah, he wants the girl. All I'm saying is that if you want that baby back in one piece, you're going to have to give the girl up. Manny gets her, we get the baby back. Then we'll deal with him."

"She's not ours to trade." Quist said.

"Says who?"

"I say."

They all turned and looked at Roy standing in the doorway.

38

She stays. And I'm still holding you to your word," Roy said, approaching the table.

The two of them stared each other down for a moment before Sam broke into a grin.

"Sister, you might not have heard me, but down here, when somebody goes missing, you don't just find them. To get them back in one piece you have to pay. And if you've got it in your head to try starting up some kind of manhunt and get the locals involved, well, I can tell you right now. You do that and you won't see that baby anymore. I don't want to sound callous, but getting that baby back means a trade."

"I'm not trading her."

Sam shook his head in amusement and glanced over at Quist. "You better talk some sense into your woman," he said, his mood suddenly grave. "It's the girl or the baby."

"Hold on," Quist replied. "We haven't heard from Manny. What's the harm in waiting to see what he's got in mind."

"Does he want money?" Zenner interjected. "I can come up with…"

Quist held up his hand to stop him. "First, we see what Manny wants. If nothing else, it'll buy us some time to come up with our own ideas." He looked over at Roy. "Are you okay with that?"

"I'm not giving her up. No matter what you or this shit bird here says."

"My, my. I doubt you learned that kind of language in the convent," Sam said, his face still somber. "Makes me sorta wonder what kind of shit I could dig up on you."

Quist motioned to Roy with his hand for her to back down. "Time out. All I'm saying is if it comes down to a trade, then we'll have time to think about some things. Maybe figure out something to give us an advantage. Agreed?"

Sam stood up, his irritation obvious. "Okay, play it your way." He started to walk off.

"Where are you going?" Quist asked.

He turned and gave each of them a hard glance. "Fair warning. If you're smart, you won't get the local cops involved. For all you know, they might've been the ones that took her. I told you I'd get you your daughter. You got her, so I figure I did my part."

"Then we make a new deal," Roy said, stepping in front of him.

"I don't renegotiate, not unless your boyfriend Quist here has some more dirt to shovel." He turned and looked at Zenner. "How about you? Got anybody you wanna sell out? No? Well then keep me in the loop, why don't you?" He brushed past Roy and walked out.

"Look," Zenner said after a moment, "If it comes to it, I can come up with a fair amount of cash." He glanced at Ximena before looking up at Royale. "I should've done something for Luna a long time ago."

"Her name's Lana. How many times do I have to tell you that?" Roy said.

"Did you tell her?" Quist asked.

Roy shook her head. "I think she remembers something. But it's not a good time. Not yet." She dropped into one of the chairs. "Sam's a snake. You don't trust him, do you?"

"Let's just say that I think he's got his own agenda. All we have to do is..." He paused as they heard the front door slam. A moment later, Frieda strolled into the kitchen.

"Sam says I am to do what you tell me," she said simply, making her way to the pot of coffee on the stove.

They all watched Frieda in silence as she poured herself a mug of coffee before turning to look at them. Quist rose from his seat and walked over to her. "We need to talk," he said, taking her arm and guiding her out into the courtyard. He glanced at Roy who shot him a questioning look.

"So what do you think happened to your other man?" he asked once they were out of earshot. "His name was Flavio, right?"

She took a swallow of coffee and cocked her head. "*Quizás muerto.* Mebbe he just go away. *No sé.* There was no blood on the passenger seat, so I think he was not in the SUV."

"Or he was the shooter."

This gave her pause. "*Posiblemente.* When I go back the SUV is gone. Sam maybe had someone take it away. I looked on the road, but I did not see any more blood. Just the tire marks."

"Do you have any idea where Sam was? Did he say anything?"

"He told me he went to El Cuervo to look for us, but he doesn't find us."

"Do you believe him?"

She took a sip of coffee, and then another, buying time for her answer. "I work with him for only *cuatro meses.* Four months, yes? He is like many of you Americanos who does what you call ...¿*Qué? Encubierto.* The undercover, yes? *Es muy dificile.* Very difficult to know when a man like Sam tells the truth."

"So you don't believe him?"

"Do not put words in my mouth, señor. Is that not how you say it? "*¿Las palabras de la boca?.* Words in the mouth, yes?"

Quist studied her for a moment. "Who do you really work for?"

She sucked her teeth and flexed her shoulders in an eloquent shrug. "I work for many people. *El gobierno.* The goberment. People who do business with the goberment."

"And Sam knows this?"

She smiled and tilted her head, but unless Quist misread the gesture, the smile was not one of amusement.

"I am someone Sam finds useful. Does he know who I really am? Or who I work for? Perhaps he does not care." Her eyes shifted at the sound of the manic chirping of a gecko somewhere behind him. "*Es muy complicado,*" she said, looking back.

"Don't underestimate him, Frieda. You wouldn't be working for him if he hadn't checked you out. So where did he find you?"

He could see her editing her reply in the back of her mind. "The Federales. The drug police. They give Sam my name. They tell him I work for them sometimes."

She paused again as if she were considering any further explanation. "They told Sam they will send me back to prison if I don't cooperate. If I don't help him. Just like I help them," she added.

He was suddenly aware of the change in her diction, the softening of her accent. "So you're an ex-con?"

She cocked her head in amusement, a hint of a smile curling her mouth. *"No exactamente.* No."

"What does that mean?"

"I wasn't a criminal. I was in prison because I was in someone's way. I was *suerte.* Fortunate. It is more common to be killed. When you are in the way. *¿Entiende?"*

"So, maybe you work for the Federales. Or not," he said when she didn't offer more. "I'm guessing you're working both sides of the fence. Is he really that stupid?"

This made her laugh. "No, not stupid, he is just ... How should I put this? I think you Americans have a saying. How a man often thinks with his...*verga.* His dick, yes?.."

Quist grinned. "You're sleeping with him."

A look of affliction crossed her face and then she smiled. "I have proven my loyalty to him in other ways. He thinks I want to leave Mexico and come with him to the States."

"So are you working for your government or not?"

"I think I am much like you, Señor Quist. Freelance is your word, yes?"

"Does that mean you go to the highest bidder? Or do you occasionally let your conscience get in the way?" He sensed her stiffen.

"You ask if I have a conscience? *Por supuesto.* Royale told me everything."

"So you would help us? No matter what?"

Again, the eloquent shrug. *"Eso depende,"* she said so softly he almost imagined it. She downed the last of the coffee and set the mug on a nearby table and then reached into her shirt pocket and took out a pack of cigarettes and a Bic. When she tilted her head to light the cigarette, Quist caught the scent of her hair; something coconut.

"So what do you think he's up to?"

"Up to? What is his game as you like to call it?" She shook her head. "I don't know. Not yet. I know Sam wants this Manny. I do not pretend to know everything Sam does or how he works. And there is one other thing. I know he did not go to El Cuervo tonight. I had people watching. Front and back. He was not there."

"But he told you he went there looking for us?" Quist turned and glanced back at the kitchen. Zenner and Royale appeared deep in conversation. "So what now?" he asked, turning back.

"As you said. We must wait."

"You'll be honest with me?"

"You ask me if I can be trusted?" She offered him a smile. "Sam, he say you were also once an undercover agent. So, when you did this work, did you trust anyone? Perhaps I should be asking if I can trust you, Señor Quist."

"I think you know why my friend and I are here. We're not interested in anything else but getting the girl and the baby out of here. Whatever game you and Sam, or you and someone else are playing, it has nothing to do with us."

She didn't reply, but reached into her bag and handed him a couple of full clips for the Glock and a cell phone. "My number is programmed. I have one thing to do and I will be back," she said, turning and walking away.

39

Royale tilted her head to look past Zenner at Quist and Frieda who seemed engaged in what appeared to be an almost intimate conversation. She still wasn't really sure whether she trusted Frieda. The fact remained that she worked for Sam. She assumed Sam had told her why they were trying to find Lana. Earlier that day, while sitting in the courtyard of the small church where Frieda had taken her to escape the frantic street life, Royale had inexplicably revealed everything that had transpired from the moment she had been notified of Charly's death; how Quist had become involved, and the events of that last night in San Miguel; everything except her own sordid part in how she had failed her daughter. Finally, exhausted by this catharsis, Royale fell silent.

"I understand," Frieda said. "This loss you speak of. Without such loss there can be no love, no forgiveness. Such pain becomes who we are. It cannot be ignored. Does what I say make sense, yes?"

Royale had nodded and wondered at the depth of Frieda's losses. Were her own scars what allowed someone like her to work for someone as deceitful as Sam?

Now as she watched Frieda speaking to Quist, she felt an unfamiliar and wholly unexpected twinge of jealousy. What secrets might they be sharing? What bond might they be forming? She had to accept the fact that she didn't trust men, this in spite of her burgeoning attachment to Quist. Was what she was feeling for him a modicum of affection or merely just the need for his help in finding Lana? She shook her head in frustration. One would think that after so many years spent divining the depths of human emotion, she would not feel like such an innocent when it came to her own feelings.

"Is something wrong?' she heard Zenner ask.

She cast one more glance at Quist sand Frieda before turning to Zenner. Perhaps Quist was merely worming his way through Frieda's carapace in much the same way he had done with her.

"I'm sorry. What were you saying?"

"I said she had nowhere else to go. She was strung out, scared. And with a kid. Ximena may sound like a cold-hearted bitch but she was the one talked me into taking her in."

"I guess I should thank you," she replied, still distracted. She glanced back at the courtyard and saw that Frieda had disappeared. Quist sauntered over to the stove and poured himself a cup of coffee.

"Where's Frieda going?" she asked,

Quist took a seat at the table and sipped his coffee, ignoring her question. "I need to talk to Lana," he said after a moment.

"She's not in any kind of shape to talk. We have to give her some time."

"Something about all this doesn't make sense," he said, ignoring her objection. "They could've just waited, or looked around some more. I mean why just take the baby?" He glanced at Zenner. "If they really wanted to, they could've forced your friend Ximena to give her up. But they didn't. How come?"

"Maybe they were worried Sam's people would show up," Zenner said. "We saw the SUV down on the road. Maybe they thought the Feds were coming."

"It's not just that. The way I see it, kidnapping the baby's a needless complication. They'd be risking getting other people involved. The cops. Sam." He looked at Royale. "I need to ask Lana some things."

Royale sighed and nodded in resignation. "Okay, but if I want you to stop, you'll stop, right?"

Quist looked at Zenner. "Do you have a decent security alarm?"

"Halfway decent, not that I ever turn it on. I used to have a dog but he died."

"Do you own a gun?"

"That I do have. Several in fact."

"Good. You may need them. Let's go see Lana," Quist said, getting to his feet.

"You won't tell her? I mean, who I am?" Royale asked as they made their way up the stairs.

He turned and looked at her. "Roy, the sooner you tell her the better. We may need her to stay focused. You tell her, and sure she might be pissed. But we might just have to use that. You understand?"

Royale nodded. Quist was right. There was no point in putting it off. She'd let Quist ask her some things and then she'd tell her. She hesitated at the door before knocking. "Lana," she said, knocking softly on the door.

A few seconds later, the door opened. Lana wore a pair of faded jeans and an embroidered peasant blouse that hung loosely over her small frame. Her hair was wet and Royale could now see her dark roots. It also appeared she had made a rudimentary effort to apply some eye makeup. The transformation momentarily startled Royale. It was as if she were staring at her own reflection in a mirror, albeit twenty years removed. Something in her reaction obviously stirred some inchoate emotion in Lana too, for she seemed to shrink back from the doorway.

"You keep calling me Lana. Why do you call me that? My name's Luna," she said with obvious irritation, though there was also something tenuous in her voice.

"Because Lana's your real name. Your name is Lana Aucoin. You disappeared…"

She realized there was no sense lying anymore. "Mercedes Schoenfeld took you away from us when you were five. She took you from Charly. She took you from me," she said, the words tumbling out so quickly she couldn't stop herself. "She bought you is what she did. And then she told you she was your mother. She lied to you. I'm your mother."

Lana stared at her with a mixture of confusion and horror that made Royale wonder if telling her had been a mistake, for her confession seemed to freeze them both in what seemed some sort of suspended animation.

"I don't believe you," Lana said finally. She glanced at Quist with a look of whimsy tinged with sarcasm. "And what? I suppose you're going to tell me next that this guy's my father?"

Quist cocked his head at Royale and smiled. "No. Just think of me as the mediator."

Royale took Lana's hand and dragged her to the mirror that sat atop the dresser. She turned Lana and stood beside her. For a long moment, they both studied each other's reflection before Lana finally turned away and sat on the side of the bed.

"I don't understand," she said after a moment had passed.

"You don't need to. Not yet." Royale looked at Quist. "But we need to find Bella and there may not be much time. Harlan needs to ask you some questions. Is that okay?"

"Bella's not an easy baby. If she cries, if they hurt her I couldn't live with myself." She looked up at Quist. "You'll find her, won't you? Please say you'll find her."

"Lana," Quist interjected, squatting down before her. "Listen to me. If we're going to find her, I need to understand some things. Okay?"

She nodded. There was still confusion reflected in her face but also something resembling resolve.

"Do you really think Manny would come after you? Or let's put it this way. Is there maybe some reason he'd come looking for you? Maybe some other reason than just to get you back?" Quist glanced up at Royale as if to preempt any interruption.

Lana held Quist's gaze for a moment before shaking her head. Quist sensed she was holding something back.

Royale had to know. "Is Bella his baby?"

"No," Lana replied almost too quickly. "I loved Bella's father." She looked up at Royale. "His name was Cruz. He worked at the ranch. He was the only one that ever really cared about me. And they got rid of him," she said with sudden vehemence. "Mercedes and Manny. They got rid of Cruz. He was just gone one day. That's when I decided to leave," she said, her voice drifting away. A long silence filled the room before she looked back at them. "Manny found me. Kept me locked up until I had

Bella. I tried to leave. You have to believe that."

"Lana," Royale said, sitting beside her and embracing her tightly.

"I was like his fucking exercise bike," she said, her voice cracking.

"Why does he want you?" Quist asked again.

Lana didn't reply for a long moment. "He wants me because I know things."

"What do you mean? You know things?"

"I mean things I'm not supposed to know. Things he doesn't want certain people to know."

"Such as?"

"Enough," Royale said, sensing that Lana was about to shut down. "Not now."

"It's important. We need some kind of leverage."

"I just knew some of the people he did business with. That's all."

"Okay. Just one more thing, and this is important," Quist said, ignoring Royale's look of rebuke. "Lana, do you know anyone named Sam?"

"Sam? No. Why?"

"He may have known either Manny or Mercedes. He might've come to her ranch. He's an American. Six three maybe, heavy set. Gray colored eyes."

"Lots of people came to the ranch. People I didn't always know."

"He had a U-shaped scar on this side of his head," Royale said, pointing above her left ear.

Lana seemed to flinch and then averted her gaze to the side. "I don't know. Maybe. Like I said, a lot of people came to the ranch."

"You're sure?"

"Christ! I told you. I don't know him."

Quist studied the girl for a moment and then stood and pulled Royale aside. "Stay close to Zenner. He'll protect you."

"Where are you going?"

"I need to talk to Sam again and find out what team he's really playing for. Take this," he said, handing her the cell phone Frieda had given him. "Frieda's number is programmed if you need her. And don't let Lana out of your sight." He turned and walked out.

Royale glanced at Lana who sat on the edge of the bed, seemingly lost in thought. Royale sat next to her and put her arm around Lana's waist. "We'll find her. I promise."

"Who's Charly?" Lana asked, her eyes still fixed on the floor.

"Charly was your aunt. My sister. I gave you to her to raise. Because I couldn't. I'm so sorry," she said, taking Lana's hand.

Lana held her hand for a moment before reaching over and tapping her fingers over the tattoos on Royale's hand. "The shooting stars. I think I remember them. I used to touch them. Oh, god." She turned away and when she looked back, her eyes registered a flow of bewilderment, some startling recognition and then something Royale could only interpret as pain.

"You remember something, don't you?"

Lana seemed to disappear for what seemed a long time before she looked at Royale. "You never told me your name," Lana said.

"Royale, but Charly called me Roy."

"Roy." She seemed to ponder this for a moment before asking, "And where's Charly?"

"She died. Looking for you."

"Manny killed her?"

"No. She…" How to tell her how Charly had died? There was no point. "I think something just gave out. I know she wanted to find you. It was because of her though that I found you."

Lana considered this for a moment and then stood. "Okay, you found me. Now find Bella," she said, and then stalked off into the bathroom and slammed the door.

40

Royale found Zenner on the rear patio. Here the grounds consisted of nothing more than clumps of low growing shrubs bordered by scrubby forest. The lone flood light only seemed to accentuate the yard's shadows. Zenner had situated himself on a rattan recliner beneath a large potted palm. He nodded at her appearance and gestured for her to sit in a lawn chair beneath a neighboring palm.

"Try to stay in the dark," he said quietly. "Although if they have any of that high tech night vision shit we're probably screwed anyway."

He cradled what looked like a hunting rifle in his lap. Propped against the palm plant was another rifle of some sort. A shotgun perhaps, the profile and bulk of which reminded her of the .12 gauge her father kept stowed beneath the bar.

"Do you really think they'll come back here to look for her?" she asked.

"Not likely, but *cholos* like the ones that took Bella... Well, if they want to come back and take another go at it, then that's what they'll do. This time they won't fuck around, pardon my French. I'd lay odds they're watching us right now. I thought I might've even spotted one a while ago over there behind that thorn thicket. I hope you told her to stay put," he added, reaching for a bottle at his feet.

"I think the last thing she wants is to be down here with me."

Zenner handed her the bottle. "Don't take it too personally. She doesn't trust anybody."

She screwed off the top and smelled it. Mezcal, maybe.

"She trusted you," she said taking a sip of the liquor. It tasted of burnt earth and a sweetness she found at first off putting, though the after taste filled her mouth and nose and left her wanting more. "What is this?"

"Something Ximena distills in the basement. She calls it La Orina del Diablo."

"The devil something."

"Devil's piss to be exact. It's mezcal distilled with some kind of herbs she gets from up in the mountains." He raised a pair of binoculars and slowly surveyed the brush at the edge of the lights. "I saw this jaguar out here one night. Just over there by that big tree. He was biding his time, too," he said, lowering the binoculars.

"You asked me earlier what it was about Mercedes that kept me there for five years. The hedonist in me would like to say it was all about the high life. The first class travel. The dinner parties in these outrageously gauche penthouses in Polanco. Now that I think back on it, I'm not sure why in the hell I ever put up with those slimy assholes with their trophy wives and six bodyguards. But then there were those beautiful fucking beach houses. I do have this thing for beach houses," he said with a wistful sigh.

He shook his head as if to rid himself of some memory. "I didn't judge at the time. I used to think it was only because I used to be a lot like them. Then I came to realize I was never like them. It was part of why I left." He reached over and took the bottle from her grasp. "You didn't know her. Mercedes, I mean. Well, she wasn't what you'd think. She was one sexy, intoxicating, bright and shining, evil piece of work." He took a long pull from the bottle before passing it back to her.

"I never really was into drugs other than a little weed now and then. She was the closest I ever got to any kind of addiction. She was like a drug, and shit if I didn't main line her. She really didn't do drugs either. Her drug was control. Control over her business, her lovers, her horses. And Luna. Lana," he said, correcting himself. "Lana was nothing more to Mercedes than some exotic pet she could pamper or ignore at will. There're plenty of reasons that girl's the way she is."

She felt like telling him what she did for a living, but in the end decided to let him ramble on.

"I don't know a damn thing about being a parent or a father. And that's what she probably needed. She needed a father more than a friend. I wasn't that good at either. I tried to teach her some things. About knowing who people really are. What they might want from you. That kind of stuff, The Way of the World 101. I doubt it ever took."

"Did Mercedes even care about what happened to her?"

"Of course she did. In her own way. That was why she got rid of that boy who knocked her up. It was her way of caring. You have to understand that there were plenty of reasons Mercedes was fucked up, too. But for her, it all came down to control. It was how she kept the lid on." He reached for the bottle and took a long pull before handing it back to her.

"Mercedes and I used to go ride horses at sunrise. She was quite the horsewoman, you know. In the mornings, she'd ride with nothing on except her riding britches and a flimsy night gown. The last time I rode with her she told me Lana wasn't really her daughter. She told me she bought her with the intent of grooming her to be some high dollar hooker. It wasn't about money though. She was looking to make someone over in her own image. Teach Lana to be like her. Somebody that used her looks and her sex to control people. Right after she told me that was when I decided to leave."

"And you left Lana with her? How could you?"

"It's easy when you're gutless. Look, no one's ever really given a shit about Lana. No one's ever loved her or treated her like something different than what Mercedes was making her into."

"I loved her. My sister loved her."

"Maybe, but you have to realize Mercedes was the only mother she knew. Or at least remembers."

Royale took another swallow of the mezcal and the set it on the ground between them. "That may be, but I'm her mother now."

"Good luck with that."

"I think I've had enough of your inspirational platitudes," she said, pushing to her feet. "I'll be upstairs with Lana if something happens."

"Then take this," he said, holding out a handgun he picked up from the table beside him. "You know how to use one? Safety's up…"

"I'll manage," she said taking it from him. It was heavier than she expected.

"Twenty in the magazine. Hopefully, you won't need 'em all. Oh, one more thing," he said as she started to walk off. "You knew it was Lana that pushed Mercedes down the stairs, don't you? I heard she beat Mercedes half to death with a riding crop, too. I have to admit the girl's got spunk. Mercedes at least taught her that."

Royale smiled. "No, she's just a biter."

"She's what?"

"I meant to say maybe she's her mother's daughter after all."

"Yeah, well, you'd be wise not to turn your back on her."

"I don't plan to. Not anymore," she said and walked inside.

41

So how many safe houses does he have?" Quist asked, turning to glance at Frieda. In the dark interior of her SUV, he could just make out her profile. He wasn't sure he entirely trusted her and wished he could see what her eyes or mouth might reveal.

She shrugged. "One other that I know of."

"And you're sure he's in there?"

"That is his truck. I have been to this house many times before. He is there."

"Alone?"

She seemed to shrug. "That I cannot tell you. He is *un solitario*, yes? A loner I believe is how you say it."

They were parked on a narrow, cobble-stoned street in a neighborhood that clung to a steep hillside overlooking the city. A contiguous but dissimilar block of houses lined one side, their multi-colored stucco walls concealing any appreciation of the interiors. The other side of the street dropped off sharply, revealing only a terrace of rooftops of differing heights. The cathedral they had passed on the drive up the hillside loomed up through the darkness, its spires illuminated by flood lights. Some sort of pageant was being held in its courtyard, and even now, Quist could hear music and scattered applause wafting up the hillside in the still night air.

"So I guess I just go knock on the door and surprise him?"

"There are many dogs in this neighborhood. He will know someone is coming."

Neither said anything for a few moments. "What do you think is going on?" he asked.

She seemed to carefully consider her answer before replying. "It is difficult to say. Perhaps, Sam is helping this Manny.
Perhaps, Sam just doesn't know what to do. Maybe he is merely
una innocente, like you and I."

He saw her teeth flash in the dark as she smiled.

"I think mostly he waits to see what happens," she added.

"He'll know you brought me here."

She smiled again. "Of course. It was what he wanted, yes?
You do not have to worry about the dogs. I will drive you to the
door."

Quist shot her a look of appraisal. He still wasn't sure what
to make of her, but the only way he would know if she could be
trusted, would be to trust her.

"You'll stay?"

"You mean do I have your back? Isn't that how you gringo
cops say it?" She nodded. "He wants me to stay. You want me to
stay. So I stay."

The ambiguity of her response didn't exactly make him feel
secure. He nodded and she started up the SUV and drove slowly
up the street before stopping before a simple wooden doorway
recessed into the stucco wall. She reached up and unscrewed
the bare bulb of the SUV's overhead light before gesturing for
him to get out. He climbed out, stuffing the Glock into his back
waistband. The dogs in the adjoining courtyards on either side
began baying. Almost immediately, the small portico was bathed
in light. Quist walked to the door and raised his empty hands as
if in supplication. Two seconds later, he heard what sounded like
a couple of safety bolts on the door pop open.

He took a deep breath and opened the door which revealed
large high-ceilinged room devoid of any furnishings save for
a ratty, abused sofa and a battered, dimly lit floor lamp. The
room smelled of cigarettes and mold. A jazz melody played
softly from a darkened side room. Miles Davis Kind of Blue,
maybe. He started down a shadowy hallway, at the end of which
was a room illuminated by what he could see was a single bare
light bulb hanging from the ceiling. An open refrigerator door
blocked the entranceway. Someone stood behind the refrigerator

door, only bare legs visible. An instant later, Sam's head poked over the top.

"Would you eat an omelet if I made one?" he asked.

"I prefer fried, over easy. But I'm not picky."

Sam grunted and closed the door, a carton of eggs clutched in one hand, a large handgun in the other, and a six-pack of beer stuffed beneath his one arm. He wore only a T-shirt and a pair of ragged cargo shorts. "Frieda's waiting?" he asked, turning away.

"I take it you told her to. Tell me something. Where did you find her?"

Sam shot him a look of surprise. "She hasn't told you? She's bought and paid for. More like borrowing. She's on the Federales' payroll. Seems she was doing time for what we might call a political crime. Crossed swords with some well-connected real estate developer. She burned down his house and threatened him with castration. All over something the guy must've done to her folks. Screwed them out of their house, I think. Her mother died of a broken heart is the pity line she used on me."

"No shit. She told me you recruited her off the street. Saved her from a life of petty crime and guys taking advantage of her."

"You can't believe half the shit she says," Sam said, tossing the egg carton on the counter. "But she's got her uses. Sit," he said, gesturing at a rickety looking Formica table surrounded by six mismatched chairs. Quist pulled up one of the chairs, and Sam joined him, carrying the six-pack of Pacificos. He laid the handgun, a large caliber Magnum, on the table next to him.

"How about you removing that knife from your boot or wherever you tuck it and put it on the table. Same goes for that Glock Frieda loaned you. Hey don't look so disappointed. I asked her if she gave you one and she knows better than to ever lie to me," he said, plucking what appeared to be a half-smoked joint from an ashtray brimming with cigarette butts. Beside it sat a black ceramic skull atop of which Sam had stuck a small partially burned candle.

He waited as Quist placed his knife and the Glock on the table, and then reached over and dragged them onto his side of the table. "Ease your chair back a little, too" he said. "I don't like to be crowded."

Quist raised one hand and slowly retrieved one of the Pacificos before scooting his chair back. "I'd say you've got some trust issues."

"Occupational hazard," he said, lighting the joint with a gold Zippo he retrieved from the pocket of his T-shirt. He took a deep drag before offering it to Quist.

"No thanks," Quist said. "I'll stick to the *cerveza*." They looked at each other while Sam took another couple of hits.

"The way I see it, you've got a problem," Quist said, taking a long pull of the warm beer.

"Oh yeah? A problem? Only one? Shit. I got a raft of 'em. Woman problems. Too much of this shit," he said, holding up the joint. "And way too many assholes I have to contend with on a daily basis. On top of that my doctor back in Houston says I may have prostate cancer. Those greaser peckerwoods that took that baby hardly show up on the list."

"You really expect me to believe that?"

Sam grinned and stared at the inch of joint he clutched between his thumb and index finger. "You know I've been doing this job for going on nine years. And before that I did ten years as a vice cop in Dallas. I stick it out one more year and the Feds promised me a pension. So it got me to thinking about retirement. Plan A, I've got this place in Nicaragua all bought and paid for. I figure I'd fish all day and chase poon tang all night." He took a final drag on the joint and then flicked the butt in the general direction of the kitchen sink.

"And Plan B?"

"Make myself scarce. Meaning empty my bank accounts and see how long it lasts before that tumor in my ass gets me. But then again." He shook his head. "The best laid plans," he murmured, exhaling and squinting at Quist through the smoke.

"It sounds like you want to tell me about it."

Sam's snort of amusement segued into a wet, raunchy hacking cough that lasted the better part of a half-minute. "This guy Henry," he wheezed and cleared his throat. "The dead guy in the SUV up at Zenner's? I've known him for six years give or take.

A stand up agent. He was rock solid, never questioned anything I did. He saved my ass more than once. Whoever shot him maybe doesn't realize what righteous retribution I've got planned for him."

"What about his partner? This Flavio guy?"

Sam studied him, his eyes half-lidded and bleary. "Hasn't shown up. If he's not dead yet then he better wish he was."

Quist took a swallow of the warm beer and waited.

"Manny's a snake in the grass," Sam said finally.

"Funny, but Roy pretty much used those same words to describe you."

"Did she now? Tell me, you two..." He made a little circling motion with his fingers. "You know. Getting it on?"

"I'm just the help. Look, let's not waste each other's time. What's happening here?"

Sam considered his reply, started to say something, and then hesitated and started again. "Manny is... or at least he used to be my informant. He kept me abreast of Schoenfeld's business dealings. Like any snitch, you can only trust them so far. If you figured that he sold her out to his cartel friends, you'd be right. He went dark after that. I only found him again six months back. About then is when I found out he had the girl with him. I watched him for a while. Let him go about his shady little ways. He was careful though, like he might've known I was watching. Although that didn't keep him from doing business with the cartel boys. There was nothing you could nail him on though. Not in the States at least. After the girl high- tailed it was when I reached out to you. If you ask me why." He smiled . "Who knows? Maybe I've just got a soft spot for young mothers."

He fell silent, and after a few seconds passed, he gestured at Quist with his chin.

"Your shirt. Open it."

Quist smiled and unbuttoned his shirt. Sam, obviously not satisfied, reached across the table and flicked open Quist's shirt front, exposing his torso. Apparently satisfied Quist wasn't wearing a wire, he sat back and took a swallow of his beer.

"You know just before you walked in the door I was contemplating what to do about you and the nun. My thoughts didn't end with you two coming out on the happy side."

They both stared at each other for a moment. Sam picked up the Magnum and studied it as if it were something he had never seen before. He looked back at Quist. "If I tell you some things, I may just have to listen to my dark side and go ahead shoot you."

"Then maybe you shouldn't tell me."

Sam grinned. "Yeah, except I need someone to talk to. Maybe offer me advice."

"How about I advise you not to kill me?"

Sam seemed to consider this before going on. "Manny Fontenot's been skimming money from the Sinaloa cartel. The only reason I know that is he told me. He told me because he needed me to cover his tracks. To make it look like my guys were screwing with their shipments, when in fact Fontenot was hijacking them and selling the stuff to some gangbangers in Phoenix. It wasn't exactly a fool proof plan. Of course, I could've told him that."

He popped open one of the beers and took a swallow. "He was supposed to pay me two hundred grand to throw the cartel off his trail. I say was because I have yet to see the color of his money. So he comes to me with this new deal. He'll give me what he owes me and all I have to do is get him the girl."

"Do you know why he wants her?"

Sam didn't say anything at first. "Because he's a pervert."

Quist shook his head. "You don't really believe that's all that's to it?"

"I've seen people do stupider shit for stupider reasons."

"She's got something on him."

Sam considered this for a moment and grunted. "Well, that might explain some things." He took another draw from the beer. "Look, no one was supposed to get hurt. But they fucked it up when they took the kid and killed Henry. I guess it comes as no surprise that these pricks down here are short on finesse."

"Back up a minute. When did you make this deal? Was it before or after you got Roy and I involved?"

"I told you. I felt bad about what happened in San Miguel. You know, almost getting you killed and what I thought might've happened to the girl." He paused as if gauging how much to say. "He offered me this new deal three days ago. I figured I didn't have much of a choice."

"And what? You were supposed to just hand her over?"

"I was supposed to make sure you were out of the way when they came to take her from Zenner's. Leaving me with plausible deniability and a fat bank account."

"So he knows we're here?"

"Of course. I had to tell him. I also told him why you and the nun were looking for her."

Quist let this tidbit digest for a moment before asking, "So what happens now?"

Sam smiled and shrugged. "If I was smart, no one would ever hear from you and the Sister again."

"You really think that's smart? I don't think so."

Sam picked up the Magnum again and casually pointed it at Quist. "You forget I've got a retirement plan."

"And I bet someone like you has a Plan C and probably a D. Am I wrong?"

"And none of those plans has you coming out on the long end, amigo. I need my money, and the only way I figure I'll get it is to play ball with Manny."

"And you trust him to hold up his end?"

Sam lowered the gun an inch. "Do I trust him? Hell no. But I figure he's my only option, though I do admit Plan D involves just shooting the oily cocksucker and taking my chances with the ass cancer."

"What if I told you I can get you enough money to maybe satisfy you? How about I call it our trust fund?"

Sam thought for a moment. "How much do you have in this so called trust fund?"

"Let' say I can come close to matching what he owed you."

He snorted and pondered this a moment. "You're good for that kind of money?"

"I'm not, but I know where I could get it. It wouldn't be that difficult."

"And I'm supposed to trust you?"

Quist shrugged. "Look at it this way, my deal's easier on the conscience."

Sam placed the Magnum back on the table and pulled a fresh joint out of his pocket.

"I admit I would surely like to shoot that coon ass."

"Do you have any idea where he's keeping the baby?"

He leaned into the flame from the Zippo and fired up the joint. "No. Like I said, that wasn't part of the plan."

"So why hasn't he reached out to make the trade?"

Sam took a long drag and exhaled. "*No se.* I hate to say this but I wouldn't be counting on seeing that baby again."

"I thought he wanted to trade."

"I wouldn't believe anything he says. I'm thinking he's waiting to see which way I jump."

"Then call him. Make the deal. Lana for the baby. You offer to be the middleman."

"And you'd make that trade? Come on, I know you cowboy types."

"There aren't any cowboys in West Virginia."

"You know what I mean. I'm guessing you're planning on trading the girl and then trying to get her back later."

Quist said nothing. The less said the better.

"And you think you can sell that to the Sister?"

"I'll tell her it's our only choice."

Sam took another hit of the joint and reached into the pocket of his shorts and pulled out his cell phone. He hit a number on his speed dial. "Hey. You see anyone? *¿Nadie?*" He listened for a moment. *"Buena."* He put down the phone and thought for a moment.

"Frieda's gonna drive you back. Stay put, and in the meantime, I'll reach out to that cocksucker and see what he's got in mind. Best you not tell the girl anything. From what I've heard, she's a might unstable."

He slid the Glock and the knife across the table. "Don't disappoint me."

"Same goes for you," Quist said, rising to his feet and stuffing his knife into his boot.

"Is that what you used on those old boys in that *casita* in San Miguel?"

"Only on one of 'em. The Sister stoved in the other one's head with a table lamp."

"What kind of nun does that kind of shit?"

"The kind you don't want to double cross. Best you remember that," Quist said, picking up the Glock and turning for the door.

42

He no sooner had stepped out the door before he heard Frieda crank the ignition. He glanced down the street in both directions before climbing into the darkened interior of the SUV. The truck smelled of cigarettes and Frieda's coconut shampoo. She made a quick U-turn and started off without so much of a glance his way.

"Your meeting. It was productive, yes?" she asked as she floored the accelerator.

"You could say so."

His mind flashed back to Baghdad and another meeting and another deal made with someone he didn't entirely trust. That deal had cost the life of someone he loved. Was he in over his head again? How many people might pay this time for his over inflated sense of self-confidence? And could he really live with himself if a trade with Manny resulted in Roy losing Lana? He didn't even want to think about the plight of Lana's baby. Face it. He had no plan. All he saw ahead of him was treachery and uncertainty.

He rolled down the window as Frieda sped through the now mostly deserted streets. The air held the sweet pungent smell of burnt sugar and wood smoke. He tried to pay attention to the route Frieda was taking in case he had to find his way back. His only landmark was the cathedral below them and a large billboard at the bottom of the hill that advertised tires. Just as they reached the intersection, Frieda's cell phone chirped.

"*Si.*" She quickly glanced at Harlan and then handed him the phone. It was Roy. She was shouting his name.

"Harlan! Are you there? Where are you?"

Roy's voice sounded muffled but he could still discern her anxiety.

"Roy?"

Before she could reply he heard what a series of popping sounds in the background. "Shit! Is that gunfire? Roy?"

"They're back. Get back here, Harlan."

He could hear someone shouting in the background. A woman. Ximena, maybe.

"We're probably ten, maybe fifteen minutes away. Okay? Tell Zenner we're on our way."

He tossed the cell phone on the seat and reached for the Glock in his waist band.

"Manny's men, yes?" Frieda said, downshifting and stomping on the accelerator. She reached beneath the seat and pulled out the Uzi. "There is a shotgun on the floor behind me. How many?"

"She didn't say," he said, retrieving the shotgun.

Frieda skillfully maneuvered through the crowded streets, taking several detours to avoid the traffic. It was only once they had turned onto the road leading to Monte Alban that the traffic thinned.

"You and Royale. Are you...how do you say? Together? As lovers?" Frieda asked.

"No," he replied, as much as he wished he could answer the opposite.

"But you care for her? That I can see," she said as they sped up the winding road.

He didn't bother replying.

They turned onto the side road to Los Ibanos and almost immediately came up behind a pickup truck over laden with melons. He braced his feet against the dash as Frieda braked hard and swung around the truck, almost losing control.

"*Mierda!*" She shot him a glance. "This is not good. None of this. Manny, he takes the baby. Why? Why is this *pinche culo* doing this? It is stupid."

"Just get us there," Quist said, fastening his seat belt and pumping a round into the shotgun.

They were perhaps fifty yards from the entrance to Zenner's drive when a black SUV swung wildly out onto the roadway from the entranceway and began speeding towards them.

"Hold on," Frieda yelled as she flicked a switch that turned on a pair of powerful fog lights. The other SUV appeared to swerve for a second, its driver perhaps momentarily blinded. A second later, the two vehicles collided in a glancing blow, each of the vehicles' driver's side scraping violently against each other in an explosion of busting glass and screeching metal.

Before Quist realized it, they were sideways in the road, their headlights illuminating the trees beside the road. In the sudden silence, he heard the other vehicle's ignition cranking as the driver desperately tried to get the SUV started. A second later, their own SUV's back window exploded. Quist instinctively ducked and then rose and fired off two rounds from the shotgun through the shattered opening. The other SUV's engine roared to life and its tires squealed as it sped off into the night.

He fired off another round and glanced at Frieda whose head rested on the steering wheel. She let out a groan as he reached over and touched her shoulder.

"Are you okay?"

She pushed his hand away and fell back against the seat, her one hand clutching her forehead. *"Joder!"* she muttered as she took her hand away and looked at it. Quist could see she was bleeding from a cut on her forehead. *"¿Dónde están?"* she yelled, fumbling for the Uzi in her lap.

"They're gone." Quist pulled out his cell phone and punched in a number. When there was no answer, he flung it onto the dash. "We need to get to the house. Can you drive?"

Frieda swiped at her forehead and looked at him. "You are not hit? Yes, I can drive," she said, turning on the ignition.

One of front tires rubbed loudly against the crumpled wheel well, slowing their progress up the drive. Zenner's house was bathed in light. As they drove up, Quist could see the front door was wide open, leading him to think the worst. Shotgun in hand, he raced up the steps. A man's body lay sprawled in a pool of blood just inside the entranceway. Relieved to see it wasn't Zenner, he edged along the wall. The air was heavy with the smell of cordite, the only sound was that of some dogs barking in the distance.

"Zenner! It's Quist."

A second later, Ximena rose from behind a planter in the patio holding a shotgun. "They are gone?" she yelled, her voice hoarse.

"Yeah. Is everyone okay?" He was suddenly aware of Frieda beside him.

Ximena shrugged. "Mateo. *Venga*," she yelled over her shoulder.

Frieda leaned down and rolled the dead man onto his side. "I have seen this man before. Talking to Sam two days ago."

"Great. You're sure you're okay?"

She reached up and touched the trickle of blood from the gash on her forehead and nodded. A second later, Zenner appeared at the door leading to the kitchen clutching a hunting rifle. He acknowledged them with a tentative smile and embraced Ximena.

"Looks like you ran into them," Zenner said. "Did they get away?"

"Afraid so."

"Don't worry, They didn't get Lana."

"Where are they?'

"Upstairs." He glanced at the dead man in the foyer. "I might've winged another one."

"Are we going to have cops coming?"

"I doubt it. An hour ago there were a lot of fireworks down in the valley. Our nearest neighbor is probably passed out by now. Even if he heard it, he won't call the cops."

Ximena walked up to Frieda and offered her a napkin she had taken from the table. Zenner walked over to inspect the body lying in the hallway.

"No word from Manny?" Quist asked.

"Not yet, but I'm sure now it's just a matter of time."

"Call Sam and tell him what happened," he told Frieda, handing her the shotgun. "Tell him to get off his ass and make that deal."

He took the stairs two at a time. It took a few seconds for his eyes to adjust to the darkened hallway before he saw Roy hunched on the floor with her back against Lana's bedroom door. When she saw him, she leaped to her feet and ran to him and threw her arms around him. Surprised by her embrace, he half-stumbled backwards. She clung to him, her face buried in his chest.

"Thank God, you're okay," she said. "I thought the worst."

Still somewhat unsure of how he should respond, he embraced her clumsily, his arms loosely wrapped around her waist.

"What's this?" he said, patting the pocket of her jacket. He pulled the handgun out of her pocket and held it up to the light. A Beretta Px4. At least Zenner had given her something easy to use. He held it to his nose. "Who gave you this? Zenner?" he asked, leaning over and placing the Beretta on a small lamp table.

"Don't worry. I never had to use it," she said, her arms still encircling his waist.

She leaned back and reached up and touched his face. He hesitated before taking her hand and holding it against his cheek. They stared at each other, her eyes indecipherable in the dim light. Ever since that night he had kissed her in the restaurant in San Miguel he fantasized about what it would be like to be this close to her. That time he had been merely testing her. Or so he told himself.

She touched her hand to his lips, her eyes holding his. It was an awkward gesture but this unexpected display of affection left him momentarily speechless.

"We need to talk," he said, gently taking away her hand.

43

Royale felt herself flush, taken aback by what she had just done. Had her caress been merely a gesture of concern? Or was there something more to it than that? It had been years, decades in fact, since she had allowed herself this sort of physical reaction to another human being, much less a man. She had hugged clients, held them in a gesture of solace, but she had not truly held someone out of her own need. She took a deep breath and stepped back. In the dim light, she sensed more than saw Quist's own discomfort. She looked away in embarrassment.

"Are you okay?" he asked.

"I'm a bit raw. I could use a good night's sleep and a decent cup of coffee."

"The coffee I can get you. Sleep's going to have to wait."

"Why? What's happened?"

"Manny's frontal assaults haven't worked, so I figure it's time for him to come to the table."

"I told you. There's not going to be any deal. There has to be another way."

"And what about the baby?"

She slumped back against the wall. "Shit, Harlan." She used to pray for answers, for solutions to some client's dilemma. Not that she ever really believed in such a thing as divine intercession. "God, how about just this once," she muttered under her breath. She looked back at Quist. "I don't know what to do. All I know is I'm not giving Lana back to that bastard. I can't."

"Do you trust me?"

She snorted. "No, not entirely."

"Fair enough. I've been with Sam. He's going to try to make

230

a deal. Hold on," he added in response to her look of dismay. He reached for her but she pushed him away.

"I won't do it. You're asking me to choose between Lana and Bella. You can't make me do that. Please. You can't."

"I'm not asking you to choose. I'm just asking you to trust me. We get the baby back. Then I get Lana back."

She shook her head. "No. I won't do that to her. Don't you get it? I can't do that."

Quist seemed to think about this for a moment. "All right. I'll call Sam and see if he's been able to reach out to Manny."

"And make sure and tell him if something happens to either Lana or Bella a shit storm will surely rain down on him."

"You're beginning to remind me of this gal I knew once back in San Miguel."

She offered him a smile and then shook her head. "You know I used to think if I just helped enough people nothing bad would ever happen to me again. It would be a sure path to salvation. Kharma-like. Doesn't work that way though, does it? When this is over, would you take me somewhere? Some place where no one has any problems."

They held each other's gaze in the silence that followed before Quist finally sighed.

"You need to talk to Lana and find out what it is she's got on Manny. How's she holding up by the way?"

"She's like a stick of dynamite. Before she was anxious, pissed off and loaded. Now she's anxious, pissed off and sober. I'm not sure which is worse."

"Do what you can. But if we have to bargain, I need to know what cards we're holding. Okay?"

She watched him walk off. Was she really willing to place the fate of her daughter and granddaughter in his hands? In any of their hands? Not Zenner's. And surely not Sam's. There was no way she would give up Lana. Or Bella either. She stood there a minute sorting through her options before retrieving the Beretta from the table and walking into Lana's room.

Lana lay on the bed, her legs tucked beneath her in a fetal position. Royale sat on the bed beside her. "We need to talk." When Lana didn't respond, Royale took her shoulder and roughly rolled her over.

"Leave me alone," Lana said, pulling away.

Royale took Lana's face in one hand and squeezed with perhaps more force then she intended.

"Listen to me! Manny wants to trade Bella for you. Do you get that? You have to tell me what you've got that he wants. We can trade that. It's the only way. Lana. Come on. What is it that you have that he wants?"

Lana stared at her and then quickly turned away. "You don't understand. It's not that simple," she muttered. "He wants to kill me. Even if I give him what he wants, he's not going to let me alone. I know too much."

"Give him what? And what is it that you know?"

She gave Royale a cold glance, her nostrils flaring as she breathed. "I took his money."

"His money? Dammit, Lana! How could you be so stupid?"

"Sure. You think I'm stupid. That I'm some strung out, slutty dimwit who's fucked up everything she touches. You see me in that painting and you think I was another one of Mercedes' whores. That's what you think, isn't it? Well you're wrong. You're all wrong. And he's going to pay for what he did to me." She started to get up from the bed.

"Wait. God, I'm sorry, Lana. I didn't mean that. Please, I didn't mean that. I..." She reached for her, but Lana pulled back. "Don't. Lana," she pleaded.

Lana fell back on the bed and glowered at her. Maybe now was the time to tell Lana about her own past. Maybe then she would understand. She looked at Lana who still regarded her with abject defiance.

"There're some things I have to tell you. About myself. Would you listen to me?" she yelled as Lana rolled away, her back to Royale. "Dammit! Look at me!" Lana didn't move. "Okay. Just listen. Some of it I've never told anyone. I just want you to know I have no right to judge you. But maybe you should judge me." Royale slipped off the bed and dropped onto the floor, her back against the door. "I was fifteen when I had you. Yeah, fifteen," she said as Lana craned her neck to look at her. "It was something that just happened. I wish I could say I chose you." She paused for a few seconds to gather her thoughts. "Life's about choices. And I made a lot of bad choices. I'd like to say I made some good ones, too. But sometimes there just aren't any choices."

Royale's monologue drained twenty minutes off the clock and the weight of twenty years of guilt. She told Lana about the boy who fathered her, about the drugs, the men, the misspent life, and she told her about Charly and what occurred that night on the boat. She also told her the circumstances of Charly's death. Lana never once interrupted, but studied Royale the whole time with more a look of curiosity than shock. In the brittle silence that followed, Royale felt herself trembling. Was it from relief? Or shame? It was Lana who finally spoke.

"You know I never posed for that painting. She just used my face. I want you to know that. After I saw it I knew what she wanted me to do. What she wanted me to be. Then they took Cruz away from me and I knew I needed to leave."

Royale reached over and took Lana's hand. Neither of them spoke for a long moment.

"I used to fantasize about my real mother. About a real family," Lana said finally. "Mercedes bought me this doll house once. I was maybe six. I'd pretend I had a mother and a father and a baby brother. Mercedes threw it all out when I turned nine." She looked away, seemingly strangling on some emotion. When she looked back, her eyes were moist. "I just wanted a mother. And a family."

Royale nodded, but said nothing, drained of any meaningful refrain.

"I took his money," Lana said, reaching for something under her bed. She pulled out a battered aluminum Samsonite. "It's almost three hundred thousand dollars. I took it because once I got cleaned up, Bella and I were going to disappear. Some place he couldn't find us." She popped the suitcase open to reveal stacks of bound currency; from the looks of it a mix of US greenbacks and pesos.

Royale stared at the pile of cash for a moment and said, "You can still do that. There are ways. Just give him the money and we can get Bella back."

233

"You don't get it. The money's not all I have." She again reached beneath the bed and pulled out a laptop. "He wants this, too." She waited for it to power up before stroking a few keys. She tapped a button and turned the screen for Royale to see.

Royale crawled over to the bed and stared at the two people on the screen. "I can't hear what they're saying."

Lana reached around and tapped another button. Royale took the laptop in both hands and held it close, straining to hear the muted conversation.

"The guy Manny's talking to. He's the guy your friend Harlan was asking if I knew, right? I know him. I know their business. And if Manny's friends in Guadalajara ever saw this, he's dead. This Sam guy. I'd imagine he'd like to get hold of this, too. I heard him downstairs talking to you. He wants me. Him and Manny both want me and this," she said, taking back the laptop. "You say you're my mother. So I'm asking for your help. Mom," she added with a touch of sarcasm.

Royale heard a door slam somewhere below, followed by voices in the courtyard. She glanced at the window and saw a smudge of orange on the horizon, and felt a flood of exhaustion as she thought of all that had transpired in the past twenty four hours. She struggled to her feet and walked over to the window. There was just enough of the dawn's light for her to see Quist and Zenner climbing into a Jeep Cherokee. As they backed up and drove away, she realized she would have to make her own deal, and she could think of only one person who might help her. She picked up the laptop, turned it off and placed it on top of the cash.

"What are you doing?" Lana asked, sitting up.

"I'll make the trade." Royale snapped the Samsonite shut, picked up the Beretta from the dresser and started for the door.

"I'm going with you."

"No. You can't. It won't work that way."

"I'm Bella's mother. I won't leave her."

"You mean like I left you?" She thought for a moment and then shrugged. "Alright, come on. But you're staying out of sight."

44

The truck stop was a good ten miles out of town and consisted of little more than a clutch of shabby food trucks and a small palapa clinging to the edge of a rutted dirt lot littered with food cartons and crushed glass. The signage on most of the food trucks advertised pretty much the same thing: *cerveza, pollo asado* and *frijoles negra.* A half-dozen or so eighteen wheelers, their beds groaning with the weight of their loads, lined the edge of the asphalt highway. Zenner had parked about fifty yards past the truck stop, the Jeep partially camouflaged by some overgrown bougainvillea. It had been Zenner's idea to scope out the site before Sam and Manny showed up. Even though Sam had assured Quist that he and Manny would come unaccompanied, they wouldn't take the chance they'd end up hostages. Or something worse.

They sat there for a while in the burgeoning dawn sharing a thermos of espresso that Ximena had brewed and inexplicably exchanging stories about deer hunting.

"Not to change the subject, but why didn't you want to take the Mexicana gal with us?" Zenner asked, scanning the road on either side of the truck stop with his binoculars. The rising sun had just breached the horizon and was to their backs as had been Zenner's intention.

Quist thought for a moment. "Too much of the wild card, I guess. Besides, Ximena could always use a little extra firepower since it seems we brought along most of your arsenal."

"I like to plan for the worst," Zenner replied, turning the binoculars to study a plump young woman in a mini-skirt climbing out of one of the truck cabs.

Quist added up in his mind how many weapons they had brought with them; a handgun apiece, a sawed-off shotgun, an AR-15, and Zenner's deer rifle. Even then, if they were outnumbered, all the guns were unlikely to provide them enough leverage. Face it. He had no leverage. All he could hope for would be that Sam might negotiate a hand off that provided Quist with a ghost of a chance to keep Lana out of Manny's hands. There were simply too many moving parts and too many players to formulate any kind of plan.

Roy's welcoming embrace back at Zenner's kept bubbling to the forefront of his mind. It made him uneasy, if for no other reason than his feelings for her stirred up a nagging sense of dread. He couldn't help but think about what happened in Baghdad, and how much those intrigues had cost him. Ever since then, he had avoided this sort of conflict of interest. A client was only a client and nothing more. The problem was Roy wasn't just a client; not anymore and perhaps never had been. Much to his dismay, this wasn't the kind of situation that lent itself to clarity and prudent judgment. Quist glanced over at Zenner. Something told him Zenner was no stranger to open ended, dodgy deals.

"You lasted quite a while doing this kind of stuff."

"What do you mean? This kind of stuff?"

"Dealing."

"I don't deal. Never did. I was the delivery man. Nothing more."

"That's what all you guys like to tell yourself. You were just a businessman providing a service. The people on the other ends were the ones doing the dealing."

"Jesus, if that doesn't sound like the party line," Zenner said, shooting Quist a look of mild contempt. "You have to realize the drug business was a lot different back then. It was just pot. The weekend entertainment for college kids, mostly. I knew the farmers down here that I bought it from. Shared dinner with their families. Made out with a few of their daughters. I knew the guys I passed it on to like they were my brothers. Hell, nowadays Forbes would be calling them entrepreneurs. I'll wager that lots of 'em are successful. Captains of industry. I know one of them to be a goddamn Episcopal bishop. No, all the coke and the hard shit and the bloodletting came long after I got out."

"But you still ended up getting cozy with someone like Mercedes Schoenfeld."

Zenner clicked his tongue. "And I guess you've never been guilty of indiscretion. I know you Fed types. You cut corners. You get dirty. It's all part of the game, isn't it? I met one of you ATF agents once. He was just as dirty as those DEA bastards. All that time spent with Aryan Nation meth heads and gun runners has a way of rubbing off on you, doesn't it? Which brings me around to that prick Sam. Whose team is he really on?"

"Hard to say. It probably depends on which way the wind blows. I can see his conscience and his hard on for Manny make him lean our way. On the other hand, I don't doubt he'll swing to the highest bidder."

Zenner gestured with his chin. "That could be them."

A tricked out, cherry red Toyota Tacoma with huge off-road tires and roof-mounted fog lights slowly edged its way past the line of eighteen wheelers. Zenner studied the pickup with the binoculars. "You'd think he'd drive something a little less conspicuous. " He took a moment to scan the highway beyond. "Maybe they're good as their word," he said, turning on the ignition. Zenner flicked his headlights and drove slowly to the edge of the truck stop. The Tacoma came to a stop about thirty feet away, close enough for Quist to make out Sam in the passenger seat. The driver's face was partially concealed by a large straw sombrero.

"I'll stay and keep you covered," Zenner said, retrieving the AR-15 from the floorboard.

Quist climbed out of the cab and made his way to a spot halfway between the two vehicles. The morning was cooler than he expected and there was a layer of fog in the valley that edged the truck stop. Manny had obviously taken Zenner's cue and instructed Sam to act as his own sentinel. Manny climbed out, tossed his hat on the seat, and strode slowly to within a few paces of Quist. He wore a pair of neatly pressed jeans and a black guayabera beneath a white nylon windbreaker. If he was carrying, Quist couldn't see it, but suspected a handgun tucked into his rear waistband, the same place Quist had tucked his Glock.

"Surprised to see you again," Manny said, his grin revealing his gold caps. "I thought after San Miguel we might've permanently parted ways."

"I'm sorry to disappoint."

"Quist, right? Sam said that's the name you go by now. He said you used to be a Fed. ATF if I recall correctly. "

"First thing, I want is proof of life."

"You mean the bambino?" Manny squinted into the sun and smiled broadly. Reaching into the front pocket of his jeans, he retrieved a cell phone. He tapped it a few times and directed the phone's screen in Quist's direction. Quist cautiously moved forward until he could make out what had appeared on the screen. He could see an elderly Mexican woman cradling a baby and feeding it a bottle.

"How do I know that's her?"

"You have to trust me on that. See the date and the time at the bottom? Taken just this morning."

Quist studied Manny's face for any signs of obvious duplicity, but figured any semblance of truth in his countenance had long since been culled from his retinue of facades.

"I hear you and your girlfriend got a personal investment in this. Makes no difference since ol' Mannny here is holding all the cards. You just have to decide who you're most willing to give up. To me, trading for the bambino's the sentimental favorite. But then again, you may be figuring if you don't make the trade, I wouldn't be the kind asshole that would pop an infant. You'd be right. But you need to understand I wouldn't have any qualms about letting one of these truck mamas here adopt her. Would be sorta ironic though, wouldn't it? Luna's kid getting reared by another whore like Mercedes. Or like her real mama. Though the kid wouldn't exactly enjoy the same standard of living little Luna had with Mercedes, now would she?"

Quist saw a vehicle approaching on the road behind Manny. He noticed Sam adjusting his rear-view mirror as the ubiquitous black Ford Explorer favored by both the cartels and the Federales edged slowly down the road until it drew abreast of the Tacoma before speeding up. The heavily tinted windows precluded any possibility of seeing who was inside. Manny seemed not to give it any notice until he saw Quist's attention drift as he turned to watch the Explorer disappear along a curve in the road.

"Friends of yours?" Manny asked.

"I was about to ask you the same thing. So, what are you willing to take for both of them?'

Manny shifted his gaze back from the road and shook his head. "No deal. I need Luna. Her for the kid's the only deal I'm offering."

"My guess is she's got something of yours."

Manny regarded him, his expression flat and unrevealing. "Do we deal or not?" he asked finally.

"How do we do this?"

"You know, I made the mistake of underestimating you once before. Fool me twice, well that second one would be on me. No, something tells me you're being too agreeable. My nose tells me you're wanting to work this some kind of way to keep the girl."

"You said yourself you hold all the cards. Give us the baby. I got a feeling the girl can take care of herself."

"You can sell that to her mama?"

Quist shrugged. "I figure she doesn't have much of a choice."

"You're right, she doesn't. You bring the girl. How about here? Say tomorrow at the same time? Just you and the girl. Leave that bastard Zenner behind. And tell that little bitch she needs to bring what she took from me. If not, that little baby of hers will be turning tricks here in another ten years." He started to turn away and then stopped. "I'm curious about those pendejos back in San Miguel. How'd that go down?"

"Too bad you didn't see your way to do your own dirty work."

Manny grinned and wagged his finger. "Be careful what you wish for," he replied and walked back to the truck.

Quist watched as Manny climbed into the cab. As they

drove off, Quist tried to see Sam's face but he seemed to be purposefully avoiding any eye contact.

"What did you make of that Explorer?" he asked Zenner as he got in the Jeep.

Zenner shrugged. "Who knows? Local cops. A pimp. Might've just been a couple of kids looking to sell some uppers to the truckers. Cartel wannabes. So what now?"

"We give Sam a hour and I'll call him. See what team he wants to play for. "

45

Ximena knelt in the foyer in a puddle of soapy water, a bristle brush in each hand. She gave Royale and Lana a quick hard glance before pouring more water on the stone floor. Royale could see a trail of what she assumed was blood leading out the front door. She wondered what had become of the body she had seen briefly in the aftermath of the firefight that had taken place just hours before.

"*Buenos dias,*" Ximena said, the tone of her voice devoid of any warmth.

"Where's Frieda?" Royale asked, tiptoeing along the edge of the puddle.

Ximena nodded with her head to the open front door. "Where are you going? Your friend said you must stay inside."

Royale ignored her and walked out the front door, Lana close behind. Frieda's SUV sat parked in the drive. Frieda knelt before the driver's side front fender, a hammer in one hand and a crowbar in the other. She looked up at them briefly before whacking the fender with the hammer. Royale stood for a moment and surveyed the crumpled side of the Land Rover and the shattered windshield.

"This is from last night? And what happened to your head?" she asked, noticing the bandage on her forehead.

Frieda looked up and nodded at Lana. "This is your daughter?"

"Frieda, Lana. Look, I need your help."

Frieda eyed the Samsonite and the Beretta. "Where are you going?"

"I have to see Manny. I was hoping you could help me find

him."

Frieda smiled in amusement. "You think I know where Manny is? And if I did, why would you think I would take you to see him?"

"Okay. Then take me to Sam."

Frieda shook her head. "It is not wise. What you wish to do."

"Es muy peligroso," Ximena added from where she stood on the steps. *"La mujer está loca."*

"I need to make a trade. And I'll bet anything Sam knows how to reach Manny."

"Sam told me what happened to you and Quist in San Miguel. So you must know what these people do."

"Believe me I know, but maybe you've noticed I'm here and they're not."

"Loco y valiente," she heard Ximena mutter.

"Now will you help me or not?"

Frieda looked away as if in thought. "Very well. I will take you to see Sam. But your daughter stays."

"No. I'm coming, too." Lana said, breaking her silence.

Frieda shrugged and dropped the hammer and crowbar. "Very well. Then we go," she said, forcing open the crumpled driver's side door.

They drove in silence toward town, turning past a large cathedral and then up a long hill. Frieda glanced down at the Beretta in Royale's lap. "You know how to use that?"

"If I have to."

"And you know when to use it? Or when it is wise not to use it?"

When Royale didn't reply, Frieda nodded and made a disparaging grunt. She turned down another street and slowed as they cruised past a block of adjoining stucco structures. Frieda clicked her tongue and stopped the SUV. "He is not alone."

"That's Manny's truck," Lana said, leaning over the front seat and pointing to a red pickup truck parked a couple of dozen meters up the road. "Maybe he's got Bella."

"Hold on. Maybe this is better. Lana, you stay here with

242

Frieda. I'll take the money."

"Money? What do you mean?" Frieda asked. "This is not good."

"And I'm going with you," Lana said, opening her door.

"I told you. You're staying."

"Wait," Frieda said, grabbing Royale's arm. She stared at something in the rear view mirror.

Royale looked over her shoulder and saw what had caught Frieda's attention. A black Ford Explorer coasted up behind them.

"Who is it?"

"I don't know," Frieda said after a moment's hesitation.

They watched as two men exited the Explorer. To Royale's dismay, one of them appeared to be carrying what looked like some kind of small machine gun.

"*Mierda,*" Frieda hissed. She looked at Royale. "Give me the Beretta. Quickly. I need your gun. Now," she said, snatching the handgun from Royale's grasp.

"What are you doing?'

Frieda took the handgun and dangled it out the driver's side window, one finger in the trigger guard. "I'm sorry," she said, her eyes focused on the mirror.

46

Is she doing what I think she's doing?" Quist asked as they drove up to Zenner's house.

"Most likely. She's handy that way," Zenner replied, rolling to a stop.

Ximena looked up from her task, and then leaned on her shovel and surveyed the garden for a moment before tossing the shovel aside and walking towards them.

"I bet that'll be a good spot to plant corn next year," Quist said to her as he climbed out of the Jeep. "Where's Frieda? I thought I told her to stay."

"*Ido.* Gone. She and the woman and the girl."

"What? They left? Where did they go?"

Ximena shrugged. "They take a suitcase and a...*¿Como se dice?* Laptop? Yes? Your woman says she wants to talk to that *pendejo* Sam."

"Shit!"

He started to reach into his pocket and then suddenly realized he had given Royale the cell phone Frieda had given him. He didn't know Frieda's number, but he did remember Sam's. "Give me your phone," he said to Zenner. He punched in the number and waited for a few rings until someone answered.

"*¿Qué?*

"Sam?"

He heard someone laugh before the phone went dead. He tossed the phone to Zenner. "We need to go. Something's not right."

As they reached the main highway, the traffic grew heavier. The previous night was the only time Quist had been to Sam's other safe house and consequently had only the vaguest idea of how to find it.

"I remember there was this big cathedral and a hillside above it. It wasn't that far from El Centro."

"The Basilica de la Soledad is my guess. It had a big court-yard down below and in front of it. Yeah?"

"I think. We drove past it and then turned right up a hill. There was this billboard with this big red snorting bull. It was above a tire store." He studied both sides of the road, struggling to recall any other landmarks. After a few minutes, they passed by the cathedral.

"There!" Quist pointed to a large billboard graced by the snorting red bull with the words *Toro Rojo Neumático* blazoned beneath it. "I remember now. Take a right and go up the hill." After a minute the road wound up onto a hill overlooking the cathedral. "His place is somewhere right up there on the left."

Zenner slowed as they both noticed Manny's red Tacoma pickup parked on the street. Parked across from it was Frieda's damaged SUV, and behind it sat a black Ford Explorer much like the one that had passed by them at the truck stop. Zenner shot him a look and shook his head.

"Keep driving and stop up there where that pullover is," Quist said, picking up the Glock from the seat and stuffing it into his waistband. "You stay. I may need a wheelman in case we need to leave in a hurry," Quist said as he started to get out of the Jeep.

"Do you even know what you're doing?" Zenner asked, cutting the ignition. "I mean, you go in there and you're likely to be outgunned."

"I doubt an extra gun would make a whole lot of difference. I plan on negotiating."

"Good luck with that."

Quist stood there a moment as he realized his hands were shaking. I don't want to do this, he said to himself, fighting a wave of nausea. Not again. Was it just some premonition stirred by the memory of what happened in Baghdad?

He took a deep breath and stepped out into the street and

started to walk toward the safe house, his eyes scanning the street on either side. He stepped up to the door and hesitated a moment to listen before looking up at the small camera above the door. When after a half minute or so nothing had happened, he knocked on the door. A few seconds later he heard the door lock being thrown. The door flew open and he found himself staring into the barrel of a large handgun, the bearer a bulked up Hispanic guy with a goatee, a shaved head, and a web of tattoos snaking from the collar of his shirt.

"*Orale, pendejo,*" he said, gesturing with the gun for Quist to step inside. He frisked Quist, removing the Glock and the switchblade in his boot, before shoving him into the kitchen.

Manny and Sam and a third man sat on the other side of the table. Frieda, Roy and Lana stood in a line along the wall next to the kitchen counter. Quist gave them a quick glance and looked around the room. Another man, this one armed with an Uzi, turned from the window to study Quist. Something in the lazy way the Mexican looked at him made Quist wonder if the man was intoxicated or high.

Quist looked back at the third man sitting at the table; thirtyish, well dressed and a head of well-coifed coal black hair. He peered at Quist with a look of amusement mixed with curiosity. He had a narrow oblong face with angular cheekbones and a pointed chin. His eyes almost looked Oriental. Quist dropped his eyes to the open suitcase on the table that appeared to contain bundles of cash.

The gunman who had frisked him laid Quist's gun and knife on the table next to the suitcase and then walked over and stood a few feet away.

"*¿Quién es este?*" the man at the table asked, turning to Manny.

Manny glared at Quist but said nothing.

"*El es nadie,*" Sam said.

"*¿Realidad?*" the Mexican sitting at the table said his gaze lingering on Quist. "*Creo que es uno de sus hombres.*"

"What's he saying?" Quist asked Sam. He shot a quick glance at Roy who shook her head and tried to work up a smile.

"He says he thinks you're one of Manny's guys," Sam said.

"Tell him I'm with ATF and I'd like to sell him some guns," Quist said with a grin.

The man at the table laughed. "El ATF? No shit?" he said, looking at Manny. He picked up the Glock and casually pointed it at Manny's head. "I did not realize you had so many interesting friends, amigo. Now you do business with ATF, too?" He lowered the gun and placed it back on the table next to the suitcase.

"You've got your goddamn money, Amado. Let's call it even," Manny said.

"Even? I think not. First, I would like to know how much money you have stolen from me. We must find that out before I leave. You will tell me that? Yes?"

Amado looked over at Frieda. "And you, señorita. ¿La DEA?" He pronounced it Day ah. "Or Federale? It seems you have many friends interested in your business," he said, again looking at Manny who seemed to squirm in discomfort.

Quist shot a sidelong glance at the gunman standing next to him who appeared to be more interested in his fingernails than the conversation. The other one with the Uzi had picked up a cup of coffee and turned back to the window.

"The señoritas," Quist said, nodding at the women. "They're fugitives. You let me take them and I'll make sure you get some of the reward money."

Amado laughed. "You are much the comedian, Señor ATF, but I think not." He stood and walked over to the women and stopped in front of Lana. "You, I know. You are the daughter of that *puta* Mercedes. We looked very hard for you and yet here you are. *Muy práctico.*"

"She's my daughter," Roy said, her voice almost breaking.

Amado turned and looked at Roy. "My men see you and your ATF friend at the rancho. I see your photographs with this *pendejo,*" he said, pointing with his thumb at Manny. "He is your friend?"

"No, he's not our friend," Roy replied. "He's a pig and he took my daughter."

Amado nodded, his eyes fixed on Roy.

Quist looked over at the table. Manny seemed to be shifting his eyes back and forth to the Glock on the table. Quist looked at the two gunmen. Both still seemed disinterested in the goings on. He shot a look at Sam and dropped his gaze to the Glock on the table.

Before he knew it, both Manny and Sam lunged for the Glock. In the same instant, Frieda pulled her gun from beneath her shirt and quickly proceeded to put two rounds in the gunman at the window. As the other one started to react, Quist kicked him in the side of the knee and reached for his gun, but Frieda was quicker, firing two more rounds into the man's chest.

When Quist looked back at the table, Manny had one arm around Sam's throat, the Glock pointed at Sam's head. Frieda leveled her gun at both of them but held her fire. Roy had dropped to her knees and seemed to be trying to pull Lana down beside her, but Lana pulled away and remained standing along with Amado who appeared remarkably calm.

"Everyone stop! Cool it! Sam yelled.

"So, *chica,*" Manny croaked. "What do we do? I tell you what. You drop the piece and we call it even. Consider it your reward for taking out those two *cholos.* Hold on. I've even got a better idea. Shoot that shit bag Amado and I'll let you walk out the door right now."

Frieda said nothing, her gun still trained on the two men at the table. A few seconds passed, the only sound Sam's labored breathing. And then Manny quickly turned the Glock and shot Amado square in the chest. Lana shrieked, but she remained standing, her eyes wide with shock.

Manny quickly pressed the Glock to Sam's forehead and looked at Frieda. "So I guess that deal's off the table. But I tell you what, you drop the gun and I won't blow ol' Sam's head off. What do you say? Not enough of a deal? Then drop the gun or I shoot Luna. Or Lana, whatever the fuck her name is."

Quist glanced down at the floor. The dead gunman's handgun had come to a rest about midway between him and the table. Too far for him to have any chance he could get to it before

Manny could react.

Frieda seemed to hesitate for a few seconds before leaning down and placing her gun on the floor.

"Good girl. Now kick it over here," Manny said.

Frieda glanced at Quist with a look of apology and kicked the gun toward the table.

"Now all of you go over and stand there against the counter." He stood up and shoved Sam towards the rest of them. "I like this. All you assholes in one bunch," he said, backing over to the dead guy with the Uzi. He picked it off the floor and slung the strap over his shoulder. He then reached down and retrieved the laptop from beneath the table.

"Honey, you don't realize what you had here," he said, placing the laptop on top of the cash and shutting the suitcase. "A bunch of juicy names. Bank account numbers." He walked over to Lana. "You could've traded, you know. You stupid bitch," he said, and slapped her.

Royale started for him, but Quist quickly pushed her back with his arm.

"Where's Bella?" Lana interjected, stepping forward, wiping at the trickle of blood on her mouth.

Manny looked at her. "I imagine she's getting wet nursed by some whore right about now." He backed away and picked up Frieda and the other gunman's automatic and stuffed them both into his waist band. He pointed the Glock at Sam.

"This doesn't have to go down like this," Quist said.

"And you, my friend, I think I'll waste you first," he replied, turning the gun on Quist.

Quist glanced at the table. His knife had fallen on the floor unnoticed.

"You really think I don't have any back up?" Sam said. "One of my partners knows we're here. He's watching to see who goes out the door. And the Federales know all about you. They've been watching the both of us. Chances are they're out there right now. Waiting."

"Bull shit. You're bluffing. Now everyone get down on your knees."

249

"It's one thing to kill Amado, but a couple of federal agents just isn't smart."

"They'll figure the cartel boys were responsible. By then, ol' Manny will be long gone."

"I think I hear sirens," Quist said.

Manny turned and stuck the Glock in Quist's face. "Shut the fuck up! I told you we were gonna have our moment." He struck Quist on the side of his head with the butt of the Glock. It wasn't enough to knock Quist to his feet, but he fell anyway. "I'll teach you to fuck around with ol' Manny," he said, and then kicked Quist in the ribs.

Quist tried to twist away but Manny kicked him again, harder this time, and Quist felt something break.

"Where's Bella?" Lana yelled.

"I told you," he said, looking back at her. "You're never gonna see her again." he said and turned to give Quist another kick.

Quist grunted in pain, rolling closer to the table.

"Stop it!" Roy yelled.

"And you. You're as big a whore as she is."

Roy swung at him but he grabbed her wrist and twisted it, forcing her to the floor. Quist lifted his head. The knife was still another arm's length away. He raised up on both elbows and started to scoot toward the table, only to be rewarded by Manny's boot on his neck. "Hold it, cowboy," he said and gave Quist another couple of kicks. Quist was able to protect his ribs, but now he wondered if the last kick had broken his wrist.

Panting from the exertion, Manny stepped back and glowered at the three women huddled on the floor. "You," he said finally, pointing his gun at Lana. "Get over here."

"No," Roy said, leaping to her feet. "I'll go."

Manny punched her in the face, knocking her back down.

"Stop it. I'll go," Lana said, struggling to her feet.

Manny picked up the suitcase and grabbed Lana by the hair. "Okay, here's the deal. Anyone shows their face at that door and I shoot her first." He shoved the Glock into Lana's side and slowly backpedaled toward the front room. A moment later,

Quist heard the front door open and then slam shut.

He looked over at Roy who for the moment appeared paralyzed. She made a small grunting sound and then scrambled on all fours over to the table, snatched up Quist's switchblade, and then stood and started for the front door.

"Roy, don't," Quist yelled, grabbing for her legs as she stumbled past him, but she wriggled free. He pushed through the pain and forced himself up onto his knees. "Stop her!" He was aware of Frieda, stepping over him in pursuit of Roy, and the sound of the door opening, followed by the sound of a single gunshot and someone screaming.

"No!" Quist yelled.

He fell back on all fours, overcome with rage and the all too familiar feeling of helplessness. Sam tried to pull him to his feet, but he brushed him away, the pain in his side forcing him back to his knees.

"Goddammit! Do something!" he yelled at Sam who hesitated a moment before making his way to the front door. Quist now heard voices out in the street and someone sobbing. He pulled himself to his feet and stumbled after Sam who now stood in the doorway, blocking his view. He pushed Sam aside. Manny lay face down in the middle of the street. Roy sat on the ground cradling Lana in her lap. Frieda knelt beside them, her hand on Roy's shoulder.

"Oh God, no," Quist said, holding his ribs and staggered slowly towards them. He suddenly remembered Zenner and looked up the street. Zenner stood behind the hood of the Jeep holding his deer rifle.

As Quist stopped beside the huddled women, Roy looked up at him, her eyes wet with tears.

"She's okay. She's okay," Roy sobbed.

Sam brushed past him and walked up to where Manny lay. He leaned down and picked up the Glock and the suitcase and then passed the Samsonite to Frieda before squatting beside the two women.

"The casita down the street with the blue door," he said, gesturing down the street with his chin. "There's a woman there that has your baby. She's okay," he added and then touched Lana's shoulder.

Lana gasped in relief and pushed her way to her feet and began half-stumbling, half-running down the street. Roy stood and looked at Quist. She started to say something but instead reached up and laid her hand on Quist's cheek before starting after Lana.

"Are we good?" Sam asked, picking up Quist's knife and handing it to him.

Quist grimaced as he reached for it. "Tell me something. Whose side were you planning on taking?"

Sam shrugged. "I was still playing it out in my mind until that asshole Amado showed up. Truth be told, I knew I was gonna do whatever I had to for this money."

"So if you would've come up with that gun instead of Manny?"

"You mean who was I planning on shooting first? Not sure. At Quantico they always taught you to eliminate the most obvious threat. But I would shot Manny first out of general principle." He turned and looked at Frieda. "You did good. I guess we're just lucky they didn't frisk you. You ready?" he asked her.

Frieda slipped on her sunglasses and nodded. "Tell the señoritas I wish them well," she said to Quist. They both started to walk off.

"So are you off to Nicaragua?"

Sam turned and looked back at him. "Why? Are you thinking about looking me up?"

"You never know."

Sam stood there for a moment looking at Quist before taking the Samsonite back from Frieda. He opened it and pulled out a wad of bills and handed it to Quist. "Shit. Take some more," he said, handing him another handful. "The kid might need some baby clothes. I'll see you," he said, giving Quist a two-fingered salute and walking off. Frieda closed the suitcase and offered Quist a smile and turned to follow Sam.

"Are you okay? You don't look good," Zenner said, walking up to join Quist.

Quist tried to move his wrist and winced. "I feel worse than I look if that's any consolation." He looked around. A few people had cautiously stepped out into the street to survey the goings on. A pair of young boys wearing skeleton suits and riding bicycles slid to a stop at the edge of the street and stared down at Manny's body.

"You think anyone called the cops?" Quist asked.

"Unlikely. Maybe they'll figure it's none of their business and decide to let the dead rest in peace. *Diu de los Muertos* and all that shit. Still, we better get our asses in gear. Anyone left inside?"

Quist shook his head. Zenner leaned over Manny's body and picked up the Uzi. He started to get up and then paused to take something that was protruding from Manny's pants pocket. It appeared to be a folded piece of paper. He flicked it open and glanced at it for a moment. "You might want this," he said, handing it to Quist.

Quist held it to the light and squinted at the contents. It looked to be a photocopy of some sort. Imprinted at the top of the page was the letterhead of the New Orleans Police Department. On closer inspection he saw it was a booking sheet that listed the name Royale Aucoin followed by a date of birth and an address. The black and white mug shots, both a head on and a profile, were somewhat distorted by the fold of the paper, but the images still recognizable. It showed a woman perhaps in her early twenties scowling at the camera. Something about her expression telegraphed both despair and defiance. One of her eyes appeared bruised and half-swollen shut. Her tousled hair partially concealed what looked like a bruise on her forehead.

Below the mug shots were listed perhaps a half dozen or so arrests. Two for drug possession, a couple more for solicitation, shoplifting and possession of stolen property, and one for aggravated assault.

"Why do you think he had this? It is her, isn't it?" Zenner asked.

Quist looked up and nodded. He studied the sheet of paper for a moment before refolding it.

"We need to get out of here. And I mean now," Zenner said. "There's a police station right down by the church. They might've heard the shot. Gather up the woman and I'll get the Jeep."

Quist held the folded booking sheet between his fingers. Had Manny kept this to show Lana who her mother really was? There was no way of knowing. He considered if he should give it to Roy or not. He was still trying to decide when he heard their voices as they came back up the street. Lana carried something bundled in a blanket. He hesitated for moment before wadding the paper up and stuffing it into the pocket of his jeans.

47

Three days later

The three women sat perched on the low stone wall that encircled the cemetery. The graveyard defied Royale's expectations, for she remembered the small rural cemeteries of her Texas youth; the rusted iron grating, some of the gravestones well-tended and ornamented by faded artificial flowers while others were moldering and overgrown with weeds, the tombstones tumbled and forlorn.

This place however, El Cementerio de la Paz, bore little resemblance. Surrounding it was a stony, fallow field of ragged cornstalks bisected by a well-trodden trail that presumably led to the village whose flat rooftops were just visible above the line of scrub beyond the cornfield. Ground into the dirt were remnants of the marigold petals that had been scattered there to ensure the spirits of the dead would find their way to the altars their families had erected to welcome them back.

In the cemetery's center stood a massive and solitary tree of indeterminate species, its own life long past, its skeletal but still impressive boughs looming over the hundred or so headstones, all of which had been recently cleaned and adorned.

The gravestone that lay just below their feet was no more than a pock-marked slab of flat stone on top of which someone had erected a crude wooden altar. Covering the altar and the stone were a motley assortment of fruits, loaves of bread, candles, and heaps of candy and miniature, sugared skulls scattered randomly among several framed photographs, no doubt the images of the deceased family member. At the base of the altar someone had placed a ring of Coke bottles surrounding a twelve pack of Corona and a bottle of mezcal.

It had been late afternoon when they set out on foot from Zenner's house; Royale, Ximena, Lana and Bella with Quist lingering a discreet thirty yards behind. Ximena had fashioned a sling of sorts from a blanket for Lana to cradle Bella. Now, it was nearing dusk, and a covey of women and children had descended upon the cemetery, their arms laden with bundles of red and yellow flowers. *Cresta de gallo,* Ximena had called the red ones; the yellow ones, the marigolds, she called *cempasuchil.*

"They come to prepare for the ceremony later this evening," Ximena explained. "They are completing their *ofrendas,* their offerings to their dead loved ones." She looked off somewhat wistfully into the distance before going on. "Every year I come to meet my daughter." She turned and looked at Royale. "She was taken from me by the village priest and my parents when she was only two days old. Many years later I discovered she had died of *la difteria*. Diphtheria is how you say it *en inlgés,* yes? I never knew her name." Ximena shook her head as if trying to rid herself of the memory.

"I'm so sorry," Royale said, breaking the uncomfortable ensuing silence. She looked across at Quist who stood leaning against the cemetery's opposite wall. He met her gaze briefly before shifting his attention back to the cornfields on either side of the trails. He had insisted on accompanying the women, for both he and Zenner could not rule out the possibility of some form of blow back from Amado's associates. Zenner felt once the *policia* arrived at Sam's house none of the neighbors would tell them much, not wanting to become involved. But if any cartel people came by and began asking questions, it might be a different story. They had all watched the nightly television news that made mention of a suspected cartel shooting in a working-class neighborhood in the hills above Oaxaca City. A gang war the local police captain had assured viewers.

Royale shot a sidelong glance at Bella cradled against Lana's chest, her face and arms poking from the folds of the blanket. She seemed small for her age, her features small and fine. A ring of dark curls framed her heart-shaped face, her dark eyes casting about in what seemed endless vigilance. Her mouth, fleshy and moist, resembled some exotic budding plant. Something about Ximena's tragedy and the events of the previous several days, made Royale shudder at Bella's vulnerability; at all of their vulnerabilities.

A sudden gust of wind caused the flames of the candles on the nearby altar to twist and right, the breeze carrying with it the pungent scent of copal. Lana folded the top of the blanket over Bella's head and made a tsking sound in response to Bella's squeal of protest.

"You realize death does not end life, yes?" Ximena said, nodding at the gravestones and assorted altars. "From death comes life. *Un circula.* You understand? A circle. " She looked back at Royale and smiled. "After you went to your bedroom last night, your friend Quist and I drank too much mezcal and spoke. His stories became very... How would you say? Personal? In the *telenovelas* they are called *las confesiones del corazón.* The confessions of the heart."

"In this *telenovela,* did Quist confess anything about me?"

Ximena smiled and shrugged coyly. "No, but he told me of your sister. And her death. He has much sadness about this. But I made him realize that her passing is what created this...*este vinculo.* How do you say? Bond, yes? Her death, you and him," she said, gesturing to Quist who still sat watching from across the way. "The death of your sister. You two meet. You find your daughter. And her daughter. *De la muerte surge la vida.* From death comes life. *Un circula. ¿Verdad?"*

Ximena attention wavered as she raised her hand in a vague salute to an older woman who had just entered the cemetery. The woman carried a bundle of marigolds in one hand, the other held what appeared to be a plastic shopping bag filled with oranges. "*La flor de cempasúchil.* The marigold. The flower of death, yes, but also the flower of life. *La circula,"* she said softly as if to herself. "I must go," Ximena said abruptly, lowering herself down. "My friend Aduela," she said, gesturing to the woman. "She comes to see her son. You will stay for awhile, yes? *Bien..* Perhaps, you will find *consuelo.* The solace. For your sister," she said, walking off.

Royale looked across at Quist who lifted his right hand in

response. The cast on his wrist was just visible protruding from the sleeve of the raincoat that also concealed the Uzi. Lana noticed the exchange and made a snorting sound.

"What's with him?" she asked. "Or should I say what's with the both of you? I swear I'm beginning to smell blood in the water," she said, shooting Royale a smirking look.

"Stop it. I don't know about him. Me and him. I guess there's something there. Or at least I think there is, but I'm way out of practice." She looked at Lana. "First time I met him, I could hardly bear to look at him. Because of Charly and what happened. I should never have told you how it happened. It wasn't fair. Especially to Harlan." She shook her head and found herself smiling. "He's an acquired taste. And he's my friend."

"That's all? A friend?"

Royale shrugged. "Stay tuned."

Lana sighed and leaned over and kissed Bella on the head. "I don't know what I'm doing. You've figured that out by now, haven't you? I mean me and this whole mother thing."

Royale put her arm around her and pulled her close.

"Every day I tell myself I don't deserve this," Lana went on. "What I mean to say is that sometimes I think I don't deserve Bella. When she looks at me a certain way I can't help but feel like I'm cheating her. Does that make sense?" she asked, her voice breaking.

"God, I doubt I ever had that feeling," Royale said, smiling. "Someone told me once that you don't have to be a perfect mother, just a good one. I remember thinking, sure, like it was really that easy. I wish I could promise you that Bella's going to turn out alright. That there'll be more light than darkness in her life, but it's a big gamble. It's scary, isn't it? But you're going to do fine." Royale offered Bella her finger which Bella immediately pulled to her mouth. "She's going to be a biter."

Lana shot her a questioning look.

"A family trait. You'll see," Royale said.

Lana rested her head on Royale's shoulder. "I guess the hard part is not knowing what's going to happen next."

"What happens next is you do your best. One day at a time. You just remember Bella's got her grandmother to help lead the way. Scary as that sounds. Don't worry. We'll make out alright. No matter what, we do it together. Ximena told me we could stay here as long as we want. We can go to New Orleans. Anywhere you want. You'll be safe."

"Safe? What does that feel like?" Lana took Royale's hand. "I'm glad you're here," she said, swiping her eye.

They sat in silence for a moment before Lana slipped to the ground. "I think I'll walk around," she said. She stood on her toes and gave Royale a peck on the cheek. "I want to remember all this." She smiled and walked over to where Ximena and the old woman were placing flowers on the altars.

Royale stood and brushed the back of her jeans and then walked slowly in a roundabout way around the cemetery wall until she came up behind Quist. "See any signs of life?" she asked.

Quist turned and gave her a pained look. She could tell the effort hurt his ribs.

"You mean people I should be trying to save?" he asked. "I think I'm done with that. Seems every time I try, I just end up getting a good beating. " He nodded with his chin at Lana. "You two look pretty tight."

"A work in progress, but I think we'll make it."

They both watched in silence as an elderly couple knelt stiffly beside a crudely adorned grave that might've been a child's gauging from its size. In most respects, it was no more than a small mound of dirt encircled by some rocks. The woman, her face concealed by a black veil, placed a bouquet of marigold and coxcomb on the grave. The old man made the sign of the cross before leaning over and placing his hands on the pile of dirt.

"I never asked you, but what did you do with Charly? You know, her body?" Quist asked, studying the old couple.

"I cremated her. I scattered her ashes on a beach on Bolivar Island. Just up the coast from Galveston. Charly and I used to catch crabs there when we were kids. We took Lana there once. She might've been two, maybe three."

A moment of silence passed before she reached into her purse, and after rummaging a bit, retrieved the small crystal salt shaker. She held it up to show Quist. "I scattered all of her ashes except for this. I wasn't ready to let her go," she said, struggling to control her voice. "So I keep her with me."

Quist smiled and nodded.

She rolled the shaker in her hands for a moment, and then slowly and deliberately, unscrewed the cap of the shaker and unpeeled the tape on its rim. "It's time I let her go," she said, half-trying to convince herself. She hesitated a second or two and poured the ashes onto the ground before them. A fine gray mist billowed and then disappeared in the soft breeze.

Quist reached over and took her hand with his good hand. "Who knows? Maybe you could come back here next year and see if she shows up."

She nodded in agreement. "What about us?" Royale asked after a moment had passed. She hoped the tentativeness in her voice wasn't too obvious.

Quist tilted his head as if considering his answer. "Let's call it a work in progress."

They held each other's gaze as if each were deciphering the other's thoughts.

"I asked you once if you would take me somewhere. Somewhere warm. Some place where people don't have any problems. Have you ever come across a place like that?"

"No, I can't say I have, but Mateo told me about this place over on the coast. A fishing village he sometimes goes to. The beer's warm but the fish are fresh and there's always a breeze. Can you settle for that?"

"For now? Sure. Can you?"

Quist smiled. "Settle? I don't know. That word somehow conjures up a low bar."

"You might be disappointed."

"I doubt it." Quist glanced up at the sky. "It's going to be dark soon. Shall we head back?"

"No. Let's stay. There's signs of life here," she said. She took his hand and pulled him into the cemetery.

The End

76824500R00151

Made in the USA
San Bernardino, CA
17 May 2018